Suddenly the peace of the evening was shattered. Wanda and Anthea were screaming. Gomez had leapt from her side into the border and was flat on his stomach in it. Teresa, following suit, was cursing her husband's politics as she realized that his fears were not imaginary, the danger was real. The ambassador was shouting, "Lie down, Celia." But it was too late. By the time Celia had worked out that the strange rattling noise she could hear was fire from some kind of machine gun, there was a tearing pain in her shoulder, and blood was running down the front of her pink evening dress.

FLOWERS OF EVIL

A CELIA GRANT MYSTERY

John Sherwood

BALLANTINE BOOKS • NEW YORK

Library of Congress Catalog Card Number: 87-20013

ISBN 0-345-35342-0

This edition published by arrangement with Charles Scribner's Sons, an Imprint of Macmillan Publishing Company.

Manufactured in the United States of America

First Ballantine Books Edition: March 1990

❧ ONE ❧

"Hey, that man is drunk," said Harriet Wilson, the women's page columnist of one of the more respectable London tabloids.

Tim Price, a young but far from innocent reporter on the local paper, was standing next to her in the roped-off press enclosure.

"Drunk? Which one?" he asked.

"The third from the end."

Price looked along the line-up of notables waiting to be presented to royalty. The third man from the end was tall and strikingly handsome, with luxuriantly waved white hair, and his trendily tailored menswear made the formal suits of the municipal dignitaries on either side of him look dowdy and shapeless. His brilliant silk necktie made no concession to the solemnity of a royal occasion and—yes, when one looked closely, one could tell. He was swaying gently backwards and forwards on his heels and having trouble keeping his eyes open. Harriet Wilson was right.

"Who is he?" she asked.

"I've no idea," Tim replied untruthfully. He did not intend to linger unnecessarily in this provincial backwater, and was already knocking on editorial doors in London. If anything newsworthy resulted from Richard Galliant's drunken obeisances to royalty, he would sell the story to one of the national dailies while the competition was still finding out who Richard Galliant was.

He moved away. The Southern Television cameraman nodded to him and murmured, "Galliant's drunk again."

Tim wondered, not for the first time, why the head of an internationally known firm at the luxury end of the textile trade needed alcohol to get him through an occasion like this. Thanks to his flair for design, the firm's ranges of dress materials were style leaders, competed for by exclusive couture houses all over the world. Prestigious interior decorators draped even more prestigious residences with Richard Galliant furnishing materials and his distinctive "RG" on your tie meant that you had no cash flow problem. But something must be very wrong. Twice recently Galliant had been, to put it mildly, not himself in public. An after-dinner speech to the Rotarians had been eccentric enough to cause surprise, and the reporter's account for the local paper had been heavily tidied up "for policy reasons" in the privacy of the editor's office. On another occasion he had gone missing when due to address an international business audience in Brighton, and had been discovered making a confused version of his intended speech to casual. onlookers in a municipal car park a mile away.

He was muttering to himself now under his breath. Had any of the officials noticed? If so, they must have decided that he was not behaving oddly enough for it to be alarming, or else that he was too important a local dignitary to offend by ejecting him from the receiving line at the opening of the East Sussex Leisure Centre for the Disabled. He had subscribed massively to its building fund, as he had to other charitable causes. Tim suspected that he was keeping a high public-service profile in a bid for a knighthood.

A clattering noise heralded the arrival of the royal helicopter. The people in the receiving line drew themselves up in readiness, some trying to look blasé about royalty, others wearing nervous smiles of anticipation. Galliant was still muttering quietly under his breath.

The helicopter deposited itself in the exact centre of a tarmac area intended for the disabled to play games of wheelchair hockey on. Officials advanced towards it across the tarmac. There was a pause. Nothing more could happen until the rotors had stopped revolving and threatening windy disturbance of the royal hair.

When they were completely still, the fairytale figure of the Princess of Wales emerged from the helicopter like Snow White from her glass coffin. The waiting officials welcomed her and a small boy was persuaded to hand over a presentation bouquet whose maximum dimensions had been prescribed in advance by the Palace; if already lumbered with unwieldy vegetation, she would have trouble accepting the wilting bunches of flowers held out by children in the crowd, which were one of the hazards of her job. To make sure the fairytale went smoothly from start to finish, the Palace laid down detailed instructions about everything, from the proper mode of address, to her taste in food and drink, so that the magic would not be shattered by down-to-earth enquiries about sugar or no sugar in the royal tea.

Tim Price had mixed feelings about these occasions. They were really media events dramatizing aspects of the nation's life, in this case its care for the disabled, and he wondered how useful they were. Was Britain a caring nation, or had caring become a spectator sport? The public subscribed huge sums when a well-publicized disaster or famine caught its capricious fancy, but was it guilt-money? A substitute for doing something about the bedridden old woman next door?

The schoolchildren behind their barrier raised a cheer. The Princess did her duty by them and their flowers, then started making her way down the line of dignitaries waiting in the entrance to the building. As she went she exchanged a pleasant word here and there, but avoided asking questions requiring a long answer which would delay her progress. Soon she was three away from Galliant, who seemed to have pulled himself together and was looking more or less normal. The TV cameraman from Southern was taking pictures, but without enthusiasm. Shots of a formal receiving-line seldom made it to the screen unless something odd happened or some celebrity was being presented. There would be better footage later in the visit of the Princess bending compassionately over wheelchairs.

He was about to lower the camera when the fairytale ground suddenly to a halt in confusion and alarm. It was all over very quickly. As Galliant was presented to the Princess he plunged forward, almost knocking her over into the arms of the lady-in-waiting behind her, and made a determined attempt to plant a smacking kiss on both her cheeks. Her security man sprang to the rescue. In the resulting scuffle Galliant's flailing arms dislodged the small pillbox hat which crowned her brushed-up hair-style. It fell to the ground amid cries of horrified disapproval. The ultimate outrage had been committed. It was almost as bad as spitting at the Pope.

Tim Price did not wait to see what happened next. Almost anything about the Princess of Wales was hot news. This was banner headline stuff. He knew where the only pay telephone in the building was, got to it first and rang a man he knew on a London evening paper.

The TV cameraman raced to his car, carrying with him the TV equivalent of treasure trove. The videotape sequence he had just recorded rated world-wide distribution, it would be bounced from satellite to satellite, repeated over and over again in newscasts throughout the world and seen by countless millions. He had caught the whole thing, partly in close-up: the collapse of the fairytale smile into panic; the relief when the assailant's intentions turned out to be amorous rather than lethal; the suppressed fit of the giggles, transformed by stern self-control into an official smile to get the fairytale performance re-started. Then came a splendid shot of Richard Galliant standing in front of the Princess of Wales with a fatuous grin on his face and his foot on her hat.

Back in the entrance hall, officialdom had reacted characteristically. No automatic gear change could have been smoother than the way all concerned entered into a conspiracy to make it appear that nothing untoward had happened, or alternatively that, if it had, it was wholly without importance. Galliant was spirited away out of sight into the administrator's office. The three appropriate members of the official party fell behind for a muttered consultation about what to do with him. This took only a moment, because the answer was so obvious: smuggle him off the premises before the media fell on him like a pack of starving wolves.

By the time the Chief Constable had absented himself unobtrusively to attend to this, Tim Price had almost finished dictating his story to the copy-girl in London. "... Since the firm's headquarters moved to Sussex three years ago comma, Galliant has been prominent in local affairs and has made generous donations to charity stop. On two recent public occasions he has appeared to be under stress for no known reason stop. That's all."

His newsroom contact came on the line again. "In other words he was as pissed as a newt, but he'll have us for libel if we say so. Nice piece, that wraps it up very tidily. Get a statement from him, can you, for the late edition?"

"I'll try."

"Fine, and find out if they're beheading him in the Tower of London or what."

"Okay, will do."

Leaving three excited newsmen scrambling for the phone, Tim checked the car park. If the royal entourage had reacted true to form they would have arranged to whisk Galliant away out of sight, and his chauffeur-driven Rolls Royce would no longer be in the car park. It wasn't. Hunch suggested that unless it had slipped away already with Galliant in it, it would be round at the back of the building, by the kitchen door of the canteen. It was, and the chauffeur was holding the door open. The Chief Constable was trying to get Galliant into the car and he was waving his arms and arguing. Mrs. Galliant, an assisted blonde with pleasantly plump curves, looked on with grimly pursed lips.

It was now or never if Tim was to get a statement. As he ran towards the group, he heard the feet of another journalist pounding along behind him. But they were too late, Mrs. Galliant had seen them. Her pursed lips opened and uttered a few short words of command. Galliant looked round dazedly, but did not move. She gestured to the chauffeur, who seized Galliant and threw him head first on to the floor of the car. Mrs. Galliant said something to the Chief Constable without a moment's loss of poise, and climbed in after him.

If Tim was to follow the Rolls when it moved off there was no time to lose. He charged back through the building to the car park in front. The footsteps behind him proved to belong to Harriet Wilson, who caught up with him as he reached his dilapidated Ford. As he started it up she wrenched the passenger door open and climbed in. "You don't mind, do you? I came down by train, I've no transport. You're local, we're not in competition, okay?"

There was no time to argue, the Rolls had appeared from behind the building and was making off down the drive, titupping at speed over the ramps installed to slow traffic down. Mrs. Galliant was in it but there was no sign of her husband. Presumably he was on the floor where the chauffeur had deposited him. Her fixed expression suggested that she had her heels planted on his chest to keep him down.

Outside the gate the Rolls turned left towards London. Tim was puzzled. He had expected it to head southwards towards the Galliants' home base at Faringfield. He followed, and four other cars turned left behind him. The rest of the media were following his lead.

If Galliant was in the car, there was still no sign of him through the rear window. "This could be a decoy operation," Harriet suggested, "with him left behind in the building."

"No," Tim decided. "That's Mrs. Galliant in the car,

she wouldn't leave him behind in that state."

"I would, if my husband behaved like that. But you're probably right, she seemed to be taking charge. A dominating lady, she looked."

"Well, her father is a retired general and I think her grandfather was some kind of Lord."

Harriet gave a cackle of laughter. "Is she the second wife or the third? No, don't tell me, let me guess. Wife number one was a cosy little northern lass who he married while he was having his humble origins in Manchester or wherever—"

"Macclesfield, actually," said Tim. "He started up in a converted garage. I wouldn't know about any wife."

"If there was one he got rid of her when he moved to London and married—let me see. A trendy textile designer with long earrings and great big cushions on the floor."

"You've been cheating. You looked him up."

"No. I'm right, though?"

"I don't know about the cushions or the earrings, but she was a textile designer who used to work for the firm. There was a lot of aggro when they divorced."

"And then the business really took off," said Harriet. "And I know just what happened, it always does, it's the fault of the damn British class system. When they've made their first million they don't say to themselves 'okay, but I want more, where's the next million coming from?' They put in a manager to look after the business and move to the country and subscribe to all the right charities and try to make the grade as country gentlemen."

"He does that all right."

"So he gets himself a gracious Georgian house in Sussex, it's what the investment brokers call the Old Rectory syndrome, and he marries a new upmarket wife to match the architecture, right?"

"Not quite," said Tim. "He didn't put in a manager."

"He *commutes*? To London? You can't commute and make it socially in Sussex."

"No, he moved the head office down here. I went there

once when there was a freebie. The design studio's in the stables and there's a lot of telecommunications equipment. He runs the business from there."

"In the intervals between drunken orgies, and not for long if he goes on making sex-fiend attacks on royalty. He's made himself invisible socially in Sussex and the stock market won't like it either, drunken textile manufacturers have no investment appeal at all."

"Hey look," Tim interrupted. "What the hell's happening?"

The Rolls Royce had swung off the main road into a maze of winding country lanes, with side turnings every few hundred yards. "They're trying to lose us," he decided.

The convoy of press cars was still following Tim. They all plunged into the maze after the Rolls, but it soon became clear that the Galliants' chauffeur was no slouch when it came to hide and seek. The Rolls was no longer in sight and the convoy was following Tim blindly. He halted beside a village phone box and got out.

"What's now?" Harriet demanded. "What are you doing?"

"Pretending I want to phone." The other press cars rushed past, still intent on the pursuit. "That's better, we don't want them breaking off and following us instead."

"Why? Where are we going?"

"Faringfield. Where the Galliants live. They may head there when they think they've shaken us off. We'll wait for him there and try for a statement. If they don't show we'll get one from someone else."

He set off again, taking short cuts through the lanes till he came to a picture-book village in a fold of the Sussex Downs: Faringfield. The houses, mostly ranging from the fifteenth to the eighteenth centuries, were grouped harmoniously round a village green. The whole place reeked of the sort of wealth which distances itself from crude modern money-making behind a period facade.

"That's the Galliants' place," said Tim. "The big white house on the far side of the green."

Harriet unleashed her unnervingly loud laugh. "Next to the church? I don't believe it, it can't be what I think!"

"Actually, it is."

The Old Rectory at Faringfield had been built in the spacious days when the parson was always the younger son of the squire and had ten or a dozen children and several servants to accommodate. Since the last rector but three had moved out into his comfortable little parsonage, the Old Rectory had been owned by a succession of chartered accountants, company directors and management consultants, who had titivated it into a state of spick and span graciousness which was awesome to behold. Tim drove in through the wrought-iron gates and parked on the immaculate gravel. There was no sign of the Rolls; if it had arrived it must be in its garage. He rang the bell in a pillared porch ablaze with white paint.

After a longish wait the door opened a few inches on a chain, and a Chinese woman dressed in black peered out through the crack. "Sorree, no one at home," she announced happily in a sing-song voice.

Tim put his foot in the crack of the door. "D'you know when they'll be back?"

"No," she said with an inscrutable oriental smile, and tried to shut the door. He blocked the attempt with his foot.

"Where are they, d'you know that?" he persisted.

She made another attempt to shut the door. When this failed, she said, "Wait, please," withdrew for a moment and returned armed with a heavy walking stick with which, still smiling charmingly, she attempted to bore a hole in his ankle. He withdrew his foot in dismay, and the door slammed shut.

"She could be lying," Harriet decided. "Let's look round the back, see if they're here all the time, or there might be someone else."

To one side of the house, an archway led into a spacious stable-yard, built for an eighteenth-century rector of Faringfield who kept a few hunters as well as a carriage and horses for his wife, a hay-wain for the glebe and a donkey cart for the children. The carriage house had been converted into a design studio, with great north-facing windows where the double doors had been. The stables and tack room were now offices. Their entrance porch was marked with a name plate bearing the firm's familiar logo, Richard Galliant's elegant signature. But the door was locked. It was after office hours.

An archway at the far end of the yard proved to lead through into the garden at the back of the house. Harriet stomped into a flowerbed under one of the windows and shaded her eyes to see in. Tim followed.

"A library!" she shouted gleefully. "How pretentious can you get, I wonder if the books are real."

"Probably," said Tim with his nose against the glass. "Galliant's quite an educated man really."

"Can I help you?" asked an icy voice behind them. "That is, apart from pointing out that *Fuchsia magellanica versicolor* does not benefit from being trodden on."

They turned. A tiny woman with white hair, a china-shepherdess complexion and a youthful figure stood glaring at them like the Queen of the Fairies in a tantrum. Beside her and towering over her was a muscular young man with very fair hair and blue eyes, so good-looking that it amounted almost to caricature.

"Why hullo there, are you members of the family?" Harriet asked.

"No," said the china shepherdess.

"Of the household, then? Or do you work for the firm?"

"We are the gardeners. Will you please get out of that flowerbed before you do any more damage?"

Ignoring this, Harriet said: "Would you describe Richard Galliant as an eccentric man?"

"I wouldn't describe him at all," said the china shepherdess.

"Why not, for heaven's sake?"

"As I have never met him, the description would not be reliable."

"But you say you're the gardener," Harriet snapped.

"I am the managing director of Archerscroft Nurseries, which maintains gardens under contract. Mr. Wilkins here is my head gardener. I took over this garden last Monday. Mr. Galliant returned yesterday from a business trip abroad. I think I saw him for a moment looking out of a window, but cannot say on such slender evidence whether or not he is eccentric. And now will you please get out of there, if possible without trampling on too many of the petunias we have just planted? If you have business at the house you should ring the front door bell."

"We did," said Tim. "They said no one was home."

"Then you'll have to come back some other time."

"Damn it, there is no other time," said Harriet. "Galliant is today's news, not next week's."

"And here comes the competition," said Tim as the garden was invaded by a rabble brandishing tape recorders and cocoon-like microphones on the end of sticks.

"Ah, the media, I might have known," said Celia Grant. "But in rabid pursuit of what?"

❦ TWO ❦

Confronted with the newly arrived horde, Celia's first thought was that in dealing with the media, as with hijackers, half the battle was to keep them calm.

This meant that Bill, who had a very quick temper, must be prevented if possible from hitting anybody, although the way they were trampling on his freshly dug borders was enough to try the patience of Little Bo-Peep. A photographer, aiming his lens at the Galliants' newsworthy luxury residence, had backed away from it in his search for a good camera angle and overturned one of the stone urns on the balustrade of the terrace with his bottom. Others, intent on peering into the house, were treading on the newly planted petunias under the windows. Celia had grasped dimly from the questions put to her that Richard Galliant had created some disturbance on a royal occasion which was serious enough to require national coverage. Although she kept repeating that this was a matter she could throw no light on, the intruders refused to disperse.

"They'll be setting fire to the hedges next," Bill muttered gloomily as one of them tripped over cotton protecting newly sown grass seed.

"Isn't there anyone around for them to interview?" Celia asked.

"Someone's in that staff cottage beyond the veg garden. I saw them go in."

"But Bill, it could be anybody."

"Anybody's better than nobody to keep this lot quiet and out of the petunias."

Celia clapped her hands to command attention. "Ladies and gentlemen, we think we know where to find someone connected with the family for you to interview. If you'll wait round at the front of the house, we'll get them to come and meet you as soon as possible."

Unfortunately Susie, the Galliants' Chinese cook, chose this moment to create a diversion by appearing at the library window and making violent signs to the media to go away, whereupon the media made violent signs to her to open the window and be interviewed. Celia left Bill to deal with this and hurried away in search of a higher-powered interviewee.

Between the vegetable garden and the swimming pool some recent owner of the Old Rectory had built a staff cottage in the dolls-house mock-Georgian style, the sort of dwelling known to architectural snobs as Georgette. At her urging knock the door opened to reveal a pale, unshaven young man in jeans and a dirty sweat-shirt who blinked at her unhealthily.

"Is any member of the Galliant family here?" Celia asked. "Or anyone connected with the firm?"

"There's me."

"Then will you come, please? Something seems to have happened to Mr. Galliant, and the media have arrived in force. They want a statement from someone."

"Not me. I'm Paul, the unsatisfactory son who dropped out. You want my step-brother Charles, he's the solid citizen in the business suit."

"I see, where is he?"

"Shouldering the white man's burden at the London office, I imagine."

Which is a fat lot of use, Celia thought. "Then I'll tell

the media there's no one here to make a statement," she said, "and with any luck they'll go away."

"No, wait," said Paul Galliant. "What has my foolish father done now to attract their attention?"

"I'm not quite clear, they all talked at once. There was something about him knocking off the Princess of Wales' hat."

"How fascinating," said Paul, grinning. "Come in for a moment."

Celia hesitated. The public-relations problems of Richard Galliant and company were no business of hers. "My only concern is to get the media out of the garden, they're trampling it to a morass."

"My sister Wanda works for the firm, come in and have a word with her."

Wanda, with a dogged expression, was ironing shirts in the tiny living-room of the cottage. She had the same pale colouring and mousy hair as her brother, and a delicate oval face made pixie-like by steel-framed granny glasses. The room smelt partly of cannabis and partly of humanity. A scantily dressed but heavily tattooed young man, who lolled in the only armchair smiling dreamily, was probably responsible for both.

When Celia had explained the situation, Wanda said: "Oh dear, we'd better phone Charles at the London office."

"It's after office hours," Celia objected.

"Then you can't reach him," said Paul. "This is the happy hour when solid citizens drop in somewhere on the way home to drink or fornicate, or both."

"We could try," said Wanda indecisively.

"True," said Paul. Seizing the tattooed young man by the ankles, he bumped him down out of the armchair on to the floor. "Out of the way, Fred, so my masterful executive sister can get at the phone."

While Celia wondered what was happening in the garden and whether Bill had managed to keep his temper, Wanda yielded to her brother's urging and applied herself nervously to the telephone. But step-brother Charles could not be reached at office or home, nor at various likely intermediate haunts.

"I don't understand, what has happened to poor Father now?" she asked Celia.

Celia repeated the media's allegation about the Princess and her hat. "They seem to think Mr. Galliant was drunk."

Down on the floor, Fred suddenly came to life and gave a hoot of malicious laughter.

"Oh dear, oh no, not true! He drinks next to nothing!" cried Wanda. "He must have had another of his dizzy spells, we ought to explain to them."

Fred sat up. He and Paul exchanged looks of conspiratorial mischief.

"That's right. Wanda," said Fred solemnly. "We should."

Despite herself, Celia felt bound to interfere. "Should you be in such a hurry? The London office may have issued a statement, or there may be one from Mr. and Mrs. Galliant when they arrive wherever they're going. You don't have to make a statement just because the media say they want one."

Wanda looked anxiously to her brother for guidance.

"We ought to say something at once to protect his image," he decided. "We can't let them go on thinking he was drunk, can we, Fred?"

"That's right, Paul," said Fred.

The atmosphere of mischief was unmistakable.

Wanda hesitated. "You go and talk to them then, Paul dear."

"No no," Paul urged. "It has to be you, you're a director of the firm."

"But I only deal with the design side," she objected. "Public Relations comes under Charles."

"You're family. It's in order for you to reinforce whatever Charles puts out. The media may find out you're here, if you don't rush out and say 'it's a lie, darling daddy never touches a drop,' they'll decide there's something in it."

Wanda still hesitated. "You don't think Charles will be angry if I butt in?"

"Of course not, he'll expect it of you, off you go."

"That's right, Wanda, you should," said Fred.

Wait, you silly well-meaning girl, Celia thought, don't listen to them, don't you see what they're trying to do? But it was too late to interfere, Wanda had already gone. And what business is it of mine anyway, she asked herself, I shall probably be out of here tomorrow never to return.

Archerscroft Nurseries was under contract to bring the garden of the Old Rectory into a state of dazzling display in time for a huge garden party to be held in the middle of June. Richard Galliant and Company had paid lavishly to become a Corporate Patron of the opera season at Glyndebourne, fifteen miles away towards the coast, and the apparent purpose of the party was to ensure that no one of note in the County of Sussex was left unaware of the fact. But if half of what the media were alleging about Galliant's behaviour was true, he had covered himself so thoroughly with shame that for some time to come all social occasions in the county would be, to put it mildly, complete without him. If he had any sense he would plead ill-health and cancel the garden party, in which case her efforts to make the garden presentable in time for it would not be required; and if the media chose to charge about in it like a herd of bison the damage hardly mattered. Cheered by this reasoning she decided to find Bill and shake the dust of the Old Rectory off her feet. Leaving Paul and Fred to exchange the gleeful looks of intriguers who have succeeded marvelously in making mischief, she followed Wanda through the vegetable garden and back towards the house.

Bill had somehow managed to herd the media into the stable yard and lure Susie out of the house as interview fodder, though she refused to be drawn beyond saying that the Galliants were "velly nice gentleman" and "velly nice lady." But Wanda was a different matter. At the centre of a jostling crowd armed with video cameras and microphones, she declared that her father was a most abstemious man. He suffered occasionally from dizzy spells. One of these, not drink, must have caused the unfortunate incident that afternoon.

Tim Price, the young reporter that Celia had found flattening his nose against the library window earlier, proved to be odiously well informed, and asked Wanda whether the "dizzy spells" accounted for his making an incoherent speech to the Rotarians last week, and talking nonsense to passers-by in a Brighton car park the week before. Was her father seriously ill, someone else asked, and if so was he in a fit state to go on running the firm? He was in good general health, was he? The giddy spells were not serious? But if they were not a symptom of some serious disease, what was causing them if not drink? What had Mr. Galliant had for lunch before leaving to attend the ceremony? A prawn cocktail, followed by biscuits and cheese? A very light lunch. Was it perhaps too light, if accompanied by a glass or two of wine on an almost empty stomach? No wine? Was she sure? A quick dry martini or two before lunch, then?

As Wanda stumbled about among the traps set for her by the media, a hotted-up Metro with tinted windows and de luxe trimmings swept into the stable yard. A thick-set young man with dark hair and heavily marked eyebrows got out. His business suit and neatly trimmed moustache made Celia decide at once that this was step-brother Charles, the solid citizen in charge of public relations.

He identified himself to the media as Charles Langley, the financial director of Richard Galliant and Company, and took a paper out of his breast pocket. It was a copy, he said, of a statement issued an hour earlier from the firm's London office. He would read it out to them:

Mr. Galliant profoundly regrets the disturbance which took place today at the opening ceremony of the East Sussex Leisure Centre for the Disabled, when he suddenly felt faint and stumbled towards the Princess of Wales. He wishes to explain that he returned yesterday from a strenuous tour of his firm's export markets in Latin America. In addition to being very tired, he was still suffering from an attack of food poisoning contracted during his trip and had eaten nothing for forty-eight hours. He has always taken a close interest in the Centre, and has made a substantial contribution to its building fund, and naturally wished despite his condition to attend its formal opening. He is only sorry that an unexpected return of his indisposition should have marred the occasion, and wishes to apologize most sincerely to the Princess for the embarrassment which the incident must have caused her.

As he finished reading a bedlam of shouted questions broke out. Paul's and Fred's mischief-making had produced a total public-relations disaster, and Celia had to admire the dead-pan calm with which Charles Langley faced it. Smiling courteously in the direction of Wanda Galliant, he maintained stoutly that there was no contradiction between what he had just read out and what she had said. A "dizzy spell" was a fainting fit by another name. He was not aware that the head of the firm had suffered similar upsets on previous occasions, but of course Miss Galliant knew her father better than he did, and some people were more susceptible to food poisoning than others. As for the prawn cocktail and the cheese and biscuits, they resulted from a misunderstanding. No doubt something of the kind had been served at lunch and perhaps Mr. Galliant had toyed with them, but according to him he had eaten virtually nothing. Needless to say he would have been mad to touch alcohol with his stomach in that condition, and Langley could vouch personally for his abstemious habits. Apart from this passing episode he was in perfect health and fully in charge of the firm. He had come back from Latin America with an order book which much larger firms might envy.

Celia caught Bill's eye and beckoned. He skirted round the crowd of journalists and joined her. "There won't be no party, by the sound of it," he prophesied gloomily. "He'll be in a drying-out clinic or some such dog-house, hiding hisself for shame."

"And we'll have six dozen pots of Regale lilies and twenty-four dozen scarlet geraniums left on our hands, and goodness knows what else." She had a nightmare vision of all this redundant vegetation being unloaded from a truck. "Mrs. Galliant will have to honour our contract whatever happens."

"Oh Celia, she won't. She's real old-fashioned gentry, they can be very mean."

Celia thought about Joan Galliant's firm little button of a mouth and privately agreed. She had summoned Celia at short notice and explained what she wanted done. But she proved to know nothing about gardening, and made it clear that like many people of her social background she despised it as a suburban preoccupation of the middle classes. Celia had to explain that it was far too late in the season to buy trays of seedling annuals and bed them out, the display would not be ready in time for the party. The only way of getting her neglected garden into colour by mid-June would be to bed out pot-grown plants and shrubs bought at astronomical expense. How astronomical, the button mouth asked. Celia, who hated instant gardening and was snobbish about bedding plants, named a formidable sum in the hope of being turned down. But it was agreed to without hesitation, and she had placed the orders. They must be cancelled at once if the party was off and instant gardening was not called for.

"Better see the TV news," Bill suggested. "He'll be on it."

Bill was right. What had Galliant really done to the Princess of Wales? Were the media exaggerating? They must get to a TV set.

"There's one at Anthea's cottage," he said. "We can go there."

Anthea Clarkson was Bill's girlfriend. He was devoted to her, and fanatically faithful. He was a puritan in sexual matters and reacted furiously against the frequent invitations to promiscuity to which his good looks entitled him. They were an oddly matched couple, for she was a hard, ambitious business executive with little in common with Bill. Her pet-name for him was "Gorgeous," which seemed significant. Celia suspected that she valued him mainly as a status symbol, to be flaunted when it was nice to be escorted by the handsomest man in sight.

Anthea had left her London job a year ago and moved to Faringfield to take up a post as executive assistant to Richard Galliant. It was she who had suggested to Mrs. Galliant that she should call in Archerscroft Nurseries to deal with her garden. She seemed to think she had done Celia a great favour, but she was wrong. Now that raising and marketing unusual plants was proving profitable as well as interesting, Celia was trying to phase out the garden maintenance contracts which had kept her afloat at first. She had longed to tell Mrs. Galliant that she wasn't interested, but how could she? Bill obviously felt that his beloved had done the firm a good turn, and Celia feared she had not always been careful enough to hide from Bill how much she disliked Anthea. Besides, the advantages for him were obvious. He and Anthea would have chances to get together during the week as well as at weekends, in fact this was already happening. Today he had even sloped off to her cottage for lunch and had returned smelling strongly of the expensive scent which she used in unladylike quantities. Lunch must have been partaken of, if at all, in bed.

The Archerscroft Nurseries van was boxed in by double-parked press vehicles, so they walked across the village green to Anthea's rented cottage. Celia decided to be very nice to her, and had to admit, when Anthea let them in, that she was a dramatic looking girl with regular features, bright green eyes and a loose mop of dark curls which did not, however, suffice to soften a determined chin.

"Hi Gorgeous, hi Mrs. Grant, you've heard?" she said tensely as she let them in. "My God what a shocker, the radio's been talking of nothing else."

In the living-room, heavy with her scent, the TV was

already switched on, dispensing advertisements with the sound turned down while she waited for the news bulletin to start. She poured drinks, and they settled nervously to watch.

It was the fourth item, and even more damaging than Celia had imagined it could be. Galliant's determined assault on the Princess could not conceivably be explained away as a result of dizziness or faintness. As he lunged at her, her terrified face dominated the screen, and Celia wondered if the royal family thought about the possibility of assassination all the time while they were appearing in public. The brave way the Princess hoisted the official smile back into position made Galliant look a heartless brute as he stood grinning and trampling on her hat. The unfortunate impression was made even worse by what followed. The smirking news reader introduced a clip of Charles Langley reading out his fable about food poisoning, followed by one of Wanda looking half-witted in her granny glasses and contradicting him at every turn.

"What a shambles, far, far worse than I thought," said Anthea. She switched off the TV and began stalking up and down the room. "It's a tragedy, he's ruined himself."

It seemed to Celia that this was an over-dramatic view. She suggested mildly that social embarrassment did not necessarily entail utter ruin.

"It will for him," said Anthea. "Don't you see, he's a genius. He has this sure-fire colour sense, knows just what the fashion colours will be two years from now. And I *don't* mean he knows which colours ICI Dyestuffs Division will be flogging to the cheap end of the market, so that all the multiples come out with godawful dingy purple in their window displays one year and cruel lemon yellow the next. He knows which colours Calvin Klein and Louis Féraud and Bruce Oldfield and a dozen others will want to launch two years from now to make everything else look old hat."

Celia wondered whether an acute nose for the latest vagary of high fashion really made the grade as genius, but said nothing.

"He's built up a fabulous business, and now this, it's mind-blowing," Anthea lamented.

"Whatever possessed him?" Bill asked. "He'd been in the boozer indulging hisself and no mistake."

Anthea rounded on him with anger in her green eyes. "No, Gorgeous. Damn it, I work for Richard, I've been on sales trips abroad with him. A thimbleful of wine with his dinner and that's it. When we're here I'm in and out of his office all the time. I've never smelt drink on him."

Celia refrained from pointing out that it would be a miracle if Anthea ever smelt anything other than her own overpowering perfume. "If that's so, Anthea, how d'you account for that very odd carry-on this afternoon?"

"I can't, Mrs. Grant, I'm stunned."

"He seems to have behaved oddly in public before," said Celia. "One of the journalists mentioned a speech he'd made that was incoherent, and another time he's supposed to have made a scene in a car park. Something must be very wrong."

"There is, but I don't know what," Anthea burst out. "The damn family don't tell me anything, they've built a huge wall of silence round him to protect him and the business. I'm not allowed to say anything to outsiders, none of the staff are, I shouldn't be talking to you. But they'll have to think again after that freak-in this afternoon. Handing out a lot of public-relations crap won't keep the worms in their cans any more."

"So now what happens?" Celia asked.

Anthea was near to tears. "Disaster. This morning Richard Galliant and Co. was worth about ten million on the Unlisted Securities Market. But it's paper millions. I hate to think what will happen when the market opens tomorrow morning. The firm's a one man band, Richard's carrying the whole thing on his shoulders. If he has a heart attack, or if something like this goes wrong with his image, the market panics, the shares are worthless and the banks start quaking ten to a dozen on the Richter scale and call in their loans, and Richard Galliant and Co. is in the trash can."

"So what on earth possessed him to behave like that?" Celia persisted.

Anthea thought about this. "He's always been a hair-trigger man. Can't stand sudden loud noises, and he flies into a rage if anyone stands behind his chair while he's working. It's only lately that it's got serious enough to give me the heebie-jeebies."

"How d'you mean, serious, Anthea love?" Bill asked.

"For days he's perfectly normal, I mean normal for him. Just the usual hysteria if you do any of the things that annoy him. Then when he's in the middle of telling you something, the words suddenly don't add up into sentences, nothing makes sense, he's like a computer with the wrong software fed into it. And you realize he's gone off the damn rails again."

"How long does this state of affairs last?" Celia asked.

"At first it wasn't very long. I'd leave him alone for an hour or two, and by the next morning, say, he'd have all his marbles back, perfectly okay."

"And later, it started to get more serious? When did you first notice that?"

Anthea thought. "Last month in London, I think. He was supposed to be giving drinks at the Hilton to a lot of top brass from Paris and Rome who were here for London Fashion Week, and they'd all arrived and I was at panic stations because I couldn't get Richard to come across from the London office and host the thing. When he did come he had that silly grin on his face like he did just now on the TV, and he wouldn't pay attention to anybody. He just sat in a corner while all these top names quacked away at each other in French and Italian and knocked back his champagne and whisky and ignored him. And when I said 'Richard, for God's sake, these people are your bread and butter, they're supposed to be placing orders,' he said, 'Anthea my dear, I don't care an ant's fart whether they place orders or not.'"

"How long did it take him to get back to normal after that?" Celia asked.

"Much longer than before. He was drowsy and talked nonsense all that evening and wouldn't go home. I had to phone Mrs. Galliant to come and collect him, and cancel all his engagements for the next day."

"You sure it's not the booze, Anthea love?" Bill asked. "Sometimes they stay off it for weeks, then break out."

"Dead sure. I'd tell you if it was, Gorgeous. I'm not selling anyone a PR line about this any more."

"Drugs, then?" Celia suggested.

"I thought of that," said Anthea. "He doesn't shoot up. I had a good look at him the other day in the swimming pool, there are no needle marks. Not that that proves anything."

"No, maybe he puts other things up his nose besides his fingers," said Bill.

"If drugs are the answer, it's not anything addictive," Celia argued. "He's not drug-dependent because there are these intervals when he's normal."

"Normal for him," Anthea corrected. "I agree it's not drugs, but what is it? Some kind of off-and-on nervous breakdown?"

"Do nervous breakdowns work like that?" said Celia doubtfully. "'Normal' for him seems to mean tiresome but not certifiable, and from time to time he breaks out."

"My gran was like that towards the end," Bill put in. "Bright as a button one day, loopy as a kite the next."

"There's another possibility," said Celia. "Someone's doping him without his knowledge to make him behave oddly and ruin himself and the firm."

"I was wondering when you'd think of that," said Anthea.

❦ THREE ❦

"Oh Anthea love, that's naughty," said Bill, when the implications of her remark had sunk in. "You know how I try not to let Celia get involved in mysteries and neglect the business."

There was a silence. Anthea put on a hangdog face in mock apology for guilt.

So that's it, Celia thought. There are a dozen garden maintenance firms based nearer here than we are. But this devious little bitch has given the Galliant woman our name and lumbered me with six dozen pots of Regale lilies and twenty-four dozen scarlet geraniums in an intrigue to get me involved in a mystery that I shan't be investigating because in the morning Mrs. Galliant will send for me and tell me to go to hell and take my lilies and geraniums with me, because the garden party's off.

She bit back her annoyance out of consideration for Bill. But there was a question she wanted answered, and she tried to put it without sounding shrewish. "Forgive me, Anthea," she said gently, "but I don't quite see why you wanted me in on this."

"I had to know what's going on," cried Anthea harshly.

"Yes, but why exactly? The family obviously know

25

what's going on, and want to keep the knowledge to themselves. What use would it be to you?"

"Don't you see? I was frightened."

"Afraid he'd turn nasty and bash you? Oh Anthea," said Bill.

She rounded on him. "Shut up, you thick oaf, you don't understand a thing."

"Nor do I, I'm afraid," said Celia. "Frightened of what?"

"Of not making it," she snapped. "Of falling through the damn floor and landing back at the bottom of the pile where I came from. When I left school at sixteen, I was the junior typist in a solicitor's office, the slave that makes the bloody tea."

"Everyone has to start somewhere," said Celia soothingly.

"Don't you ever have nightmares of landing up where you started? I took a huge risk when I threw up a steady job in London and came down here. It was interesting and quite well paid, but there was a promotion block and any management vacancies that cropped up went to men. Then I had this offer from Richard and he said the firm was expanding and he'd probably have a directorship for me in a year or two, so I decided to take the risk. Then Richard started playing up and it looked as if things might fall apart. I had to know whether or not they were going to, don't you see?"

"So that you could get out in time before it happened," Celia murmured. "I do see."

"And now they have fell apart, good and proper," said Bill. "After this afternoon's caper."

"Bill Wilkins, I hate you. It's boring to say obvious things in a bright intelligent voice like that. Of course it's fallen apart and I shall have to creep back to London with my little tail between my legs and go round begging for jobs with a black mark against my name because of what happened here."

"I wouldn't be in too much of a hurry to abandon ship,"

Celia suggested. "You might be better off if you stayed on the burning deck in a heroic attitude till the last moment. Someone has to tidy up after this latest catastrophe."

"The family will do that."

"So far they haven't tidied up very successfully," said Celia, thinking of the hash that Wanda Galliant and Charles Langley had made of their dealings with the media.

"Oh hell yes." Anthea looked even more panic-stricken at the memory of their disastrous television appearance. "It was Wanda's fault, of course, she makes a mess of everything."

"Wanda didn't strike me as an intellectual giantess," Celia murmured.

"No, but let me show you something." Anthea went out into the hall and came back with a heavy silk scarf in a geometrical design of brown and sharp lime green and purple, a beautiful thing made even more desirable because the shock of an unusual colour combination was a triumphant success. "This is one of Wanda's. She's head of design and she's brilliant at it, inherited all her father's flair, in fact he leaves that side entirely to her nowadays. Apart from that she's a subnormal dimwit, with no business sense and no idea how to handle people. Press statements come under Charles Langley who's in charge under Richard on the executive side, but she hasn't even grasped that."

"She wasn't sure whether to interfere, but her brother egged her on."

"Typical, Paul's always putting banana skins under Charles Langley, he hates him."

"Langley's their step-brother, is that right?" Celia asked.

"Right. Joan Galliant's first husband was killed in the Falklands war, Charles is their son."

"Who came into the firm when she and Richard Galliant were married?"

"Right."

"And his arrival caused a lot of resentment?"

"Right again. They fight like cats in a bag when they're

by themselves, but where the interests of the firm are concerned they stand shoulder to shoulder and lie like troopers."

Except when Paul wields his banana skins, Celia thought. This was quite an interesting little problem, she would enjoy playing with it for a moment. "You've noticed the pattern in Mr. Galliant's fits of odd behaviour?" she said. "All the really damaging episodes that we know about happened when he'd got a public appearance scheduled: a meeting with buyers, two speaking engagements and now this royal thing. In other words, he was being doped at times when there was a good chance that it would make him behave oddly in public."

"It doesn't follow that he's being nobbled," Bill argued. "It could be just his nerves brought it on, at the thought of having to talk to all those people. Eh, Anthea love?"

She thought about this. "He does get uptight before a difficult meeting or when he has to make a speech. It could be that."

"Do people have off-and-on nervous breakdowns?" Celia asked. "I thought you did the job thoroughly or not at all."

"Anthea says it came on gradually," Bill pointed out. "That could be just his nerves getting worse as time went on."

"Or it could be the poisoner experimenting with the dose and gradually upping it," said Celia. "Has he ever had one of these attacks abroad, Anthea, or anything like it?"

"I don't think so, Mrs. Grant, not that I know of. I went to Rome with him last month and he was marvellous, talked to them in a sort of kitchen Italian he's learnt and they loved him and placed a mountain of orders."

"Then you see what that means (and do call me Celia, by the way). The poisoner, if there is one, can only operate when he's at home, and doesn't have access to him when he's abroad."

Anthea seemed not to be listening. She was away in a

panic world of her own. "What's going to happen to him? What will happen to the firm?"

Celia suddenly remembered that she had decided not to let herself get involved in this problem; and also that she had had a long day and was very tired. She rose. "Time for me to go home."

"But you will help, you will think about it?" Anthea insisted.

"I'll try, but if the family won't take anyone into their confidence there's very little I can do. Goodnight, Anthea, and thank you for the drink."

Bill had not moved from his chair. He was cocking an eyebrow at Anthea, asking permission to stay the night.

"Off you go, Gorgeous," she said.

"But—"

"No, damn you," she snapped. "I'm tired and I have work to do."

She pushed him out of the house with a perfunctory kiss, but held Celia back. "I know you don't like me, Mrs. Grant. You think I treat Gorgeous like dirt. I do. I can't help it though I love him dearly and he's an angel to put up with it, he's the only thing that keeps me sane. I'm not a nice person at all, I'm horribly selfish. But please try not to hate me too much."

Celia dealt with this as gracefully as she could, and urged her again not to be in too much of a hurry to leave her job and return to London. Then she walked back across the village green to the van with Bill, pondering on this new light on his love life. Other thoughts followed, mostly in the form of questions. Who would benefit from the ruin of Richard Galliant's reputation? The intruding Charles Langley, brought into the firm on the coat tails of an ambitious mother? A rival firm? Richard Galliant's vengeful first wife, urging on their son Paul to strew his path with banana-skins?

I must control myself, she thought, I'm mad to be constructing these scenarios, what a waste of mental energy.

It's not my problem, and I could kill devious little Anthea for involving me in that hellish garden.

Suddenly she felt very sorry for Anthea, and less inclined to be cross with Bill for sticking to her. One must not be nasty to lame ducks, she thought, and green-eyed dramatically handsome Anthea had surprisingly turned out to be a lame duck dressed up as a bird of prey. Why didn't I spot it before, she asked herself. Goodness, am I subconsciously in love with my head gardener, who is half my age? And am I jealous of Anthea's relationship with him? What a hoot, I could make it sound very plausible and pull some fool of a psychiatrist's leg with it. The thought made her giggle aloud.

"What's so funny?" Bill asked crossly as he strode along beside her.

"Nothing . . ." The truth of the matter was, she was fond of Bill in a motherly way and could foresee that sooner or later that tense, selfish little tramp would hurt him horribly. But for the present she made a firm resolution: she would do her best not to be nasty to Anthea.

"Yes, Mrs. Grant, what is it?" said Joan Galliant in an ostentatiously patient voice which meant "I am very busy and the less I hear about that boring garden the better."

She was at her desk in the library, between long windows opening on to the terrace. The room bore eloquent witness to Richard Galliant's colour sense and flair for design. A Chippendale style mirror and superb antique furniture blended happily with a modern chandelier like a bursting rocket, shot silk curtains and a carpet in a striking geometrical pattern. What looked like Joan Galliant's contribution to the décor consisted of a no-nonsense architect's desk-lamp on her elegant satinwood escritoire, and a framed photo of a superior-looking horse.

Celia had been kept hanging about for an hour waiting to see her, and wasted no time in stating her business. "I was wondering if you wanted to cancel your contract with us."

The button mouth contracted and the eyebrows shot up. "Why?"

"I read this morning's papers and wondered if you intend to cancel the garden party."

"What on earth made you think that?"

Celia was at a loss for an answer. When she arrived the media were still picketing the entrance to the Old Rectory drive. Galliant's attempt to ravish the Princess of Wales had continued to reverberate through the breakfast-time radio bulletins and the press had been merciless to him. All the papers had pictures of him standing on her hat, and the botched attempt at a cover-up by Wanda Galliant and Charles Langley had been a godsend to the cartoonists.

"What put such an idea into your head?" Mrs. Galliant persisted. "Why on earth should a stomach upset of my husband's, now, make me want to cancel a party in three weeks' time?"

"Fair enough, but I felt I ought to point out that if you were thinking of it, now is the very last moment to tell me. There's still time for me to cancel the orders for plants. If it's left any later, I'll have to charge you for them."

Mrs. Galliant glared. Celia decided that she must once have been very pretty in a vapid blonde way, and perhaps still was when she was not making aggressive faces. The button mouth could probably double as a rosebud.

"I've told you, Mrs. Grant," she said, "there's no question of a cancellation. So now will you go out there and get on with it? I've not seen much result so far."

"I had four gardeners working here all yesterday," Celia retorted, "dealing with the consequences of several months' neglect. You don't want me to bed out on top of a lot of weeds, do you?"

"I don't care what you do provided you get a move on and stop bothering me."

Celia stalked to the door, hoping to get out of it before she exploded.

"Wait, Mrs. Grant, there's one more thing. I gather that your interference was partly responsible for the muddle yesterday, when two statements instead of one were issued to the press. The affairs of the household and the firm are no concern of yours, in future would you please mind your own business?"

"A rabid herd of media people trampling on newly planted petunias was my business. It was the household's responsibility to deal with them, so I fetched someone. Look here, Mrs. Galliant, we obviously dislike each other very much. Wouldn't it be wiser to cancel our contract for the garden by mutual agreement?"

The mouth was no longer a button. Its corners had turned down, and it was trembling. "No. Please. I know it must be difficult for you, the garden's been neglected, but that was because of . . . special circumstances. Richard's set his heart on having it looking marvellous in time for the party and I don't want to disappoint him. Please do carry on, I'm sorry if I was rude."

"That's all right. You have a lot to worry about."

The defences were up again at once. "I'm perfectly capable of dealing with any worries I may have. You concentrate on that damn garden."

Celia decided as she left that she rather admired Joan Galliant. Her determination to keep the flag flying despite everything was brave though probably doomed, and her moment of collapse had shown what a strain she was finding it.

Resigning herself to concentrating after all on "that damn garden," Celia went out into it for another look. It was a perfectly good garden really. Some previous owner with an eye for landscaping had given it a sensible basic layout, it would look rather good when it was properly planted up. The stone urns which edged the terrace would have to be filled with something, but the problems really began four steps down from there, where a wide grass path ran away from the house with a long, straight border on either side of it.

Much work and shockingly lavish expenditure would be needed to bring these two neglected borders into luxuriant bloom in three weeks' time. They had once been well planted, and had probably been well looked after by the gardener whose disappearance had made it necessary for Archerscroft Nurseries to be called in. But he had left some time ago, the spring tidying-up had not been done. The soil was infested with bitter cress, and the dismal remains of last year's Michaelmas daisies and day lilies had not been cut down and cleared away. To judge from the look of things the defecting gardener must have walked out on the Galliants early in March. Why had a replacement not been found sooner? What were the "special circumstances" that Mrs. Galliant had muttered about to account for the garden's neglect?

At the far end the vista between the borders widened to accommodate a small waterlily pool set in the grass, but nothing could be done about that. The water would not have warmed up enough by mid-June to bring the waterlilies into flower, and she was revolted by Joan Galliant's suggestion that she should buy plastic ones at a supermarket and float them on it. Beyond the pool, steps led down to a wide sweep of lawn. This was where the marquee for the party would be set up, and the shrub borders surrounding it presented no problem. All that was needed was a few bold plantings of azaleas and hydrangeas to give colour. She was already in touch with the firm which forced hydrangeas into flower early to decorate the royal box at Ascot, and was enquiring in the trade for azaleas held back in cold store with a view to exhibition work in June. The most ghastly headache was a rose garden full of disease-ridden snaggy bush-roses expiring miserably in soil which was obviously rose-sick. Her mind had gone blank with horror when first confronted with this problem. On recovering her senses she had told two gardeners to dig out all the pestiferous roses and burn them in the adjoining vegetable garden (a neglected waste of cabbage stalks but no concern of hers, thank goodness), and ordered twenty-four dozen scarlet Paul Crampel geraniums to replace them.

They would look very municipal but that could not be helped.

She went back for another look at her main problem, the long borders. Work had started on them, tomorrow they would finish clearing them and forking them through ready for planting. Some of the things there already could be left and worked into the display, notably four tall shrub roses, two each side, which would be useful to give height at the back. Luckily they were all the same rose, a stunningly beautiful relative of *Rosa moyesii** called Nevada. When the flowers appeared they would be creamy white and four inches across. They could be fitted quite happily into her carefully worked out colour scheme, which started with cool blues and whites and mauves at the end nearest the house, and culminated in a riot of scarlet and orange where the vista opened out into the main lawn.

But were those huge, elderly shrub roses Nevadas? A horrid thought hit her. What if they were Marguerite Hillings?

Marguerite Hilling was a pink sport of Nevada, less popular and well-known, but readily available from the larger rose nurseries. Celia looked again at the chocolate brown stems and fresh green foliage. At this time of year the two roses were indistinguishable. It was anyone's guess whether the four-inch flowers would be creamy white or what the catalogues, understating the matter grossly, described as "a pleasing deep flesh pink."

The thought of this giant display of shocking pink looming over her carefully planned colour scheme horrified Celia. Whichever they turned out to be, she would have to keep them, because the main trouble about this border was giving it height at the back and the amount she was already

---

*Leading geneticists have suggested that despite what the breeder says Nevada cannot have been fathered by *Rosa moyesii* because its chromosome count, the botanical equivalent of a blood test, is wrong. *R. moyesii fargesii* and *R. spinosissima hispida* have been suggested as possible pollen parents. The pink sport first appeared in about 1954 in England, and in New Zealand in 1958. It was introduced by Hilling in 1959 and named after his wife.

having to spend on container-grown shrubs for this purpose shocked her. Which were they? She must find out. How? Mrs. Galliant would not know, and would behave shrewishly if asked. Who else was there? The defecting gardener, perhaps. Was he still living in Faringfield? And would not an enquiry about shrub roses form a convenient introduction to him, after which his observations on other aspects of the Old Rectory set-up could be enquired into?

Clearly this came under Mrs. Galliant's ban on "not minding one's own business" so it would be unwise to ask anyone at the Old Rectory where the ex-gardener was to be found. But refraining from losing her temper with Mrs. Galliant had given Celia a thirst, the Red Lion across the village green looked inviting, and what were village pubs for if not to act as information centres? She decided to leave her car in the stable yard and walk there.

The media had given up their mass picket outside the gate, but Tim Price from the local paper was still there, and she had to say "no comment" seven times before he left her alone to walk across the grass to the Red Lion. It was still early, and the bar was empty apart from a very fat landlord polishing glasses behind it. Celia ordered herself a lager and settled down to gossip about the deplorable effect on vegetable gardens of waterlogging in March, followed by the drying winds over Easter. Five minutes of this made it possible to ask where the ex-gardener at the Old Rectory was to be found, what she wanted to ask him, and why.

"Ye can ask him," said the fat man. "He's lodging with his sister now, it's the house next to the post office. But he won't tell you nothing, George Belling won't."

"Why not?" Celia asked.

"He don't want anything to do with them lot up at the Old Rectory. Not after what happened."

Little prompting was needed to bring out the story of "what happened." George Belling, who was in his seventies, had gardened for the last rector to inhabit the house, and had been passed on from owner to owner ever since. He was therefore "used to all sorts" and had "rubbed along with them pretty well," which probably meant that he had done what he liked in the garden and pretended to be deaf when asked to do otherwise. But in the Galliants he had met his match.

"It was him, not her," the fat landlord explained. "Usually it's the ladies give trouble, but he was the one that fussed, saying how it was a crime to plant this flower next to that one because the colours clashed, and he was to move it at once. Then she'd come out and tell George to take no notice and not bother and he wouldn't and then he'd get it in the neck from Mr. Galliant for not moving it. And that Mrs. Morris kept on at him—"

"Mrs. Morris? Who's she?"

"The little Chinese woman that does the cooking, Susie her name is, that's married to Morris, the chauffeur. She kept on at George in her squawky little voice, telling him to grow all sorts of fancy vegetables that he'd never heard of, and George got more and more fed up."

"So in the end he left," Celia put in.

"Not him! It was his garden, he'd looked after it for fity years, he'd never have gone of his own accord. They sacked him."

There had been an almighty row, it seemed. George had arrived one morning to find Galliant wandering round the garden in his dressing-gown and muttering to himself. When he saw George, he had "created and carried on something awful" about the state of the paths in the rose garden, to the effect that foot-high weeds in the gravel were tangling themselves round his ankles and tripping him up. Admittedly there were a few weeds in the gravel and George would have got round to them with his can of weed-killer in time, but there was only an inch or so of growth on them and it was nonsense to make such a fuss. George had pointed this out and insults had been exchanged. To make matters worse, Galliant's dressing-gown had floated wide open, revealing the fact that he was wearing nothing underneath it. George, a stickler for the decencies, had been deeply shocked by this and had told him

36

brusquely to "cover himself." When Galliant refused he had taken it as a deliberate outrage directed against himself, and stormed into the house to protest to Mrs. Galliant.

Joan Galliant had reacted calmly at first, telling George to take the rest of the day off to cool down, and promising to speak to her husband. George had stomped off, leaving Galliant apparently asleep in a long chair on the lawn. The shock had come that evening, when Joan Galliant had called at George's cottage and told him that her husband denied having said or done anything untoward, apart from making a legitimate complaint about the weedy state of the gravel. She had talked it over with him, and they both felt it was time for him to take a well-earned rest and retire on his old age pension. Horrified at this development, George had begged her to change her mind, but she had been adamant.

"She wouldn't hear of it," the landlord explained. "She said she and her husband were tired of these constant rows over nothing at all. So they'd decided to make other arrangements for looking after the garden, and they'd be needing his cottage, but they'd give him a week to get out."

"Which cottage? Where?" Celia asked.

"The one Paul Galliant's in now, that's the son by the first marriage. It was a put up job, see? They'd planned it together. Mr. Galliant was to create at George and make a scene, so she could sack him for being quarrelsome."

"When did all this happen?" she asked.

"Beginning of March some time."

"But they hadn't made 'other arrangements' about the garden. Nothing's been done to it since."

He winked. "They had, but the 'other arrangements' didn't work out the way they expected. It was to do with Paul, see? A real wild lad, and he'd been in trouble in London. So they got him down here and he was supposed to do the garden for them."

"But does he know anything about gardening?"

"According to George there was a horticultural college

somewhere that he dropped out of, he may have learnt a bit there. After that he had a business doing window boxes in London. He used to come down here with a girlfriend, dirty little creature she was, and pinch plants off of George for his window boxes. Then something happened in London, no one knows quite what, and they got him down here and turned George out of his cottage to make room. All for nothing, because he's in here morning, noon and night and never lifts a finger in the garden."

This is the sort of thing families do, Celia thought. They set the problem child up in a little business in London and hope for the best. When that doesn't work out they decide that the responsibility of looking after their garden will probably be the making of the boy at last, and everything will be different when they have him under their eye. So they sack the gardener and turn him out of his house to give the black sheep of the family a chance to turn over a new leaf. It doesn't work. What will they try next? Anything rather than admit failure . . .

The landlord was making discreet signals to her. She turned. Paul Galliant had just come in, followed by Fred, his tattooed and cannabis-drenched boon companion. Celia picked up her glass and sat down at a table out of sight round the corner of the bar. If it were reported to Galliant headquarters that she had been seen in tête-à-tête conversation with the landlord, Joan Galliant would undoubtedly conclude, rightly, that she had not been obeying orders and "minding her own business."

The Belling saga was very interesting, especially Galliant's highly significant complaint to him about the "foot-high weeds." And there was another detail of the story that didn't add up, but she would have to think about all that later. A new development called for her attention. Tim Price had come into the bar and was making determined conversation with Paul and Fred about the weather and the opening of the cricket season. As soon as decency permitted he changed the subject casually to the Galliants and their troubles.

A fascinating situation developed. Price thought he was passing himself off successfully as a casual enquirer with no connection with the press, but Paul and Fred knew perfectly well who he was and were bent on mischief. Richard Galliant, they said, was an alcoholic with a violent temper who knocked his wife about and was always in and out of mental homes. The attack on the Princess of Wales was nothing to what went on in private and had been hushed up. For instance? Price enquired eagerly and was rewarded with a long and detailed story about an employee called Frances Worthington, who had been raped by Galliant and complained about it. Threatened with the sack for lying, Frances had proved a very awkward customer, and Galliant had had to pay out a huge sum to hush the thing up . . .

Tim Price swallowed this fable unsuspectingly until Paul mentioned in passing that *Francis* Worthington was male. "Are you sure about all this?" he asked.

"Of course," said Paul. "Richard Galliant's supposed to be my father."

". . . Supposed?"

"Yes, my mother slept around a lot and she isn't sure. It could be the Duke of Edinburgh or it could be Noel Coward, but don't put that in your nasty little newspaper, will you?"

Paul and Fred collapsed in mocking laughter, and Price withdrew in confusion to go and phone. Celia realized that her immediate problem was still unsolved. Was the display in the long borders going to be punctuated by nightmare outbursts of man-eating pink? Who could she ask, since the disgruntled Belling had sent everyone connected with the Old Rectory to Coventry?

Wanda Galliant, perhaps. She lived in the house, if she was such a brilliant textile designer she must have some colour sense, she ought to know. Celia walked back to the Old Rectory, and asked for Wanda at the Richard Galliant and Company reception desk in the stable yard. The receptionist made enquiries but was sorry, Miss Galliant was "tied up at the moment." If Mrs. Grant would wait, she would come through and see her as soon as possible. Celia explained that she only wanted to ask one simple question; could she not go through to the studio for a moment and ask it?

The receptionist was shocked by this suggestion. No one, absolutely no one, was allowed into the studio unless they worked there, not even employees of the firm. Why not, Celia asked, had there been trouble over copying of the firm's designs? Instead of replying the receptionist threw her a horrified look and buried her nose in her word processor. Evidently there had indeed been trouble, so awful that the whole subject was taboo.

Celia slotted this distressing fact into her growing picture of the woes of the Galliant family and firm, and waited for Wanda to appear. There was plenty to look at. The reception area did double duty as a show-room, with softly lit wall-cases displaying the firm's range of fabrics. They surprised her. Smart little Anthea had given her the impression that Richard Galliant's main talent was an acute fashion sense. He had far more than that, a deep creative feeling for colour and line. These textiles had a unity of style, like the classics from the William Morris workshop. They would be beautiful long after they ceased to be fashionable.

But whose style was it nowadays? Richard Galliant's or Wanda's? Did Galliant mind the design leadership passing out of his hands? Or was his grip on the business so loose that he did not care?

Suddenly Wanda Galliant stood before her and peered uncertainly at Celia through her granny glasses. She seemed to be having trouble making the transition from the world of the drawing board, where she knew just what she was doing, into the everyday world where she did not. "I'm . . . sorry to have kept you waiting, I had the computer on line to the factory in Slough . . ."

"That's quite all right," said Celia.

"We put all our designs for printed fabrics on a computer, you see, and the computer at Slough inks the rollers and prints the design. . . . What was it you wanted to know?"

Celia put her query about the colour of the shrub roses. But it soon became clear that Wanda was one of those people with no bump of locality who cannot visualize from a description in words where something is.

"Oh dear, I'm not sure which roses you mean," she said. "I'd better come and see."

As they crossed the stable yard, Celia explained how anxious she was to make a success of her colour scheme for the garden. "I was afraid the party would have to be cancelled because of . . . your father's illness."

"Oh *no*, Mrs. Grant, father wouldn't hear of it. He's in a nursing home for a few days for tests, but I'm *sure* he'll be perfectly fit in a day or two and ready to come home." It was impossible to guess from her tone whether she believed this, or whether it was the fiction that the whole family was peddling to enquirers.

They entered the garden through the archway from the stable yard. Wanda stepped up on to the terrace and peered short-sightedly down the grass path between the borders. "What's that down there?" she enquired mildly. "A balloon that's blown in from somewhere? . . . a football?"

Celia looked. There was indeed a round object bobbing about on the surface of the waterlily pond at the far end of the vista. It was neither a balloon nor a football, but a human head. "How extraordinary," she said. "Someone's having a dip in your lily pool."

Wanda gave an unnerved gasp. "Oh *no*! I can't bear it." She screwed up her eyes behind the glasses. "It's not him, is it, can you see?"

"Yes. It's Mr. Galliant."

❧ FOUR ❧

"It's happened again, I can't bear it," cried Wanda in a voice which rose into a shriek of uncontrolled panic. She ran down the grass path to the end of the vista, to see for herself that it was indeed her father in the lily pool, then turned and dashed back towards the house, shouting "Morris! Mother! Come quick, father's back from the nursing home, it's happened again."

Left to her own devices, Celia decided to go and see what Galliant was doing in the pool, and found on arrival that he was lying on his back in it. He grinned up at her fatuously. "Hi!"

"Hullo," she replied.

He heaved himself up from the water, looking like a heavily built statue of Neptune in an Italian fountain. His hair was wild, he was unshaven and stark naked.

He nodded in the direction of Wanda's receding outcry. "People who shout in that disgusting shade of purple have no aesthetic sense."

As Wanda was dressed in mousy shades of brown, this puzzled Celia. "Are you enjoying yourself in there?" she asked.

"Oh, immensely. As you see, I'm looking for red-nosed dolphins."

"Isn't the pool a bit small for dolphins?"

He peered down at the water doubtfully. "What an extraordinary remark, why d'you say that?"

"Dolphins are quite large, and the pool is rather small."

His mood changed, and he glared at her accusingly. "You're a devil with steel eyes. Oh yes, that's what you are."

"No, really. Nothing of the kind."

"Liar. You're ravishingly pretty, I grant you that. But you don't deceive me, all you nurses are devils with steel eyes. Without exception. Oh yes."

A hue and cry was approaching from the house, consisting of Morris the chauffeur, Wanda and Mrs. Galliant, whose shouts of indignation echoed down the vista. ". . . walked out of the nursing home . . . damn careless of them . . . no idea where he'd gone . . ."

As the hue and cry grew closer, Galliant lay down again in the water, as if hiding in it for self-defence. "I hate these disgusting purple noises," he complained.

Mrs. Galliant reached the pool first. "Oh really, Richard, starkers again! I wish you wouldn't."

"But my dear, I'm looking for red-nosed dolphins," he protested.

"You might as well say you're looking for middle-cut salmon," she retorted. "Please get out at once."

He made a hangdog face like a scolded child, then thrust his private parts up defiantly at her among the floating leaves of the waterlilies.

She frowned. "Don't be silly, Richard, no one wants to see *that*."

"Father, don't," moaned Wanda.

"Morris, you'll have to deal with him," Joan Galliant decided. "For Pete's sake get him into the house before anyone sees him and put him to bed."

"Very well, Madam," said the burly chauffeur, and took off his jacket. "Now, Mr. Galliant you silly bugger, are you coming out or must I come in and get you?"

Galliant made no move, and Morris began pulling him

out of the pool with what seemed to Celia rather unnecessary brutality until she realized what a powerfully built man he was.

"Where are his clothes, he must have arrived in some," Joan Galliant remarked as Morris frog-marched Galliant towards the house.

Celia had already addressed herself to that question, and had retrieved a shirt, slacks, socks and a pair of bedroom shoes from the remains of last year's Michaelmas daisies. "Here," she said.

Joan Galliant snatched them from her. "Mrs. Grant, what in hell's name are you doing here?"

"If I am to turn your garden into a miracle of beauty in time for your party," Celia retorted, "you must resign yourself to my being in it from time to time."

"Well please resign yourself to being in another part of it when that sort of exhibition is going on, instead of standing gaping. And if you sell the story to the press you'll find you have a lot of plants on your hands that I won't pay for."

"I have no intention of selling anything to the press."

"So you say, Mrs. Grant, so you say. Watch it, or I'll make damn sure you never work again for anyone within a twenty-mile radius of Faringfield."

"Oh, I think my regular customers know me well enough to ignore that sort of nonsense," said Celia and withdrew with dignity.

Her car was parked in the stable yard. Tim Price, back from the pub, was lurking near it.

"Excuse me," he said. "I believe Mr. Galliant's just got back from the nursing home."

"No comment," said Celia.

"He is back home, isn't he?"

"No comment," said Celia.

"Oh come on, beautiful, give us a break."

"My beauty is neither here nor there if you know he's back."

"I don't," said Tim with an engaging smile. "I only

know he walked out of the nursing home at eleven this morning, and wasn't missed for over an hour."

Susie was watching them from the kitchen window and uttering shrill cries of Chinese alarm. Fearful of being accused of treasonable dealings with the enemy, Celia hurried towards her car, but Tim side-stepped and blocked her way. "There was a lot of shouting just now in the garden. What was it?"

"No comment," said Celia.

Morris came pounding out of the back porch and across the stable yard. "Hey you," he shouted. "Still hanging around, are you? Forgotten what I said?"

"I only remember you talked a lot of nonsense."

Morris seized him by the lapels and shook him like a terrier with a rat. "Oh, you forgot, did you? Don't forget again: this place is unhealthy for weaselly reporters with long noses that don't want a broken one and two black eyes." He turned Tim round and landed a kick on his bottom that sent him sprawling, then rounded on Celia. "I'm surprised at you, dear. Fancy talking to that low class of person after what you was told."

"My side of the conversation consisted mostly of saying 'no comment,'" she assured him.

"I certainly hope that's true, dear, for your sake, or you'll be out of that garden on your ear."

"He's right, you do talk a lot of nonsense," said Celia and climbed into her car.

On the way back to Archerscroft she thought about Richard Galliant's behaviour in the lily pool. He had complained twice about "disgusting purple noises." That had clicked in her mind at once. But where on earth had she read about drug-induced hallucinations in which the senses got mixed up and the sound of a bell, for instance, was perceived as bright blue? Another thing, according to the landlord of the Red Lion, Galliant had complained to Belling about "foot-high" weeds in a gravel path. That rang a bell too, she had read somewhere about a man who had suffered a similar hallucination while riding a motorcycle.

There was no doubt about it, Galliant's symptoms were those of a person suffering from the effects of a hallucinogenic drug.

She had intended to spend most of the day in her office, grappling with a huge waiting list of customers wanting plants of *Helleborus* "Roger Grant," the prizewinning *Corsicus x niger* hybrid which she had raised and named after her late husband. But the blanks in her memory nagged her all the way home. Where had she read about the bright blue noise and the hallucinated motorcyclist? Probably in some botanical tome, a lot of the hallucinogens were herbal. Roger had been a leading light on the staff of the Royal Botanical Gardens at Kew and had accumulated a large horticultural library, most of which she kept in her bedroom because she never had time to read during the day. With a guilty look at her cluttered office desk she withdrew there and began pulling books out of shelves. The counterpane was soon littered with likely volumes, full of fascinating but irrelevant information.

In 1576, she read, Lobelius in his *Plantarum Stirpium Historia* had described "a pregnant English lady who having eaten ten or twelve nutmegs, became deliriously intoxicated." ... In ancient China, it seemed, cannabis was predominantly a medical plant, used to treat gout, "female disorders," rheumatism, malaria, constipation and absent-mindedness, and the task of sorting out the species in the genus *Cannabacae* had been begun by the great Lamarck himself and extended by the Russian botanist Janislevsky in 1924 ... *Cannabis sativa*, the tall plant of northern areas, was used primarily for the fibre in its stem ... what was this book she was reading? Embolen, of course.* She was sure this was where she had read about how hallucinogenic drugs made people mix up colours with sounds.

Presently she found it. Time, consciousness of self, space and the perception of the physical world, all these

*William Embolen: *Narcotic Plants.* Cassell, London, 1979.

could change under the influence of the drug. The subject became acutely sensitive to colour and sound, and a possible effect was synaesthesia, in which the senses were confused with each other, so that a perfume became red and the sound of a bell in the distance a vivid blue. Richard Galliant had perceived his daughter Wanda's shrieks as an unpleasant purple, but what was the drug involved? Unfortunately Embolen's remarks applied to all hallucinogens, which was unhelpful.

The hallucinated motorcyclist still eluded her. She was sure she had read about him recently, where though? Despair set in, coupled with a malaise which she diagnosed, on thinking it over, as hunger caused by the omission of lunch. She rectified this with odds and ends from the refrigerator, made coffee and remembered: the book was not on the shelves upstairs, it was one she had bought last Christmas intending to give it to a medical student nephew, then found too interesting to give away. Where was it? Right beside her, she discovered, on the kitchen shelf devoted to cookery books, a strange but not necessarily illogical place for a reference book on poisonous plants.†

Here was the quotation she was looking for, under the heading "Symptoms of Poisoning." "The patient stated that he had had difficulty in negotiating a path through the white lines on the road with his motorcycle, because they kept jumping about and lashing at his legs. . . . Such hallucinations occur as a rule 2–4 hours after taking the poison and may continue for several days. The occasionally observed tendency to undress and/or look for open water is probably a consequence of hyperthermia."

Hyperthermia? That meant feeling too hot, and it explained something that had puzzled her about the story of Belling's dismissal. March seemed an extraordinary time of year to wander round one's garden in nothing but a dressing gown, hanging open despite the protests of a

†*A Colour Atlas of Poisonous Plants*, by Dietrich Frohne and Hans Jürgen Pfänder, translated from the second German edition by N.G. Bisset, Wolfe Publications, London 1984.

shocked gardener, and afterwards going to sleep in a deck chair on the lawn. But all was explained if the drug had made him feel intolerably hot. To judge from the family's reaction his dip in the lily pool was not the first time he had undressed to cool off in open water. Equally significant, he had felt threatened by weeds, on the paths in the rose garden, tangling round his ankles, just as the motorcyclist had felt threatened by the white lines on the road.

What drug had produced these effects in the cases cited by the two authors? *Datura stramonium*, the Thorn Apple or Jimson Weed. There was a celebrated passage about its effects in Robert Beverly's *History and Present State of Virginia*. Published in 1676, it was one of the early references to the Thorn Apple, and all the authorities quoted it. She looked it up:

The James-Town Weed, which resembles the Thorny Apple of Peru . . . is supposed to be one of the greatest Coolers in the world. This being an early Plant, was gathered very young for a boiled Salad, by some of the Soldiers . . . and some of them ate plentifully of it, the effect of which was a very pleasant Comedy; for they turned natural Fools upon it for several days: One would blow up a Feather in the Air; another would dart Straws at it with much Fury, and another stark naked was sitting up in a Corner like a Monkey, grinning and making Mows at them. A Fourth would fondly kiss and paw his Companions, and snear in their faces, with a Countenance more antick, than any in a Dutch Droll. In this frantic Condition they were confined, lest they should in their Folly destroy themselves; though it was observed, that all their Actions were full of Innocence and good Nature. Indeed they were not very cleanly: for they would have wallowed in their own Excrements if not prevented. A Thousand such simple tricks they play'd, and after Eleven Days returned to themselves again, not rememb'ring anything that had passed.

But of course it was most unlikely that Galliant was being poisoned with Thorn Apple. To begin with, it was an American plant which occurred only occasionally in the wild in Britain. Keble Martin listed it as "introduced, very poisonous." Finding it would be the first problem, and it flowered in June and July, which meant that the thorny seed capsules, which packed most of the punch, would not be ripe till August. One had to imagine someone deciding over a year ago to poison Richard Galliant, and sowing Thorn Apple seed so that it could be harvested in the autumn ready for use this spring. And why, Celia asked herself, am I assuming that a plant poison is involved? Because of my bias towards horticulture. There must be chemical hallucinogens which produce the same effect. But how would one get hold of them?

What on earth was Joan Galliant up to? If I was in her place, she thought, I wouldn't make this great carry-on about the publicity angle. Why is she erecting this wall of silence as if hushing the thing up was all she cared about? If it was happening to my husband I'd be hell-bent on finding out who was drugging him and why, and I'd wonder whether the poisoner knew enough about the correct dosage of the drug to avoid doing permanent damage. Or was Joan Galliant perhaps so slow on the uptake that she had failed to grasp what was going on? Why had she not called in the police and moved heaven and earth to get the thing stopped long ago, instead of letting Galliant stagger from crisis to crisis and try to embrace the Princess of Wales?

Does she know who is drugging her husband? And is she protecting the culprit, unwilling to denounce him or her? Or is she after all drugging her husband herself, like a wicked royal mother plotting to oust her husband and instal her son by a previous marriage on the throne? Charles Langley looked too solid a citizen to be credible as a usurper, but he seemed competent and was probably ambitious, and appearances were deceptive. Was he in the plot with her? However that might be, the facts pointed to one clear conclusion: her conduct was only understandable if she knew and approved of the poisoning, or at least believed it was an inside job by someone close to her who had to be protected. If she suspected, for example, that a rival firm was trying to ruin Richard Galliant & Co. she would be raising the roof and to hell with the adverse publicity.

But what was the point of arguing round and round in circles like this? The whole structure was built on the flimsiest guesswork. It was a fascinating problem, but a very unsatisfactory one because the family concerned seemed determined not to have it solved and without their co-operation there was little or no hope of making progress. Celia reminded herself that her only responsibility in the matter was to make the garden at the Old Rectory look like the Chelsea Flower Show in time for the Galliants' party.

Teresa Enriquez looked again at the engraved invitation card. ". . . On Sunday 15th June, to meet Miss Teresa Enriquez and members of the cast of Mozart's *The Marriage of Figaro* . . ." Richard had always said he would give a party in her honour if ever she came to sing at Glyndebourne, and it would probably be a good one, he had the showoff's talent for giving a large party well. But the card said: "Mr. and Mrs. Richard Galliant request the pleasure . . ." and that was a disagreeable surprise. Why were they still keeping up appearances? She had assumed that they would already be living apart.

She had found the card waiting for her two days ago when she flew in from New York. There were also flowers from Richard, with an affectionate note. According to Pilar, her dresser, maid and travelling companion, someone sounding like him had phoned yesterday while she was at Glyndebourne being shown round by George Christie, the owner of the opera house, and meeting the people she would be working with. As Pilar had no English and Richard no Spanish, the conversation between them had not got very far, but he would probably phone again.

As far as she was concerned that could hardly happen too soon, they had not met since *Norma* in Rome, and that had been for only two days. It was the first time in Buenos Aires that she treasured as a special memory, though some of the meetings in between had been good too. But they had been snatched moments when a singing engagement of hers coincided with a business trip of his. This time it would be different; the rehearsals and performances would keep her here for six weeks, with long hours in between for idyllic dalliance in this green English countryside. She had rented a furnished country house for the purpose. With this morning's sunshine streaming in through the windows, it had reminded her excitingly of a set for Violetta's country retreat in the second act of *Traviata*, which she had sung in last winter in Vienna.

Singers she had met on the international circuit had spoken affectionately of Glyndebourne, and when she saw it for the first time yesterday afternoon, she had understood why. A gracious country mansion of mellow red brick stood in a very English garden of small enclosures and spreading lawns surrounded by sweeping curves of downland: compared with most opera houses a marvellously peaceful setting in which to work. When the management showed her round the theatre complex, built on at the back of the house, she was surprised to find how large it was, with a very well-equipped stage and a huge scene dock. But the auditorium was tiny, holding less than eight hundred, there would be no need to force one's voice. The stage was very well equipped and there were plenty of rehearsal rooms. Her guided tour ended in the historic Organ Room, where the beautiful proportions and fine furniture and pictures made her exclaim with pleasure. It was the main reception room of the house and George Christie, the son of Glyndebourne's founder, explained that it had seen Glyndebourne's first beginnings, in the shape of semi-amateur performances organized by his father. The idea of building on an opera house had occurred to him after his marriage to Audrey Mildmay, the opera singer, whose portrait hung in one of the foyers. She had commented that if he was going to spend all that money he ought to "do the thing properly." To judge by Glyndebourne's international standing fifty years later, he had.

She had never sung there before, partly because their scale of fees was modest compared with the enormous sums that a coloratura soprano of her international standing commanded; and partly because the three weeks of rehearsal they insisted on, followed by the three weeks of performances, would immobilize her when she could be earning good money elsewhere. But because Richard Galliant was such an attractive man and lived in Sussex, she had put out feelers suggesting that she might be available for, say, the Countess in *The Marriage of Figaro*. The Glyndebourne management was surprised but delighted, and that was that.

Riding down to Glyndebourne, in the car they had sent to collect her, she was nervous. Today was to be her first working day of rehearsals, and she wondered what lay ahead. In a sense she was slumming, but a performance was a performance and one had to do oneself credit. Glyndebourne had a high reputation musically and she had heard good reports of Karel Wenzel, who was to conduct, but the producer looked alarmingly untidy as well as young. Was he one of the tyrannical young producers who insisted that opera must be "relevant," not a museum art but one with a message for today? That was all very well, but relevance often seemed to involve singing while lying on one's stomach with one's head facing upstage. What tricks would this young man get up to? Another such young man had once made her sing the Countess in modern dress, made up and bewigged to resemble Jacqueline Kennedy Onassis, with the lustful Count and Susanna chasing each other round the stage disguised as John Kennedy and Marilyn Monroe lookalikes in a first act set which was a faithful reproduction of the Oval Office.

Costume designs were produced for her inspection, and reassured her. At least they were sticking to the right century.

"The Countess, you see her how?" she enquired.

"Is not a grandmother," Wenzel replied. "Is not a heavy

Wagner lady with big waist and solemn voice. Is light, is graceful."

"That's right," the producer added. "She was under age when she married the Count, I doubt if she's much more than eighteen now."

That was fine, as far as Teresa was concerned. She was forty-seven, but she had kept her figure and in a good wig she could still summon up enough youth and *beauté de scène* to get by on stage. But the young producer was stealing worried glances at her, as though he did not believe it.

"Our lighting man is first class," he said unnervingly.

"Countess is full of fun, Madame, is sparkling," said Wenzel.

Fine, but that view of the role ran into a difficulty at the outset. How was the unfortunate girl to sparkle during her first aria, "Porgi amor," a lament for the loss of her husband's love, set to a melody so sad and haunting that it was usually taken at a funeral pace?

"Okay, but you make 'Porgi amor' not too much *larghetto*," she insisted.

Wenzel nodded eagerly. "We take it a little fast, and after the pause, when come those semiquavers, I slow down for you."

She threw him a shocked look. "No, why? I take them *al tempo*."

Did he really think they would be too much for her if he kept to the brisk beat he intended to start with? He was wrong, with an effort she could still manage them. But the suggestion unnerved her.

The morning passed quickly, with wardrobe fittings and consultations of one kind or another. Over lunch in the canteen, with other members of the cast, she was first surprised, then pleased to find herself being treated undeferentially as a member of the club and not as an overpaid international prima donna. But she eyed her stage husband, the Count Almaviva, nervously. He was young and built like a prize ox. Would he bellow and drown her?

53

After lunch she and the Count and Susanna settled down to rehearse their first concerted number. "We take number thirteen, *terzetto*," said Wenzel, and turned to her with a trace of embarrassment. "Concerning that old problem, bar one hundred fifteen, and again bar one hundred thirty...?" He left the question hanging in the air.

She looked at the score, puzzled. "This 'old problem,' what is it?"

He looked even more embarrassed. "I think perhaps you ... find it more comfortable not to bother with them?"

She saw now what he meant. At two points the Countess had a tricky run up to a high C, and in the old days a custom had grown up of giving them to the Susanna to sing, because the heavier-voiced, less vocally agile Countesses who were then the norm found them difficult. Now that lyric sopranos like herself were singing coloratura roles there was no problem.

"No! Me, I sing them," she said firmly. "You watch me, how I sparkle."

This insulting suggestion had never been put to her, why was Wenzel making it now? He must have heard her somewhere on an off night. There had been rather a lot of them lately. Suddenly she understood, it was as if the ground had opened up under her. They thought she was on the way down, near the end of her singing career, and had offered to come to Glyndebourne because the house was small and would not put too much strain on a voice she was no longer sure of. Wenzel had looked disappointed when she insisted on taking the high Cs, thinking perhaps that it would be even more embarrassing to transfer them to Susanna when she failed to produce them.

The rehearsal began. "Brutissima la cosa," she sang. The situation was indeed *brutissima* and she was not referring to her stage predicament, with her half-undressed page locked in her dressing-room and her husband threatening to break down the door.

The terrible truth was, Wenzel was right. She had ceased to be sure of her voice, it was not what it was. She knew it, and it would soon be obvious to others. She was haunted by the memory of poor Maria Callas fussing about the lights and acting everyone else off the stage to hide the fact that her voice was in ruins, and cancelling at short notice when it was so unreliable that she was terrified to go on. She would stop before she got to that point, but it would be on her very soon, and then what was to happen?

Richard Galliant was going to supply the answer to that question; or so she hoped. She intended to marry him. That was why she had come to sing at Glyndebourne.

Celia bought every newspaper she could lay hands on at the village shop and conned them hurriedly over breakfast. They all reported an announcement from Richard Galliant & Co.'s London office to the effect that their chairman's trouble had been traced to a rare allergy, which was now under control. It was a matter of opinion whether this fiction was an improvement on the previous one alleging a stomach upset. One or two science correspondents had taken it seriously enough to provide learned background material on allergies, ergotism, migraines and other irrelevancies, but the stock market had taken a more sceptical view and the company's shares had taken a steep nosedive. According to a report by Tim Price in one of the papers, a lorry driver heading for London on the A27 had given a lift in the small hours to a man in bedroom slippers who corresponded to Galliant's description and had talked nonsense. Joan Galliant seemed to have done a workmanlike job of laughing this to scorn without actually denying it, but it could not be said that Richard Galliant & Co. had had a good press.

Having spent far too long studying the papers, Celia set out late and with a guilty conscience on an expedition into darkest Hampshire, where a rose-grower had promised her some container-grown *Madame Abel Chatenays*, *Grandpa Dicksons* and *Icebergs* in full bud, which were available because an order to decorate a fertilizer firm's stand at an agricultural show had been cancelled. There was also a hope of extorting from another firm such delphiniums as might be surplus to requirements for its stand at an RHS show in June, and she had heard rumours of violas going cheap from a grower who was bankrupt.

While she headed for Hampshire, Bill Wilkins set off for Faringfield, taking a labour force of two strapping girls with him to finish clearing the ground so that the results of her scrounging could be planted out. The girls chattered and giggled but took no notice of him, nor he of them. He had made it clear long ago that there was nothing doing, and they had even stopped sneaking hungry looks at his profile when they thought he wouldn't notice. He was in a grouchy mood. Celia was involved in a mystery at the busiest time of year at the nursery, with the extra sweat of the Faringfield caper on top of that. She was clever as a cartload of performing monkeys, but this was a hard one to crack and he saw no hope of her cracking it and saving Anthea's job. Meanwhile, the routine work of the nursery would get dramatically behind.

But the real bind was, he and Anthea were going through a bad patch, the worst since she threw up her job in London and ended up as Richard Galliant's personal assistant in Faringfield. When he heard that she'd fixed up Archerscroft Nurseries with the Old Rectory contract, he'd thought fine, that's really neat. I'll finish there for the day, go down the village to the cottage, have me home comforts there with Anthea and be on the spot good and fresh for work next morning. Weekends would be longer too. But somehow it hadn't worked out. Not tonight, she'd said, I've a rush job on for Richard, or I need to wash my hair, or I've an auntie coming for the weekend who'd be shocked, one excuse after another. They'd had two quick, hectic lunch hours together, that was all, and Anthea had spent them in his arms clutching at him hungrily, the way she did when she felt scary about herself and needed him to make her feel warm and safe. No wonder she was frightened, what with Galliant cocking everything up, and her job on the line along with everyone else's in the firm.

You'd think this would be one of the times when she needed him, so why was she making all these excuses? At lunch time today he would try to make her give sex a rest and tell him what was the matter.

Helped by the girls, he worked his way steadily along the two borders, and barrowed rubbish and weeds to a corner of the vegetable garden. He and Celia had been delighted to discover in the same corner two huge, well rotted compost heaps. If they were George Belling's work he was a pro who knew his business. Rather than return the barrows empty, they started taking back loads of compost and dumping it on the borders, ready to fork in.

Half way through the morning the Galliants' Chinese cook brought them out mugs of tea, and looked worried when she saw that they were helping themselves to compost. "You leave me some, I need," she said. "Come. I show you."

She led them to the far end of the vegetable garden. A patch had been cleared of weeds and rotting cabbage stalks and dug over. Shoots of some vegetable that Bill did not recognize had begun to appear. "I do this, need vegetables," she explained, then pointed at the compost heaps. "Need this for vegetables."

"Okay lady, we leave you some," he assured her.

"You leave me plentee for my vegetables," she commanded, and trudged back to the house.

Bill went back to work. Presently Anthea came running into the garden from the stable yard, looking nervously over her shoulder as if she was afraid of being seen. "Don't be cross, Gorgeous, I can't meet you for lunch."

Bill struggled to keep his temper. "What's up then? Why not?"

"Panic in the office. All hands to the pump."

"Oh Anthea. What's wrong? Excuses all the time, you're not being straight. You going sour on me?"

"No, damn you, of course not and it's not an excuse, it's genuine."

"What's the big panic then?"

"Wanda's keys have gone missing again."

"So?"

"There are only three keys to the studio and she has one of them. Every so often her keys go missing and one of our designs gets stolen. Pritchard and Colson come out with a near-copy of it the moment we put it on the market."

"Who's Pritchard and Colson?"

"The firm that Richard's ex-wife works for, she thinks he behaved badly over the divorce. This is her revenge. They steal our designs and bring out something just different enough not to be sued for breach of copyright. Richard's cleared everyone out of the studio and he and Wanda and I have to take turns to mount guard up there till the locksmith arrives to change the lock on the door."

"Oh Anthea love, I'm sorry I grouched, that was naughty of me. But there's things I don't understand, we must talk."

"Oh Gorgeous, must we really? Come to the cottage then, for a drink around six."

"Why only a drink? One of the girls can drive the van back, I can stay."

"No, Gorgeous love. Sorry."

"Why the hell not?"

She thought for a moment. "Mrs. Galliant says the village doesn't approve of people living openly in sin, and she's not having Richard's personal assistant setting a bad example."

"What right has she got?" Bill shouted. "Anyway I don't believe it." But Anthea had darted away.

Thoroughly upset by her behaviour, he went to the Red Lion with the two girl gardeners for a snack lunch, but could not stomach their idiotic chatter. As soon as he had bolted his sandwich and half-pint of bitter, he left them and wandered back to the Old Rectory. Cutting through the stable yard to the garden he heard music he approved of coming from somewhere close at hand, and went nearer to listen. A tricky rhythm track, more like jazz-funk than rock, with a lot of slick instrumental breaks and a vocalist who took up the rhythm and did interesting things with it instead of belting out a straight one two three four. He recognized the group from its style. Its name was Dark Speedway and the vocalist was Caradoc Watney.

Whoever was listening to this had taste, Dark Speedway was one of Bill's favourites. Exploring, he traced the sound to its source, the open front window of the staff cottage. He looked in. There, watching a video of himself in action amid flashing lights and banks of synthesizers, was Caradoc Watney in person.

"They'll never catch me," his videoed image sang in a high, terrified wail, "'cos I don't know who I am."

Brilliant, Bill thought. He had felt just like that ten years ago, when he left home for the first time to work in London: not sure who he was, terrified of "them," consoled by a vague hope that "they" wouldn't see him because he didn't really exist as a person.

The vocal ended, and the lead guitarist took over, reinforcing the mood in a panic-stricken instrumental accompanied by agonized cross-beats on the drums and guitar.

"That's great," said Bill, and meant it.

"He does an even better one later," said Watney without taking his eyes from the screen. "Watch out for it after the middle eight."

He was right, it was even better, ending in a strange echoing wail on the synthesizers.

"How do they do that?" Bill asked.

"You can programme a Yamaha DX to do anything on a cartridge. This is the promotion video for my new single, being released next month, you like it?"

"It's great. You're Caradoc Watney, right?"

"Right, but Caradoc is for onstage. Offstage I'm plain Fred. Come on in."

"You live here?"

"No." He made a sweeping gesture. "My squat's a dirty great manor house that my agent bought for me five miles away over there, but my cow of a wife went off with the guitarist from Holy Terror and I come here for company.

This is Paul Galliant's place." He raised his voice. "Hey Paul, we got a visitor."

Paul Galliant appeared from the kitchen, carrying a frying-pan full of something that gave off blue smoke. "Hi, whoever you are. You want some?"

"I'm Bill. No thanks, I've eaten."

"You into singing or playing?" Fred asked.

"No. I garden."

Paul Galliant looked at him. "Oh yeah, I saw you around. Clearing up after my shocking delinquent behaviour, disgraceful, wasn't it? His poor parents wanted their dreadful drop-out to look after their bloody garden and turn over a new leaf and grow a halo, so they set him up in the staff cottage, not wanting him in the house because of his insanitary habits—"

"He smokes," Fred explained with a put-down intonation.

Paul threw him a sharp look, then went back to the kitchen to transfer the contents of the frying-pan to plates. While he was doing this Wanda Galliant came rushing in.

"Paul? Oh my God, where is he? My keys have gone again, father's furious. Are they here?"

Paul appeared in the doorway carrying two plates. "I dunno, dearie, have a look." He put the food on the table and he and Fred started to eat.

"They were here last time."

"I know, Wanda dear, you must try not to be so careless."

"It's not carelessness, you know that. Someone takes them and gets into the studio and steals our designs, and then the keys turn up in places where I could easily have left them."

"But Wanda dear, if you weren't so careless no one would have a chance to take your keys."

"I know, but I can't help it. I get interested in something else and I forget. You can't spend your whole life watching your keys. Oh, do help me, father's in one of his states and he sent me to see if they're here."

Fred and Paul exchanged shrugs. Paul picked up the platefuls of food with a martyred look. "I'll put these back to keep hot, but really Wanda dear, you are a fiendish nuisance."

He and Fred began an exaggeratedly thorough search, sniggering as they peered between the pages of pop magazines and in other unlikely places. Embarrassed, Bill followed Wanda into the kitchen and helped her search there and in the bedrooms upstairs. The keys were not to be found.

"They wouldn't be, would they Wanda dear?" said Paul heavily. "The joker that takes them always keeps them for twenty-four hours before he leaves them around for you to find, he wants to use them first. You didn't think of that, did you? Go and tell our silly old father to calm down and stop creating."

Wanda gave a gulp of despair and went. Bill noticed the time with a shock and returned to the garden, where the two girls had seen no reason for starting work again without him. He started digging again fiercely, feeling very sorry for stupid meek Wanda Galliant and very angry with the two men.

Presently he was attacked by a furious Susie, who complained shrilly that he and the girls had helped themselves far too greedily to the compost and left too little for her vegetables. This was nonsense, they had left enough to mulch twice the area that Susie had planted up, but she was not to be pacified and trudged away into the house muttering ominously.

Bill was embarrassed. Celia had impressed on him that Archerscroft Nurseries could not afford to be on bad terms with the Galliant household. She would have the hide off him if he got on the wrong side of Susie. Fortunately there was another compost heap in the far corner, not rotted down yet. Fresh kitchen refuse had been dumped very recently on top. He poked about in it, and decided that the bottom half was usable. "We'll turn it over for her," he told the girls. "Take the top off and put it on one side and leave her the rest."

All would have been well if this had been explained to Susie at once, but a diversion made him forget. Celia arrived with her pickup full of horticultural loot which had to be admired. Shortly afterwards a truckful of Regale lilies appeared and had to be unloaded at once. By the time he and Celia had sorted all this out it was too late. Susie, returning to the vegetable garden with a basinful of kitchen refuse, had found one of the Archerscroft girls decapitating her precious heap, with the obvious intention of stealing the good stuff underneath and using it for her wicked purposes in the flower garden. Unstoppable screams of rage rent the air as Susie, gesticulating violently, snatched the fork from the thieving girl and began to put the unrotted top back on the heap.

Bill began to explain to Susie, and tried to calm her down. He would have liked a bit of moral support from Celia, but she seemed to be otherwise engaged.

Celia was staring down at something lying among the scattered kitchen refuse from the top of the heap. Flowers large, pendulous, she murmured to herself. Calyx spathe-like or toothed, not circumscissile at the base . . . there were two of them. They were pendulous, so they could not be Thorn Apple flowers which were upward-pointing, and anyway Thorn Apples would not be in flower at this time of year. But they were unmistakably flowers produced by a member of the same family. There was foliage too, and chopped up bits of a woody stem.

Had Susie seen all this too? She was forking everything back feverishly on to the top of the compost heap. Celia was too astonished to stop her. It was unbelievable. If appearances could be relied on, someone in the Galliant household had chopped up a healthy specimen of one of the tropical tree daturas and thrown it out to rot down among their kitchen refuse.

❧ FIVE ❧

Celia had hurried home and surrounded herself with reference books. The more she read about the genus datura, the more alarmed she became. The daturas were all *Solanaceae*, a family which also included among others mandrake, deadly nightshade, tobacco (the source of nicotine, which in concentrated form could kill in minutes), and henbane or *Hyoscyamnus niger*, of which Frohne and Pfänder remarked that its old German name, "Altsitzerkraut," was "a reminder that in the country it was occasionally used to help 'useless old people who were just sitting around' into the next world," despite the fact that its "unpleasant smell and the sticky nature of the plant make it understandable why man and animals . . . usually avoid it." With the exception of the tobacco plant with its nicotine, the other lethal members of this jolly family all contained ester alkaloids of the tropane group, whatever they might be. The main ones in the daturas were hyoscyamine, said to produce "madness and terrifying sombre hallucinations"; hyoscine, which had a sedative effect on the central nervous system, and atropine, which could cause death within 24 hours as a result of coma and respiratory paralysis. The proportion of atropine in the Thorn Apple was much less than in deadly nightshade, and the likelihood of killing one's victim correspondingly less. But did this apply to the tropical daturas? Evidently not. The whole genus was notoriously lethal, the most frequently used means of murder and suicide on the Indian sub-continent, and capable of inflicting permanent brain damage on people unwise enough to experiment with them for kicks.

She was astonished to discover the variety of uses to which the whole family was put. Daturas were or had been used by Russian thieves to stupefy their victims, by prostitutes in India to rob their clients, by primitive tribes in Latin America to intoxicate adolescents during their rites of passage, by American Indians as a cure for rattlesnake venom, and by a tribe in Colombia to drug widows so that they did not make a fuss when being buried alive with their late husbands. The seeds were the part normally used, either disguised in food or in a solution derived from them which could be added to drink.

That brought one slap up against a difficulty. The plant chopped up and hidden in the compost heap at the Old Rectory was in flower. There would be no question of it producing seed for several weeks. That suggested that other parts of the plant must have been used on Richard Galliant, but they would be far more difficult to disguise. Assuming for the sake of argument that the flowers or leaves were narcotic enough to make him misbehave so grossly, how could he have been persuaded to eat them? What did they taste of, and how could they be disguised?

They couldn't, this is ridiculous, she decided. Then she remembered what Richard Galliant had had for lunch: a prawn cocktail.

A light lunch, Wanda had said, consisting of a prawn cocktail followed by cheese and biscuits. It other words a few frozen prawns mixed up with a lot of greenery and smothered in a pink vinegary gunge that would disguise the taste of anything.

Having solved that problem to her satisfaction she plunged into the reference books again. Most of the oriental mischief seemed to have been achieved with the help of the herbaceous species, notably *D. metel*. But the plant in the compost heap was definitely not *D. metel*. It was one of the tree daturas, the only tropical species normally cultivated in Britain as an ornamental. Were their leaves and flowers damaging? According to Frohne and Pfänder the flowers certainly were. They reported a case in which "... Two fifteen-year-old boys were found by the police wandering naked and delirious through a field. It emerged later that they had eaten five or six flowers of *Datura suaveolens*." That was one of the tree daturas, evidently their flowers were narcotic, but what about the leaves? The only information in the book about their properties referred only to the ordinary Thorn Apple: "Horse dealers knew early on about the sales-promoting effect of this plant," said Frohne and Pfänder. "Even the most miserable worn-out nag will become as frisky as a thoroughbred when you stick a couple of rolled-up leaves up its rectum."

She remembered now. The basic work on the datura family had been done by a geneticist called Blakeslee who died in 1954. His results were published by his team of assistants after his death, Roger must have had a copy ... Yes, here it was.*

Blakeslee had been interested mainly in *D. stramonium*, which he used as a vehicle for experiments in genetic engineering. He and his assistants had made separate analyses of alkaloid content of its leaves, flowers, seeds, roots, and stems and gave the hyoscine, hyoscamine and atropine content of each as a percentage of dry weight. They had also compiled and recorded similar analyses of the tropical daturas made at various times, but only the herbaceous ones. When it came to the tree daturas, fatigue and boredom seemed to have set in. No one seemed to have bothered to find out which bits of the plants contained what percentage of what. Of *D. sanguinea*, for instance, all that Day and Foster had discovered in 1953 was:

*Blakeslee: *The Genus Datura*, Various authors, Ronald Press Co., New York, 1959

Hyoscine	0.35 in aerial parts
	0.2 in roots.
Hyoscyamine	0.02 in aerial parts
	0.4 in roots.

Several alkaloids not characterised with certainty.

Of *D. suaveolens*, the one most commonly cultivated in northern greenhouses, Simoes (1951) merely said "hyoscyamine, 0.1."

On reading further in the reference books, she discovered a possible reason for this lack of enthusiasm for the tree daturas. They had been so messed about by hybridization that they were of no interest to serious geneticists;† hybridization not by Western horticultural man but by tribesmen in their habitat in the High Andes, who crossbred them to produce improved strains with even greater stupefying qualities. For this reason "these daturas are imperfectly known to botanists . . . each species varies with respect to the concentration of these alkaloids, but they are all in abundance in most parts of the plant." In other words there was no means of knowing how successful the tribesmen had been in hyping up the stupefying effect of whatever plant had been used on Richard Galliant.

She was still deep in the subject when Bill looked in on her to settle the work schedule for next day. It was almost nine o'clock. He had stayed on after her at Faringfield to keep his drinks date with Anthea.

"How was she?" Celia asked.

"Okay. . ." he said, and thought that's a lie, it was a catastrophe like last time, a frantic meeting of bodies and no meeting of minds. He had tried to discuss the Galliant mystery and her position in the firm, but she would have none of

†But the geneticists have been arguing since 1805 about whether they are genuine daturas or a separate genus, and what they should be called. For a time they were threatened with the insulting generic name of Pseudo-datura, but a school of thought seems to have prevailed which calls them brugmansias, a name snatched away summarily from another group of plants which have been given it "in error."

it. In the end, when he got stroppy trying to find out what was wrong, she had burst into floods of tears and screamed at him hysterically to get out. But he couldn't tell Celia that.

"She worries," he added when Celia looked sceptical. "Her job's getting dodgier and dodgier. The firm's in dead trouble and she knows it." He noticed the reference books scattered round the room. "You been looking up that plant?"

"Yes, and I want to ask you something. What did you make of Susie's behaviour when it turned up in that kitchen rubbish?"

"I been wondering about that. It was funny, how she forked everything back on to the top of the compost heap. Frantic about it she was, like the devil forking naughty people into hell."

"Why, Bill? Was she just defending her beloved compost against yet more thievery by us? Or was she trying to cover up the incriminating evidence before we saw it?"

"It was that. She'd been fussing all day about us helping ourselves to it. She would, if she knew there was something dodgy in it."

"That doesn't follow. I'd fuss if someone came along and helped themselves to too much of my compost."

"D'you reckon she knew what it was when she saw it?"

"Her face didn't tell one anything. But daturas are used for all sorts of unspeakable purposes in the Far East. A Chinese woman with centuries of peasant culture behind her would recognize one at once."

"Oh Celia, there's no centuries of peasant culture behind Susie, she's a townee. According to Anthea she comes from Hong Kong. Anthea says Colonel Langley, that's Joan Galliant's first husband, he was stationed there once and Morris was his driver. He married Susie and they went everywhere with the Colonel afterwards, wherever he was posted. When he retired he kept them on and Joan Galliant did too, after he died."

This was interesting. Morris and his wife had arrived at the Old Rectory in the retinue of the second Mrs. Galliant, like the Italians in the train of Catherine de Medici when she arrived in France as a bride. "Which means," Celia said, "that their loyalty is to Joan Galliant, not to her husband."

"That's right. Anthea says they'd cut your throat soon as look at you if she told them to."

Celia remembered that Catherine de Medici's Italians had been very unpopular at the French court. In the same way the staff at Galliant's probably regarded the Morrises as Joan Galliant's private mafia and the source of all evil, but was that justified? Again, it depended on how you interpreted Susie's behaviour during the scene of discovery by the compost heap.

"I dunno," said Bill. "Them Chinese are so po-faced you can't tell what they're thinking. Inscrutable, it's called."

"The whole gang is being inscrutable behind its Great Wall of Silence, like the Central Committee in Peking. That's understandable if they're really plotting to oust Richard Galliant to make room for Charles Langley, but are they?"

"I dunno," Bill repeated. "Would you poison someone and throw out the evidence with the kitchen rubbish?"

"I think I'd consider it a reasonable risk. It wasn't foreseeable that the remains would be brought to light before they'd had time to rot down."

"The risk would be less if someone else had put it there. They'd say, well it's a bit dodgy, but if anyone finds it they'll point the finger at the Galliants, not me."

"True enough," said Celia, "but who are the other possible risk-takers?"

"Paul, for one," said Bill promptly. "Easy as falling off a piece of cake. That cottage of his is right next door to the vegetable garden."

This reminded Celia that Bill had spent some time in Paul's cottage and she asked for details of his discoveries there. As he reported on the loss of Wanda's keys and the resulting scare about design-copying, she made mental notes of various questions she would put to Anthea about this, then made him describe the set up at the cottage.

"Are Fred and Paul what you call 'okay'?" On this question, Bill was infallible.

"Oh yes, Celia. Straight as rifle barrels, both of them. Fred had a wife, but she ran out on him."

"Probably because Fred likes his cannabis."

"No. Not Fred."

"But when I went in there that night he was lying on the floor in a daze. I smelt it."

"It's not him you smelt, it was Paul Galliant. His bedroom pongs of it, I was up there searching for Wanda's keys."

"Fred could be having it too."

Bill thought about this. "I'd be surprised. He made a remark about Paul 'smoking,' a bit contemptuous as if he disapproved, Paul didn't like that. Besides, rock musicians need to be clean when they go through customs, or they're in trouble."

"But Fred was in a daze."

"You'd be in a daze all day if you spent your nights yelling your head off under them flashing lights."

"What sort of pop star is he?"

"One of the good ones, a lot of them are rubbish. The backing's always interesting, neat rhythms and so on, and the words often mean something. I think he must have changed managements a few years back, before that he was into the Heavy Metal stuff."

"I'm sorry, could you explain?"

"A big heavy beat, bang bang bang bang, leather armbands with spikes on them and a lot of muscles showing, and words that didn't make much sense. It was very crude and brutal, they knew just what they was doing, stirring up the nastiness in people and trying to whip the fans up. And look at the name, Dark Speedway."

"'Speed' being slang for heroin or something?"

"That's right, and there was a rumour that if you played the tape backwards it was all obscene, a sort of black mass, but that may have been just a publicity story to make their image even nastier."

"But now he's a reformed character, musically speaking?" said Celia.

"Or it could be just, the rock scene's moved on and he's cleaned up the act to stay in the fashion. He's still a nasty person, look at the way he and Paul treat Wanda."

"Is he Paul's evil genius?"

"Them two are both evil, I dunno about the genius."

"But Bill, why do they bully the wretched Wanda like that?"

"She's the victim type, the sort that takes whatever her menfolk hand out to her and never complains. Nasty people enjoy handing it out to them."

"Yes. Wanda's a brilliant textile designer and he's a flop at everything he touches. Paul's jealous and he's discovered that she's easy to manipulate."

"Or it could be his way of getting at his dad," Bill suggested.

"Oh. You mean, drop-out son hates father for being brilliant and successful, so he bamboozles daughter into issuing a damaging press statement."

"Oh yes Celia, and snitches her keys off of her so he can steal copies of her designs—"

"Which he sells to a rival firm where he has a contact—"

"That's right. The first Mrs. Galliant. His mum."

The next week passed in a flash. The Old Rectory job was only one of the things clamouring for Celia's attention, and she dared not upset Bill by letting the routine paperwork get behind. She spent most of the following weekend on it, and went to bed dog-tired on the Sunday night. But at two in the morning she was woken suddenly by her subconscious mind, which brought an urgent message to her attention; tree daturas, it said, had a heavy and distinctive scent, and there was a folk legend to the effect that anyone who slept under one of them and inhaled its scent all night would be stark staring mad by the morning.

She had known that in the back of her mind ever since the discovery of the datura remains in the compost heap. Why had it come to the surface now? For a very good reason, she realized. Some time during the past few weeks, she could not remember when, she had given a passing thought to that folk legend; because somewhere, she could not remember where, she had smelt a heavily scented datura.

No, I am imagining things, she told herself. I have been reading about daturas, and have conjured up the smell of one out of my disorderly subconscious mind, Sigmund Freud would be delighted with me.

But I remember thinking: do people who go to sleep under a datura really go mad? Why would I wonder about that unless I had really smelt one?

But I only smelt it, I didn't see it. I have no clear mental picture of it. It could have been a lily. They have roughly the same heavy, sweet scent. I could have smelt a lily and let my scatty mind wander till it thought about the perils of datura-sniffing.

Anyway where was this lily-datura thing? If I had seen it I would know which it was. I must have been busy with something else and sniffed and thought "there's a datura somewhere here" without looking at it. Where, though? Indoors somewhere. No one in their senses would put a tree datura outside when there was still a danger of frost, and no self-respecting lily would have been flowering out of doors in early May.

A glasshouse? At one of the nurserymen's I went to when I was ordering the planting for the Old Rectory job? With a mass of half-hardy things displayed on stages? So preoccupied with the problem of deciding what to order that I didn't look for the datura? Possible but unlikely. I was ordering lilies, among other things. I would have thought to myself "Ah, is that a lily I can smell?" and looked for it.

Where, then? Why do I associate the datura-smell with one of my excursions to Faringfield? Bill was with me when I smelt it. I was going to make some remark to him about it, but something else happened and I didn't. Where the hell was it, my brain really is rotting. If it was when we were working together at Faringfield, it must have been quite early on, if I'd smelt it after we found the datura in the compost heap it would have rung a bell at once and I wouldn't have pushed it down into my subconscious. But he came with me on that round of nurseries when we were deciding what to order. I could have smelt it anywhere in Surrey or Sussex.

Had he smelt it too? She would ask him when she got a chance. But now she must go to sleep again, or she would be like a rag in the morning. She must put the whole datura genus out of her mind, and stop giving herself indigestion by thinking about that appalling prawn cocktail. Tomorrow was going to be very busy, and she must be ready for it.

It certainly will be busy, she told herself as she walked from Sloane Square Underground next morning. But she was determined to get her business done today, before the grounds of the Royal Hospital in Chelsea were invaded by the mob. If she failed, she would have to face the horticultural rough and tumble of the Chelsea Flower Show when it opened its doors to a densely packed mass of members of the Royal Horticultural Society tomorrow.

Since horticulture had become a booming multi-million pound business, the grounds of the hospital founded by Charles II for his red-coated veterans, the Chelsea Pensioners, had become far too small to hold the main flower show of the British gardening year. There had been talk of moving it out of London. But nothing had been decided and the show consisted of too many people trying to see too many flowers in far too small a space and too many salesmen trying to sell anything from swimming pools to secateurs to people whose main hope was not to be trampled to death in the crowd. By opening time tomorrow, the whole area between the King's Road and the river would be choked with traffic, pedestrians would be overflowing into the roadway, and the inhabitants in the area would be resigning themselves to their annual week of misery and uproar.

But today, blessedly free from overcrowding, was the

so-called Special Day, devoted to judging the exhibits, hobnobbing among pundits, the press preview and other activities which would become impossible once overpopulation had set in. As a member of Floral Committee B, Celia had a minor role to perform in the judging, and also rated an invitation to the President's Lunch in the refreshment tent. But she had other more important priorities: to pick the brains of any pundit who really knew about daturas, and to buy plants to fill the yawning gaps in the long borders at Faringfield.

But first she and the other members of Floral Committee B had to decide which of 93 new varieties of bearded irises submitted by breeders merited a test at the Society's trial grounds at Wisley. Fortunately this task was made simple by a recent trend of opinion in iris-fancying circles to the effect that any iris which could not produce three terminal blooms to each spike, plus two each on two well-displayed branches, was "rubbish." This eliminated half the contestants, and repulsive colour, lack of scent, or blooms presented in a huddled mass brought the entries down to a manageable number, leaving Celia free to go the round of the stands in the huge marquee and pursue her other priorities.

On the last day of the show, plants used to make up the exhibits would be sold off. She began making her rounds, explaining her predicament to exhibitors she knew, and asking them to earmark what she needed and keep it back for her to collect when the show closed. Nothing herbaceous, a delphinium or a lily brought to perfection of flower for Chelsea would not perform well in a border after five days of being breathed on by huge crowds in a stifling marquee. Shrubs were a different matter. They were the only satisfactory way of giving height at the back, and she bought lilacs, rhododendrons, purple-leafed pittosporums and rhus, golden spireas; also helichrysums and artemisias for the front of the border, for she was a firm believer in grey-leaved foliage plants among the blocks of colour to cool the whole composition down.

Killing two birds with one stone, she put a question to

all her contacts: did anyone know of a grower who specialized in tree daturas? But she drew a blank, even with a
large firm specializing in house plants. Poinsettias, yes.
Dieffenbachias, yes. Even Clivias, yes, there was a limited
market for them. Tree daturas, no. Why should anyone
clutter up costly hot-house space with them? There was no
worthwhile demand. People grew a few in odd corners
when they had room, but as far as the trade knew, no one
specialized.

That was disappointing. She had hoped to find an obvious source, a firm that a poisoner wanting to buy a tree
datura would naturally apply to. But no, they were grown
in holes and corners all over the place, it would take weeks
to go round them all asking if anyone connected with Galliant & Co. had made a suspicious purchase. Besides, she
had hoped to consult a grower who really knew about the
thing that puzzled her most; according to the books the tree
daturas were summer flowering. How was it then that the
remains in the compost heap had included two flowers produced well before the end of May?

She looked around the huge marquee, crammed with
everything the ingenuity of man could make plants do,
from camellias kept in arctic conditions to hold back their
blooms till Chelsea, to serried ranks of potted clematis with
only one flower on each plant, the other buds having been
removed to ensure that the solitary bloom was enormous.
Surely there must be someone who would know the answer
to her question in the collection of amateur and profes-
sional expertise which had produced all this? A former colleague of Roger's from when he was on the staff at Kew?
Someone from one of the big house-plant firms or the top
brass of the Royal Horticultural Society itself? But none of
them were about. The aisles between the stands were almost empty of people. She realized the time with a shock.
She was about to be late for the President's Lunch, and
hurried out to the refreshment tent.

"Celia! How nice," said a voice across the table as she
sat down in her place. Opposite her was the owner of a

famous garden in Devon, whom she and Roger had stayed with often when Roger came down to advise from Kew.

"Can you force tree daturas into flower early?" she asked as soon as the decencies of conversation permitted.

"Never grow them. Nasty things, send you mad if you go to sleep under them."

Her other neighbours, all equally eminent in their fields, did not know either. The general reaction was, nobody had tried, and anyway, why would anyone want to?

Someone, somewhere had wanted to, Celia thought. The question was, why? She had hoped that Chelsea would provide her with a quick answer. But she had another, more time-consuming but quite hopeful line of enquiry up her sleeve. She would follow it up this afternoon, for there was no point in hanging around after the lunch broke up. Presently the Queen would arrive, accompanied by most of the Royal Family. Nothing else could happen while they went round the stands, and there would be no getting any sense out of the exhibitors, who would be worrying for hours beforehand about how to manoeuvre the name of the firm into shot for the television cameras as they were graciously taken notice of by royalty. Recklessly extravagant, she took a taxi to the unlikely looking starting point of her new line of enquiry, the wholesale-only showroom in Great Portland Street of "Lavinia Lure, Modes."

She had tried on a Lavinia Lure dress and jacket once, and taken it off again hastily, not having realized till then how easily she could be made to look like a superannuated tart. Perhaps because of this daunting experience, her eye had often been caught by the Lavinia Lure advertisements when leafing through *Vogue* under the drier at her hairdresser's. They always consisted of five or six pages of young women scowling, pouting, sticking out their stomachs or their bottoms, kicking up their legs in the air, and in general carrying on in the frenetic manner now considered appropriate when modelling trendy clothes. And to ram home the message that the clothes were slinky and exotic there was always at least one datura in the picture, often more.

Were they artificial? She thought not. If they were, the same ones could be used over and over again. But she had bought the current issue of *Vogue*, before leaving home, and the daturas in Lavinia Lure's "High Fashion for High Summer" were definitely different plants from the ones in their "Salute to Spring" in the two-month-old issue she had seen at the hairdresser's. Yet they were in full bloom too, and so were the ones in their "Glitter for Autumn," as far as she remembered. Did Lavinia Lure photograph all the clothes for the year in a marathon session while they were in flower? If not, they must have a source of forced daturas. She marched into the shop to ask.

When she explained her business she was shown into an inner office containing a comfortable-looking middle-aged woman with no pretensions to chic.

"Oh no, dear, they weren't plastic," she said in answer to Celia's query. "I can't bear plastic flowers. Nor can Henry, that's my husband that's the head of the firm. We always use the real."

"I'm trying to find a grower who specializes in daturas. D'you mind telling me who supplies the ones you use in your advertisements?"

"No one does, dear. Henry grows them, that's my husband. We use them in all our publicity, they're part of our brand image. Henry loves them so. We have a lovely conservatory full of them at home, out at Pinner. The perfume's wonderful."

Suppressing her excitement, Celia asked what happened when they wanted to photograph one of the scowling young women with a datura in winter, when the daturas would not be in flower.

"He holds them back in the cold, then forces them, dear. We have to. There are always some in flower in case we need them."

Good gracious me, thought Celia. Her scalp began to prickle. "Do you ever sell them?" she asked.

"Oh no, dear. They're poisonous, you have to be careful." She gave Celia a sharp look. "Why are you asking me all this?"

"Someone I know was being poisoned by one. D'you have any dealings with Richard Galliant & Co. over dress materials?"

"Goodness no, they're too up-market for us, we can't afford the prices. Anyway, you can get the same sort of thing much cheaper from Pritchard and Colson." An idea struck her. "Oh my God, dear. Was it Richard Galliant, this person who was poisoned? We read about him in the paper. Was that what was wrong with him?"

"Yes," said Celia, "and the plant they used was in full flower well before the end of May."

"Oh *no*! When did the poisoning start?"

"Some time in March."

Suddenly she was in violent motion, scrabbling about among the clutter of her desk. "Oh my God, dear, we were afraid of something like this." She found her desk diary and opened it. "When was it now? Yes, here we are. On March the fifth, we had a big show at the Connaught Rooms for out-of-town buyers, and Henry brought the daturas up in his van to decorate the catwalk with, like we always do, lovely they looked. And afterwards when he loaded them up to take them away again, one of them was missing."

"You've no idea who took it?"

"No dear, it could have been anyone, we're not like the couture houses where they're afraid of copying, anyone can get into our shows. Henry reckons it was while he was loading the daturas into his van afterwards, someone was pretending to help and walked off with one into a car. We were worried, of course, very worried. There's only one reason why someone would want to steal one of those."

Celia was in a triumphant mood as she left the shop. If the top brass at the Royal Horticultural Society really wanted to know why anyone would want to force tree daturas, she could give them the answer. But the triumph quickly deflated itself as she realized that in fact, she was no nearer knowing who the poisoner was. Most people at

Galliant, and at Pritchard and Colson for that matter, would see *Vogue* as a matter of course, and would therefore know where to look when they wanted to lay hands on a tree datura. All the likely suspects had connections with the rag trade and would have no trouble getting a card for the Lavinia Lure dress show at the Connaught Rooms. Armed with this cheerful thought, she caught the train home.

At the end of a long day of rehearsals, Teresa Enriquez drove back through the green Sussex countryside to her temporary home in a dip of the South Downs. She had recovered her nerve and the rehearsals were going well, now that she and Wenzel had reached an understanding about the *appogiaturas*.* Wenzel was making sure she was not outsung in ensemble, and she was beginning to realize the value of Glyndebourne's fifty-year tradition of teamwork, thorough rehearsal and intolerance of prima donna airs. Moreover the cubicles in the ladies lavatories backstage were large enough to accommodate her in her crinoline.

Pilar came out into the hall to meet her, in her usual black dress and also, it seemed, in a black mood. Teresa listened patiently to her grievances about English cooking arrangements and the inability of the cleaning woman who went with the furnished house to understand Spanish, however loudly it was spoken. When this was over, she discovered a letter with a Miami postmark lying on the table in the hall. She winced as she recognized her husband's handwriting. Nowadays the news was almost always bad. When she had married Miguel Gomez Fernandez, she was an up-and-coming young soprano, beginning to make her name on the gruelling international circuit. He was the youngest son of a prosperous newspaper proprietor in Ciudad Antonio, with an inherited business sense, a love of her and of

---

*The vexed question of ornamentation in Mozart's vocal works cannot be discussed here. For many years the *appogiatura* was banned at Glyndebourne, apparently on the ground that whatever was done at the Vienna Opera, with its "velvet-and-chocolate" approach to Mozart, must be wrong.

music, good looks and nothing much to do. To marry him and make him her manager made sense then. But not now.

When things started to go wrong she was not alarmed at first because she did not understand what a change of government in Ciudad Antonio meant: that Miguel's family and the newspaper it had owned for four generations would be in opposition; and that because the family was in opposition there would be harassment and well-orchestrated labour troubles at the sawmills and other enterprises it owned, to prevent them from earning the profits that kept the newspaper afloat. Something of the grim reality came home to her when Miguel's father and both his brothers were killed in a "car crash" with obvious political overtones. Even so, she did not foresee Miguel's reaction: he was the only son left alive, the honour of the family was in his hands, his mother and sisters and sister-in-law looked to him for vengeance, he must keep the newspaper going at all costs.

At first he went on acting as her manager. But he was soon so involved in his political intrigues that he started making muddles over her bookings. After a very disastrous one, in which he arranged for her to sing in Milan and New York on the same evening, she told him enough was enough, and put herself in the hands of a reputable New York agency, ignoring his theatrical threats to kill himself if she did any such thing. From then on it was downhill all the way. He spent most of his time in Miami, the listening post and intrigue-centre of all the Hispanic exiles. The paper was still struggling along, and he contributed a twice-weekly column abusing the government thunderously, which it was allowed to publish provided he signed it with a pseudonym, for the government liked to preserve the outward democratic decencies. But flight delays and other mishaps on the state-owned airline soon saw to it that the paper was not distributed outside the capital and the distribution had to be done by charter planes at enormous cost. For a time, Teresa had not grudged it him when he asked for money to keep the paper going. He had served her career loyally for years, it was her turn to support him.

79

But now almost all her savings were gone and he was demanding an increasing share of her current earnings.

The first three pages of his letter consisted of endearments. The bad news came on the fourth. An attempt to raise money by smuggling cigarettes over the Colombian border had failed disastrously owing to the greed and dishonesty of intermediaries. The time was in sight when the paper's wage bill would not be met, he was sorry but he must call on her again for help. The reports from Ciudad Antonio all spoke of the government's unpopularity, there had even been a riot outside the presidential palace, it would not be long now before his darling would be rewarded for all her generosity when he returned to his capital in triumph.

She had heard all this before, and suspected that her money had been used to pay a few layabouts to stage a performance outside the presidential palace which the exiles' news sheets could describe as a riot. When would it all end? Miguel, with his eye on the money, bullying her to sign up for a *Tosca* in Milan in two years' time, followed by a *Norma* at the Metropolitan, both enormous houses. What state would her voice be in in two years' time? She could imagine the Milan audience hissing and booing after she had faked her way through "Vissi d'arte," the sour negotiations with second-rank houses to book her for the drawing power of her name, regardless of the state of her voice, because she had to have the money. Unless she did something decisive, she would go on and on downhill till she ended her days in that home in Buenos Aires for aged musicians with no money.

She saw the time, and rushed upstairs to bath and change. In half an hour Richard Galliant would be calling to take her out to dinner. He was rich, handsome and a lover of opera. He had been her lover for two years. His marriage was breaking up, his description of his cold upper-class English wife with her stiff army background was killingly funny. To marry him was the obvious solution.

❧ SIX ❧

Celia had decided to take the long borders at the Old Rectory by storm. All the plant material needed for them had been assembled, including the left-overs from last week's Chelsea Flower Show. She had her whole labour force there to do the planting. It was hot. Soon everyone was sweating and Bill had his shirt off.

At mid-morning there was a sensation: Richard Galliant appeared in the garden. He had been confined to barracks by his wife since his misconduct in the lily pool and Celia had seen nothing of him, though Bill had caught sight of him once being dragged away from the library window by Morris. Now, fully dressed, shaved and obviously back in command of his faculties, he had come out to demonstrate that this was the case and enjoy the sunshine. He stepped lightly down from the terrace and greeted Bill, who was unpotting and planting out delphiniums at the top end of the grass alley, with a cheerful nod.

"Hullo there, you're Bill Wilkins, is that right? I've heard a lot about you from Anthea Clarkson."

Bill made a face. "Not all me guilty secrets, I hope?"

"If you've got any you've been cunning and kept them from her, she thinks the world of you. You're a lucky man too, she's a pocket marvel, terrific at her job."

"She's clever as a cartload of monkeys," Bill agreed.

"Oh dear me yes, and better tempered, monkeys can be very vicious. I'm a pig to work for, but she never gets stroppy. Hiring her was one of the cleverest things I ever did."

"She likes working for you, Mr. Galliant," said Bill, wondering whether this was true.

Galliant looked round at the busy horticultural scene. "What a lot there seems to be to do. Will you finish in time for our party?"

"Not if it snows all next week," said Bill, grinning. "Or there could be a volcano erupting, that would get us behind."

Galliant grinned back. "No volcano could survive socially in Sussex. The inhabitants would look down their noses at it till it subsided in sheer embarrassment. Seriously, though, about the garden?"

"Don't you worry, Mr. Galliant. We'll have it fixed up nice for you in no time."

"Ah. Now, my wife says your Mrs. Grant plans to splash colour around quite lavishly. Could you just give me a rundown of what she's got in mind?"

Bill was on his guard at once. Here we go, he thought, Celia must deal with this. He'll want everything altered like he did with George Belling. "You better ask the boss about that, Mr. Galliant. That's her over there planting the lilies."

He nodded and moved on. "Nice to meet you, anyway."

Celia's nose was buried among the lilies. He addressed his query to the backside which she was presenting to the world.

When she explained her colour scheme he made an embarrassed face. "Oh dear. I'm going to be awkward, Mrs. Grant, and you'll hate me. Could you possibly turn the whole thing round, and put the hot colours up at the end near the terrace, and the cool blues down by the lily pool? The way you've got it, the hot colours will come forward when they're looked at from the terrace, and shorten the apparent length of the vista."

"I could, with a lot of extra work, but are you sure that's what you want? The guests at your garden party will be looking at it from the other end."

"Ah."

"Mrs. Galliant said they'd be parking their cars in the paddock and entering the garden through the wicket gate at the bottom end of the lawn. So they'll get their first view of the vista from that end, from in front of the marquee. I discussed this with Mrs. Galliant, and she thought the planting should be done with that in mind."

"How awful of me, I grovel. Joan's right as usual, and so are you." He made her a courtly bow of apology and changed the subject. "Your nice Wilkins is planting delphiniums, I see. You're obviously so good at your job that I hesitate to ask, but you will obey the immortal Gertrude's* ban on huge unrelieved masses of blue? You will break the blue up with contrasting whites and yellows?"

"Of course, but Gertrude was dictatorial as well as immortal, and I propose to ignore her veto on mixing blue and purple, and throw some *Salvia superba* into the mixture. I hope you don't disapprove?"

"My dear Mrs. Grant, the corniest of clichés rises to my lips and I can't resist it. I'm sure that when you've finished, the garden will make as pretty a picture as you do yourself."

He went back to the house and Celia went back to her lilies. Presently Bill came to work alongside her. "I got another mystery for you to solve, okay?"

"Oh dear, okay I suppose. What is it?"

"While Galliant was chatting me up, his missis was at the library window, watching."

---

*Miss Gertrude Jekyll (1843–1932) was a horticultural expert whose writings dominated British gardening taste for the first quarter of this century.

"Very natural. She wanted to make sure he'd fully recovered, and wasn't going to misbehave."

"Okay, but answer me this. Why was she laughing to herself fit to bust?"

Bill and Celia spent the lunch break in the garden instead of going to the pub with the others. Anthea had arranged to bring the three of them food from the office canteen to eat out of doors. When this was first suggested Celia had thought it tactful to make a counter-suggestion. "Or why don't I go to the pub and leave you two to picnic?"

"Oh no, Celia, relax, no problem," said Bill quickly.

His vehemence surprised her. Anthea's suggestion was an obvious device to avoid a tête-à-tête with him. If he was equally anxious to avoid one, their relations must be even more strained than she had thought.

Anthea was certainly very much on edge when she appeared carrying the three platefuls of quiche and salad. They sat down in the shade to eat, but she picked tetchily at her food and was eating almost nothing.

"I'm enjoying this," said Celia. "You're lucky to have such a good canteen, Anthea."

"It's very small. Married staff who live near usually go home to lunch. They had to organize something for the others because there's nowhere else, apart from the Red Lion with its barbaric sandwiches."

"Who does the cooking?"

"Susie."

Celia choked on her quiche and had to be hit on the back. This information connected up with something she had seen and intended to ask about: a huge catering trolley emerging from the back door of the house and trundling across the stable yard to the office block, propelled by the tiny Susie. It happened every day, just before the lunch hour. When she had recovered enough to speak she began questioning Anthea about it.

"Susie cooks the canteen food over in the house?"

"Yes. There's no kitchen the other side, only a sink and

a hotplate for soup and so on, and a machine that makes disgusting coffee. Susie puts a menu on the office notice-board the night before and you write down what you want. Next day she cooks it and brings it across from the house on the trolley."

"And comes straight back to the house?"

"No. Not till she's laid the food out and started up the coffee machine and so on."

"Which takes how long?"

"It varies. Sometimes she stays to sort out muddles about money."

"And meanwhile, what's happening about the Galliants' lunch?"

"She lays the table before she brings the trolley across."

"And their food?"

Anthea thought. "At this time of year it's usually cold, a salad or something like that off the canteen menu. I think she puts it out ready for them when she lays the table."

"In their dining-room?"

"No, that's miles from the kitchen and the table seats sixteen. They use the breakfast room off the kitchen when they're by themselves."

"What shape is the table in there? Round? Oblong?"

"Oblong. Why?"

"They're more habit-forming than round ones, you can be fairly sure where each member of the household will sit."

"Celia, what are you trying to prove?"

"Isn't it obvious? On the day when Richard Galliant was due to have his fateful encounter with the Princess of Wales, his lunch had been sitting unguarded opposite his place at table while Susie was over in the office block. It consisted of a prawn cocktail. In other words, prawns and salad drenched in that pink vinegary sauce with a lot of pepper in it. The ideal thing to disguise the taste of a few datura leaves mixed up in the salad."

"Oh Celia," said Bill admiringly.

"Okay, but that doesn't alter anything," Anthea argued.

85

"Who decided to give him this convenient prawn cocktail for lunch on that particular day? Joan Galliant. Who else?"

While they discussed the reasons for suspecting Joan Galliant, Celia studied Anthea. She was still beautiful, but the mop of dark curls needed washing and there were fatigue marks like faint bruises under her eyes. She kept glancing restlessly at her watch, as if something she expected to happen had not materialized. Presently it did.

"Ah!" she said, interrupting the discussion. "I've been waiting for this, here comes another bit of the lunchtime arrangements that you don't know about."

As she spoke, Susie came trudging through the archway from the stable yard carrying a covered plateful of food, and stomped away with it towards the staff cottage.

"This riveting addition to the routine started after the Princess of Wales fiasco," said Anthea. "Since then she's been taking Paul his lunch."

"Why's that so riveting then?" Bill asked her.

Anthea explained that Paul had nothing but social security to live on, because Galliant had cut off the money supply when he went on strike and refused to work in the garden. But Paul had persuaded Susie, who had a soft spot for him, to supply him with food from the Old Rectory and Joan Galliant, rather than play the cruel stepmother, had turned a blind eye. Paul had been in the habit of saving Susie trouble by collecting his lunch from her kitchen, but what they had just seen suggested that the Galliants had put a stop to this arrangement.

"Oh I get it, that jells," said Bill. "They've rumbled that it was the prawn cocktail sent Galliant silly, and they think Paul did it, and they've forbidden him the kitchen in case he does it again."

"Correction," said Anthea as Susie trudged back to the house. "Joan Galliant has forbidden Paul the kitchen because Richard knows now that his food's been tampered with, and she has to pretend to suspect somebody, so he doesn't suspect her. Paul's her stepson, she'd like to get him in bad with his father, so she sets him up as chief suspect."

Maybe, Celia thought. In any case Paul seemed to her credible as a suspect for the poisoning. He bullied his sister and hated his father, and the tie-up with his mother's firm made him the prime suspect over the copying of Richard Galliant designs. She asked whether that trouble had started after Paul moved down from London.

"Not really," said Anthea. "Design copying's a chronic headache in the rag trade. There was a bad outbreak in November, soon after I joined the firm. Cribs of three of Wanda's marvellous silk prints appeared in the shops while we were still showing them to the trade."

"Can't you sue for breach of copyright?" Celia asked.

"No, they take Wanda's idea and alter it just enough to protect themselves. They can't put our name on the selvedge, but it still looks like a Galliant design. And it's always the same people, Pritchard and Colson."

"Paul's Mum's firm," said Bill.

"That could be coincidence, Gorgeous. There are only two or three other firms with the specialized plant for that quality of textile printing."

"But only one with an angry lady in it that didn't like being divorced," he persisted.

"Did Wanda's keys disappear when you had the trouble in November?" Celia asked.

"No, but I think that was when they started tightening up on who has keys."

"Ah. Who does besides Wanda?"

"Her secretary. Richard. And a spare set is kept in his desk, just in case."

"In case of what, love?" Bill asked.

"Richard's away a lot. Wanda spends two days a week up in Slough, at the works. If her secretary was ill the chief accountant or I would have to get the keys out of Richard's desk and let the staff in."

"When did Wanda's keys start disappearing?" said Celia.

Anthea thought. "Just after Easter, I think."

"By which time Paul was installed in the cottage?"

"Yes. But no one put two and two together till three weeks later, when the Pritchard and Colson reps started dazzling the customers with two more lookalikes of our designs."

"Only three weeks?" said Celia, "Isn't that too quick?"

"Not really. Wanda's technical people translate the design into a computer disc that tells the machine what coloured ink to put on which rollers. You only have to copy the disc and fiddle about a bit with the programming so that it isn't an exact copy and you're home. Wanda's keys disappeared again last week, so we can expect the next Pritchard and Colson outrage before the middle of June."

After thinking about this, Celia said: "I distrust these keys."

"Oh Celia, why?" Bill asked.

"Whenever they disappear, everyone panics. They all rush to the design studio and prepare to sell their lives dearly in its defence. That's why the keys disappear, to make everyone look for the culprit in the wrong place."

"And the right place is where?" said Anthea.

"Goodness knows, but what about the plant in Slough? With an accomplice here who snitches the keys at intervals to keep you interested?"

"Does the accomplice also put stupefying foliage in Richard's prawn cocktail?" said Anthea. "And hide the remains of the datura in the Galliants' compost heap?"

"Goodness knows, the two things may be quite unconnected. Oh dear, it all seems very complicated and nothing fits. I'm probably being much too clever. We ought to settle for the simple answer, which is on the one hand a fresh outbreak of this chronic trouble over design copying; and on the other, Joan Galliant behaving like one of those horrid Roman Empresses who poisoned everyone right left and centre so that their sons would be the next Emperor."

"Oh no, Celia," Bill objected. "A Roman Empress wouldn't put the evidence on the compost heap for anyone to find."

"I've always thought leaving it there to rot down was a reasonable risk. The only point is, the risk would be more for Mrs. Galliant and her son and the Morrises than for someone from outside, because if it was found, contrary to all the probabilities, the suspicion would fall on the Galliants and not on the outsider."

"I still think it's a negligible risk for anyone," Anthea argued. "Negligible enough for Joan Galliant and her wall-of-silence mafia to take. It wasn't foreseeable that the compost heap would be turned upside down before the datura rotted, and even less foreseeable than when it was, a botanically clued-up lady with an enquiring mind would be there to say 'Ah, this plant that the ordinary person wouldn't recognize is what they're getting Richard Galliant stoned out of his mind on.'"

"If it's Joan Galliant and Charles and the Morrises doing it," said Celia, "there's one thing I don't understand. Why would they be trying to ruin the firm that butters their bread and provides sizeable slices of very palatable cake?"

"They're not. They're only making things look bad for a week or two to force the price of the shares down."

"Goodness," said Celia. "Why would they do that?"

"So that Charles Langley can afford to buy a controlling interest. He's ambitious, and his mother's so ambitious for him that it's making her ill."

"But Anthea, if the banks call in their loans, which the papers seem to think they're threatening to do, they'll have a receiver in and there won't be anything for Langley to control."

"Richard says we're a long way from that yet."

"You'd need a Niagara of cash flow to buy up a firm like this," Bill objected.

"No problem, Gorgeous. He's loaded, when he was working in the city he made a huge killing on the stock exchange. I know, because there was a rumpus about it."

"You mean, he did something illegal?" Celia asked.

"He got away with it, but the bad smell was overpowering and he had to resign. Insider trading, it was."

"Which is what, love?" Bill asked.

"Making a profit out of something your firm's been told in confidence, before the market gets to know."

"He did that?" Celia asked. "You're sure? There are always rumours about that sort of thing."

"I asked someone in my old firm to find out about him. He rang back yesterday with this story."

"So naughty little Charley gets the sack," Bill summed up, "and he rings Mum and says oh help Mum dear, I've come unstuck in the city and there's a black mark against me name and no one will take me on, so I'm on the national assistance, oh dear what am I to do? And Mum grouches at him a bit at first and says oh how disgraceful, your poor dear father would turn in his grave. Then she calms down and says 'you better come down here, your stepfather will fit you in, he'll do anything I want if I tickle the hairs on his chest nicely.'"

"That's right," said Anthea, "and she gets Charles in charge of the London office and the finances, which infuriates all concerned."

"Is there anyone who's particularly cross?" Celia asked. "Anyone who was in line for it?"

Anthea thought. "I imagine Frank Dawson's a bit peeved. He's the chief accountant. He'd more or less been promised Financial Director. He's so quiet and reserved that I wouldn't know what goes on inside him, but I can imagine a dark horse like him doing the dirty on the Galliants if he got the chance. Another thing, Charles hasn't endeared himself to the secretaries. I'm told he goes in for some quite heavy sexual harassment. They say the design studio's a seething mass of jealousy and intrigue, but of course that's directed against Wanda, not him."

The lunch break was over, and the gardeners were back from the pub. Celia left Bill to organize them and walked through with Anthea to the stable yard. The back door of the Old Rectory opened on to the yard under a porch-like structure complete with coal-holes. She touched Anthea's arm. "Before you go back to the office, would you just try that door and see if it's locked? I'd do it myself, but you can make some excuse to Susie if it isn't."

Anthea went, and came back. "Locked. It never used to be. Joan Galliant's 'protecting' darling Richard. And the big laugh is, there's no point now in her putting on a great act of locking up the kitchen. The poisoning's over, the datura's been thrown out on to the compost heap, and there's a very damaging dent in Richard's image."

Wondering what it was that made Anthea so tense, Celia returned to the garden. But she and Bill were soon back in the stable yard, helping the driver unload a huge delivery of geraniums. While they were doing this, a low sports car like a very flat flying saucer swept into the yard. Fred Watney and Paul Galliant crept out, like hermit crabs emerging from their shells. Paul saw Bill and gave him a friendly wave. "Why weren't you in the Red Lion with the others?"

"Busy," said Bill with his hands full of geranium pots.

"You should have come, it was fantastic," Paul shouted, red in the face.

"He's right, you should have been there, Bill," Celia murmured as the wicked pair sloped off towards the staff cottage. "We need to know a lot more about those two."

"The girls say they was drunk and talked to them very nasty and dirty," he told her.

"I daresay, but if they ask you again please say 'yes.'"

"Oh why, Celia? They won't tell me nothing."

"They will if you pretend to be very wicked and keep your ears open."

"Okay, but it'll be dead boring."

"No it won't. They're both play-acting, if you ask me. And I want to know the plot of the play."

Tim Price had stopped haunting the Red Lion after his humiliating experience there at the hands of Fred and Paul, and had chosen a pub in Uckfield to entertain his latest news source about the Galliants' affairs.

"She's so self-centred," said June Hamilton. "You wouldn't think it to look at her with that meek face and those glasses, but she is."

"Yes?" said Tim Price, and gazed into her eyes soulfully to encourage her to say more. Buying this dislikable girl a pub lunch was proving worth while after all, he had struck a gold-bearing seam at last. June Hamilton was a recent recruit to the design studio, and she was giving him the low-down on Wanda Galliant.

"Don't be misled by that soppy washed-out blonde look," June went on. "Underneath it she's as hard as nails. No one must have the credit for anything except her."

"She's supposed to be a brilliant designer," said Tim. "Is she?"

June considered. "She's not bad, but her stuff's all the same and we all have to copy her style. If you do anything original it's stamped on."

"Most firms print the designer's name on the edge of the material," said Tim. "Don't they let you do that?"

"Goodness no, even Wanda doesn't get a selvedge signature. I think it's because old Mr. Galliant wants the public to think that he designs everything himself. He's jealous of her, I shouldn't wonder."

"You'd think she'd stand up to him," said Tim, "if she's as hard as nails and wants to keep all the credit for herself."

"Yes . . . well you see, she's obstinate about certain things, but she's not very bright really and it's quite easy to bamboozle her."

"She's not married?"

"My God no, what an idea. But she's not gay, if that's what you're thinking. I'm sure of that, because she makes sheep's eyes at Charles Langley whenever she sees him. I think she's in love with him in a pure sort of way with no implications below the waistline. She doesn't get it regularly from anyone, you only have to look at her to see that. I don't think it's occurred to her to want it."

Even if this was reliable, it was not the sort of thing Tim

could print, so he decided to change the subject. "The atmosphere in that studio must be fairly tense."

"My dear, it's a snake pit. Especially now that we're all under suspicion of selling Wanda's precious designs to Pritchard and Colson."

This was new to him and very usable: Galliant's were having design-copying trouble, and were keeping very quiet about it. He pressed her for details. It was all Wanda Galliant's fault, was it, for not looking after her keys? Yes, he could understand how angry with her they all were. Had they been subjected to third degree questioning? How shocking. No, of course he wouldn't use her name, but she was quite right, when these things happened they had to be exposed, it was her duty to speak out. But now she must excuse him, he was due back at work.

He hurried back to his typewriter and pecked out a powerful piece about the intolerable atmosphere of pressure and suspicion among the staff at trouble-torn Richard Galliant & Co., whose eccentric founder and chairman . . . etc. He was doing well out of the Galliant story. He had made the national press three days ago with a report on the opening night at Glyndebourne, which Richard Galliant had been "too unwell" to attend, so that his guests, three world-famous couturiers and their wives, had to be entertained by his wife and stepson. And now this. With any luck it would keep the story alive for a day or two longer, to earn him another by-line and freelance fee.

June Hamilton drove back to Faringfield, pleased with the interest she had aroused in a lively and attractive young man. The lunch had lasted longer than she expected, and she arrived back at the studio rather late. Wanda was standing near her drawing-board, looking at the work on it.

"Ah, June, there you are, I was looking at this. It's very nice."

June gritted her teeth and waited for what she knew was coming.

"I was wondering if we couldn't try doing it as a drop

reverse . . ." Wanda began drawing something on a scrap of paper.

Here we go again, June thought. I was the outstanding student of my year at Central, and it's my design and that's how I want it to be. How dare she muck it about as if I was an eighteen-year-old on the pre-diploma course?

Wanda finished her rough sketch. "Something along those lines, I thought." She put her scrap of paper down on the drawing-board and moved it about. "You needed something to give a bit more interest here . . . and here."

The maddening thing was, June could see that she was right. She had put her finger unerringly on the weak spot in the design. The extra touch she was suggesting would turn a competent June Hamilton design into an inimitable Wanda Galliant one, and that was infuriating.

At five o'clock Celia straightened her aching back and reviewed progress. There was a lot still to do. Regiments of Paul Crampel geraniums had to be planted out in the former rose garden. The dingy shrubbery round the lower lawn must be brightened up with blocks of hydrangeas and rhododendrons. The stone urns on the terrace needed filling with no matter what, provided it looked expensive. The planting in the two long borders was finished. A last-minute windfall of a pink kurume azalea called "Hino-mayo" had arrived in time to brighten up what threatened to be a dull patch in the middle, and the scheme had worked out more or less as planned, with hot orange, yellows and reds at the lily pool end, graduating through to blues and pale colours up by the terrace. To her immense relief, the Nevada versus Marguerite Hilling problem, which she had lost sight of in her agitation over other matters, had been resolved in her favour. The buds were showing colour and it was not the fatal pink.

But unfortunately, the reality was a crude parody of the mental picture she had carried around for so long. She had thrown in plenty of foliage plants as an antidote to garishness, but however careful one was, instant gardening could not help looking vulgar and the result of her labours looked very vulgar indeed. However, some quick calculations last night had shown that, thanks to luck and shrewd bargaining, Archerscroft Nurseries was going to make a handsome profit on the contract.

Determined to be through with the distasteful job tomorrow, she had kept the workforce for an extra hour on overtime. The girls had just driven off in the van, but Bill had stayed behind to discuss the work schedule for next day.

"Are you meeting Anthea this evening?" she asked.

"No."

Celia did not press him for an explanation, and none came.

"That flying saucer thing's still parked in the stable yard," she said, "which means that Paul's still got the awful Fred with him in the cottage. Would you mind hanging around a bit and seeing what happens? You might get another chance of a heart-to-heart with them."

Bill threw her a sulky look and prodded the grass with his toe, but said nothing.

"Well, do you want to clear this mess up and save Anthea's job, or don't you?" she prompted.

"Okay, Celia, will do," he said dully, and walked away through the arch.

Celia went back for a last look at the long borders, to see if anything could be done to improve them, but decided that they would look even worse when various things that were still in bud came out. They were, of course, good of their kind, a real *tour de force* in fact if one liked that sort of thing. She didn't. Did Richard Galliant? She shuddered to think what he would say when he saw them.

"Do you forgive my inquisitiveness," said a mild male voice behind her. "I had to see what it all looked like."

The voice belonged to a thin, sad-looking man in his fifties with a scholarly stoop. "I work in the office here and I saw all these beautiful plants being unloaded in the yard. I just had to see what you were doing with them."

He looked along the twin borders and said "Ah . . ."

"It'll be better when the shrub roses are right out," Celia

said dishonestly. "I was afraid at first that they might not be the creamy white ones. If they'd turned out to be the pink version they'd have wrecked the colour scheme."

"Dear me yes, how fortunate that they're Nevadas, Marguerite Hilling's a very bright pink. A mysterious pair of roses, those two. They're tetraploids, the breeder can't have kept proper records. What on earth can the pollen parent have been?" He looked down the borders again and said "No paeonies?"

"The flowering season's so short. And they'd be in full sun, which makes it even shorter. I decided not to risk it."

"As far as I'm concerned, the paeony is the queen of flowers. I specialize in them." The gleam in his eye betrayed the obsession of an addict.

"You breed them?"

He nodded. "Not professionally, of course, but I've had some quite interesting results crossing the doubles with an anemone-flowered one with a petaloid centre."

"They must be in bloom now, how exciting for you," said Celia.

"If you'd be interested, Mrs. Grant, and not in a hurry to get home, I could show you them. I only live five minutes away."

This was the sort of invitation she could not resist. "I'd love to. How did you know my name?"

"I've known of you and your work on hellebores for some time. I'm on the Archerscroft mailing list."

"Oh, good. And you are—?"

"My name's Dawson. I'm the firm's accountant."

No, Celia thought. He's not a suspect, Anthea's got it wrong. He's not the sort to work himself up into a secret fury and poison his boss because Charles Langley's been brought in over his head. All he cares about are his paeonies, he can't wait to retire in five or ten years' time so that he can concentrate on them and nothing else.

They moved off. There was no sign of Bill in the stable yard. His car had gone, and so had Fred Watney's flying saucer. Wondering what had happened, she set off with

Dawson across the village green to his modest thatched cottage. As they walked up the front path, the scent from the paeonies hit her like a wave. He took her round the corner of the house and there they were, a great sea of them, the double lactifloras, the anemone-flowered, the arietinas, some new introductions from the United States that she had never seen before. She spent a long time studying the crosses that were his special pride.

"Are you thinking of taking out plant-breeder's rights?" Celia asked.

An embarrassing conversation followed. Dawson hinted that he would like a financial arrangement with her, but his crosses were not distinctive enough to be a commercial proposition. She got out of it by offering to swap two "Roger Grant" hellebores for a tray of seedlings of one of the new American anemone-flowered strains.

"Come and meet my wife and have a glass of sherry," he suggested when this had been settled, and turned towards the house. Only then did Celia notice two women sitting on the terrace and watching them silently.

She followed Dawson towards them. One of the women lay slumped in a wheel chair with her head on one side, recognizable at a glance as an advanced case of disseminated sclerosis. The other, thick-set and with badly dyed hair, must be a nurse-companion.

"Ah, Philippa my dear," said Dawson. "I'm so glad you came out to enjoy this beautiful mild evening. Guess who I've brought to see you, this is the distinguished Mrs. Grant of hellebore fame." He turned to Celia. "And Miss Miller here is our friend and helper."

Celia duly produced yet more admiring remarks about the paeonies. Both women smiled, and Mrs. Dawson said: "They're Frank's favourite flower."

When Dawson suggested sherry, Miss Miller looked at him with grimly pursed lips, then rose and went into the house. She was away for some time. Conversation languished. Celia could think of nothing to talk about other than the paeonies, which had already been admired *ad nauseam*. This is absurd, she thought. There must be something else we can discuss, and why am I feeing more and more embarrassed?

Still Miss Miller did not reappear with the sherry. Dawson was getting restive at the delay. His wife was looking frightened for some reason, and seemed to be begging him mutely to take some action. Presently he murmured an excuse and went inside to hurry Miss Miller up. When they returned, he was carrying the decanter and glasses and she looked as if she had been crying. Before pouring out Dawson shot a reassuring smile at his wife, who stopped looking alarmed and smiled back. Miss Miller managed a ghastly smile as she rearranged Mrs. Dawson's shawl, and was rewarded with a frightened smile of thanks from the invalid. There were more forced smiles as they raised their glasses of sherry.

Celia sipped hers in mounting embarrassment. The tension between the three of them was electric, what was this pantomime covering up? Did they always mount it for the benefit of visitors? And if so, did they always find it such a strain? Already they were willing her silently to go. She finished her drink as fast as she decently could and took her leave. Even the paeonies had begun to look sinister as she walked past them.

Ann Miller watched Celia turn the corner of the house, and waited till she heard her footsteps fade away down the path. Then her suppressed fury burst out. "Frankie, why did you bring her here?"

"Because—"

"Because she's pretty, that's why. How dare you? Simpering little thing, that helpless air doesn't deceive me, she's a minx if ever I saw one. Do what you like behind my back, but *don't bring them here*."

"Oh, dear, what nonsense. You really must control yourself, Ann, you're being ridiculous. If you go on like this you'll have to be shut up. In a mental hospital."

"And then who would lug Philippa on and off the commode? Who else d'you think you can get for what you pay me?"

A moan came from the wheel chair. Philippa was listening with tears running down her cheeks.

He tried to drag Ann away out of earshot but she shook him off. "I shall go and live with my sister in Canada like I said. Bringing that woman here was the last straw."

"Listen, Ann. She was interested in the paeonies and I thought I could arrange something with her about plant breeder's rights and make some money."

"Liar. She didn't say a word about that, and anyway, how much money? Not enough. There never will be enough, because you're too feeble to stand up for your rights. Why did you let Galliant put Langley in over you as Financial Director, answer me that?"

"Because—"

"Excuses, excuses, I won't listen. Do something. I give you a month to do something, or I'll go off to Canada just like *that*."

Horrors, Celia thought as she hid in the shelter of the front porch. She was not ashamed of eavesdropping, she had to know.

How many years had passed—ten? fifteen?—since Frank Dawson first tiptoed along the passage from his wife's bedroom to Miss Miller's? And here she still was, dyeing her hair and longing for the moment when she would be a wife and not that furtive, underpaid person "our friend and helper, Miss Miller." Did he still tiptoe along the passage? Did she trust him to do the right thing by her when the moment came? Was he stringing her along because she was cheap and someone had to look after Mrs. Dawson? Worst of all Mrs. Dawson, slumped in her wheelchair, knew all about those trips to Miss Miller's bedroom. She had read the message of the dyed hair correctly as a distress-signal to her husband, and knew they were both waiting for her to die.

The sherry had turned sour in Dawson's stomach. He

went into the house to vomit. There was no sister in Canada, he had checked, only a distant cousin. Ann had no money and nowhere to go. When she said "do something" she meant "find enough money to put Philippa in a home, divorce her and marry me." It was madness, there was no way his salary could be stretched to cover nursing home fees. He had never wanted to marry her, still less so now. They had drifted into it because he was a healthy man with an invalid wife and she was willing. For years he had managed somehow to hold the situation together despite her hysteria and insane jealousy. But any minute now, things would fall apart for good.

Poor Philippa, he thought as he retched in the downstairs lavatory. It was even worse for her than it was for him. But he had "done something." It had needed a lot of nerve, more than he thought he had. With luck, he would be able to hold the situation together for a little longer.

❦ SEVEN ❦

When Bill Wilkins left Celia in the garden at the Old Rectory, he faced a problem. How was he to loiter in the hope of falling in with Fred and Paul, without convincing Anthea, who was still in her office, that he was spying on her to see if her excuse of working late was genuine?

So I open up the engine and pretend to frig about with it, he decided, but not for long, Anthea would soon see through that.

Surprisingly, there was no need for it. Further along the line of parked cars Fred seemed to have had the same idea. He was frigging unconvincingly with the engine of his flying saucer. When he saw Bill he said "Hi there."

"Trouble?" Bill asked.

Fred shut the bonnet lid. "Oil check. No problem."

"Sorry I was busy at dinner time."

"You free now?"

"Depends," said Bill cautiously. "What for?"

"Come over to my place. Paul's coming. Have a dip in the pool, eat something from the freezer. Okay?"

"Okay. Thanks, I'd like that," said Bill. Crikey, he thought, celebrated glamorous Fred Watney was hanging around waiting for me, what is this? Some kind of trap?

There was a short wait while Paul was fetched from the

cottage. When he arrived it became clear that the party was not yet complete. Fred tooted his horn. A dark, scowling young woman with a sallow complexion came out of the office block and hurried towards them

"Hi June, meet Bill," said Paul.

June Hamilton gave Bill a nod, and tucked herself into the hutch-like area behind the two passenger seats of the car. Paul followed and used the confined space as an excuse to entangle his limbs with hers more thoroughly than was strictly necessary. This left the front passenger seat free for Bill.

Fred leant across from behind the wheel and held open the passenger door.

"I got my own car here, I'll follow you," said Bill.

"Run you back here after," said Fred. "No sweat. Okay?"

Not okay, Bill thought. I'm not having no magical mystery tour in that thing, and then be left without transport to get away when I've had enough.

"No, thanks all the same," he said, and turned away to go to his own car.

"Follow me, then," Fred shouted crossly, and underlined his annoyance by shooting away out of the stable yard almost before Bill had started his engine.

Bill saw no reason to rush after him in a panic, and made Fred wait for him at every intersection where he could go wrong. After a few miles they turned in at the drive of an enormous, very ugly house, red brick on the ground floor and fake-Tudor beams up above.

The door was opened with much clattering of bolts by a gorilla-like manservant who looked as if he doubled as a security guard. They trooped into a vast entrance hall with deep wall-to-wall carpeting and no furniture to speak of. The false-Gothic stone fireplace had a huge blown-up photograph over it of Fred on stage with the group. There was a poster-size head and shoulders of him on the opposite wall and a full-length one of him with a guitar over the arch to the stairs. He wandered off into one of the rooms and did something which caused the refrain of his own latest hit to echo through the house.

When he came back he was holding a copy of the *New Musical Express*. "This just came," he said and searched the pages eagerly. "Here we are, look."

He was holding the magazine open at a double page feature about himself and devouring it hungrily. Bill was embarrassed for him. Surrounded by blown-up pictures of himself, with his own voice coming from the loudspeakers, he was looking at his own photo in a magazine, with a soppy expression on his face as if he were looking at a girl he fancied. "They'll never catch me," wailed the voice from the loudspeakers, "'cos I don't know who I am." He's right, Bill thought. He don't know who he is, he has to look at his own publicity to find out, he'd be a nothing person if his image wasn't there reflecting something back at him for him to imitate.

"Swim?" Fred suggested when he had read the magazine article twice. "The pool's through here."

What had once been a huge drawing room had been turned into an indoor swimming pool. Swimming costumes were hanging over a poolside chair. June picked up a bikini.

"No need to bother with that," Fred told her, grinning. "Us lads shan't."

Paul was grinning too. June hesitated, then put the bikini down again obediently. Fred smiled coldly at Bill, making it clear that he would be chickening out if he failed to toe the nudist line.

Giving orders is what turns him on, Bill thought. He gets a kick making people jump through hoops for him like in a circus, it helps him to feel like a real person. Not just Paul, who's his zombie, but that girl too. And me, and the people who go wild at his concerts. If everyone jumps to his tune, it convinces him that he's not a nothing individual.

They swam. Fred's tattoos were a nasty sight. None of them wore bathing trunks, for Bill had decided it was too soon for open defiance of the rules. Nothing improper was said or done, because Fred had banned it. Once, when Paul got too close to June in the water, Bill heard him mutter "Lay off her, can't you? Keep her guessing. Let her get all excited and sexy wondering when the action will start."

When the group was into Heavy Metal, Bill thought, with all that nonsense about filthiness and black masses, he had his fun making a whole audience go wild and behave nasty. He's cleaned up the image, but the tattoos are still here and he's still the same underneath.

The manservant brought champagne and Coca-Cola. They drank, sitting on the edge of the pool. June Hamilton and Paul had their heads together, tearing someone's character to pieces. "She's ever so self-centred," June was saying. "You wouldn't think it to look at her with that meek face and those glasses, but she is."

They lowered their voices, but Bill managed to overhear that they were discussing Wanda Galliant and some plan for annoying her. That jelled. By normal standards the girl was a switchoff. Paul was only going with her to use her in his hate campaign against Wanda.

Bill had taken a close look at Paul while they were swimming. There were needle marks in both his scrawny thighs. But none of them looked new. When Paul and June had gone to shower and dress, he asked Fred about the marks. "When did he stop shooting up?"

Fred looked at him coldly. "It's not good manners to notice."

"It is, when you're concerned about someone. You done a lot for Paul, that's why I asked."

The flattery worked. "I look after me friends," said Fred. "He's been off it since March, I paid for the nursing home."

Why, Bill wondered. Not, surely, for an unselfish reason, but what other motive was there? To avoid scandal attaching to Fred Watney? That was a possibility. "Got hooked here, did he?"

"Him and my bitch of a wife, it was her fault he got

hooked. Silly cow, she knew I'd not stand for it. Anyone in the group that's found with it on them, he's out on his ear, and it was the same for her." He gripped the edge of the pool fiercely at the memory and his knuckles showed white. Bill decided that the wretched girl must have told him a few home truths before she left. Had she got hooked because she couldn't stand life with Fred?

"I tell people she ran away with a cheap-jack guitar player," Fred said in a strained voice. "But it's not true. I threw her out and she fixed herself up with him, he was all she could find."

"But you never threw Paul out?"

"I never knew about her getting him hooked, not then. He went off to London soon after, I didn't find out till he contacted me to say he'd had a row with his awful parents and they were dragging him down here. I thought, if that's so, he better get off it first."

That jells, Bill thought. Fred paid for the nursing home because he doesn't want nasty rumours among the neighbours about people getting hooked in his house.

"You say he's clean, but his bedroom stinks of pot."

"Yeah, well. Poor little bastard, he has to have some pleasures."

Did Fred supply the pot? Probably, as part of the ringmaster technique. He would get a kick out of despising Paul while he smoked it and making him feel guilty.

"Paul's family gave him a rotten deal," Fred went on. "Bastards and bitches, the lot of them."

"How come, Fred?"

"Take his old man, for instance. Always picking on him, even when he was a kid. Paul didn't come up to specification, oh no. What his dad had ordered from under the gooseberry bush was a handsome great bruiser of a lad who'd be good at games and clever at school, with a good business head so he'd be a credit to the firm when the time arrived. What came was a weedy little runt, no good at games and bone idle at school and not any good at art even, and then dropping out of that horticultural college. It was enough to make a respectable upward-mobile gent wild, and he didn't let Paul forget it."

"Why's Paul so against Wanda?" Bill asked.

"Wanda was clever at school, see? And good at art and she was as good as gold and never gave any trouble. She was a natural as daddy's girl, he's been all over her ever since she was a kid. So Paul had to be mummy's boy, and when the family rows started his mum used him as a cosh to beat his dad with. Between them they gave Paul one hell of a time, and his step-mum that came along after they broke up ain't much better."

"Crikey. What's wrong with her?"

"Her dad was a general and she's inherited the whole damn military bit, bar the little moustache. Wants to run the show, thinks she can smooth things over and make everyone pretend to be happy like in a fifties musical and not say how much they hate each other. What the hell good is that? Paul thinks she's rubbish, and so do I."

But Fred decides what Paul thinks, Bill told himself. And Fred has rubbished everyone close to Paul except himself, this is the ringmaster thing again. But why was he being told all this? He was being recruited into the Fred Watney circus, but what sort of performing animal was he supposed to be?

"Paul thinks the world of you," he said, hoping to learn more.

Fred smirked. "I look after me friends."

"What was the big row about, when they made him come back home?"

"Oh, that. It was to do with his bitch of a mother, when he was in London she made him have lunch with her once a month. Making up to him still, so he'd be on her side in the rows with his dad. He was having a cash flow problem like people do when they're shooting up, and he used to snitch money from her purse over these lunches. But he did it once too often and took too much, and she made a great drama of it right there in the restaurant in front of the waiters. Wanda was there too, and of course she told on him to his dad."

"Of course?" Bill queried.

"She's daddy's darling, remember? And she's been telling to dad on her naughty little brother since she learnt to pee in a pot and not in her nappy."

"Does his dad know Paul had drug trouble?"

"They asked when the big row broke, you'd have to be a moron not to when someone steals from his mum's handbag. But Paul said no no no, it wasn't that, it was on account of that window-box business of his getting into debt, and he was at his wits end for money to keep it going."

"And they believed him?"

"His dad did, or he pretended to because he felt more comfortable that way. I dunno about Mrs. Galliant, she's a sly operator."

"Was bringing Paul home to do the garden her idea?"

"That's right. Get him back into our clutches, she said, and spy on him and clobber him when we think he needs it. So I told him to say no deal unless he could have that cottage and live independent. And then his dad started coming out into the garden and saying you should have finished that job today, you idle little bastard, why haven't you, and tomorrow I want you to do this and look sharp about it. So I said to Paul, if that's how it is, you better tell him you got a bad back. And there was a big row over that, you can imagine; 'You snotty little bastard, rah rah rah, if I'd talked to me dad like you talk to me he'd have taken the strap to me etcetera.' And that's how things were till this morning."

"What happened this morning, then?" Bill asked.

"Mrs. generalissimo Galliant's decided to have another go at smoothing it all over and making it all look happy. So she sends her old man round to the cottage to do one of his weepy acts, he does them quite well. 'Oh Paul, I been thinking of you all the time I was lying on me bed of pain with me allergy'—but it was the drink, if you ask me—'and feeling so sad because you and me don't seem to get on. So why don't we have a man-to-man lunch together tomorrow and talk things over and see if we can't get to like each other a bit more, eh?' So Paul said yes he would, what a good idea, but only because he's too terrified of his father to say 'no.' He was shaking all over like he always does when his father comes near him. I told him to make an excuse in the morning and not go. It always ends up the same with the old bastard yelling at him for not being the sort of son he had in mind during the relevant orgasm all those years ago. Paul always comes out of it in shock, it makes him feel so awful that he pukes his guts up. If I let him keep that date, he'll be back on the heroin in no time at all."

Bill was feeling more and more uncomfortable. Why was he being told all this? Where were Paul and June?

They dressed and went in search of them. June was sitting by herself at the foot of the stairs, leafing sulkily through Fred's *New Musical Express*. "Looks like Paul's through with her," Fred muttered. "You want to go next?"

It took Bill a full minute to work out what he meant, and recover from his astonishment and disgust. "No thanks, I got me own arrangements."

"Oh yeah, with Anthea Clarkson, I could tell you a thing or two about that little bird."

"No thanks, I don't want to hear."

Fred grinned at him contemptuously, then called to June. "Where's Paul?"

"He went, ten minutes ago. He said to tell you he'd taken the Jag, he'll bring it back in the morning."

"I must be away too," said Bill.

Fred gave him the cold stare treatment. "You were invited to eat here, remember?"

"Sorry, I changed me mind, I got to be at work early tomorrow."

"Listen Cinderella, I don't like guests that say they got to go for no reason."

"I have plenty reasons."

"Ah, but you better stay unless you want to walk. I got your car keys."

"I know that. I saw you snitch them from me clothes while I was swimming, so I helped meself to the keys of that thing you came here in. Want to swap, or do I drive meself home in it?"

"I'd phone the police and say you'd stole it," said Fred, white with fury, and moved towards the bell to ring for the gorilla-shaped butler.

Bill stood between him and the bell-push. "Don't act silly now. Want me to dump you in the pool with two black eyes and all your clothes on?"

Fred could be seen thinking about Bill's size, and how inconvenient two black eyes would be professionally. Deciding to make the best of a bad job, he broke into an unconvincing smile. "Hey, you crafty bastard, I like you," he said. "Catch."

A bunch of keys flew through the air. Bill threw back the keys of the flying saucer, then wondered what to do about June.

"Want me to drop you off?" he asked her.

She shot Fred a sultry look and went back to her magazine. "No thanks."

"Bye then," said Fred. Strangely, he seemed to be suppressing a snigger, as if at some secret joke.

So that was it, Bill thought as he drove off. I was supposed to have a go with that nasty little piece, who would blab about it in the office so it got round to Anthea and I'd be in the doghouse with her. What was the point, though? Was it just a malicious little ringmaster's joke, like prompting Paul to organize nasty little June into playing some dirty trick on Wanda?

How was it that brilliant music could be made by a very disgusting person? He was pondering this problem when another thought hit him. Why had Fred wanted to stop him leaving? And why had Paul slipped away? Was there another angle to the malicious joke? Was there any connection between him being kept there and what Paul had slipped away to do? On a sudden hunch he turned off from the direct route home into the lane leading to Faringfield. It would be interesting to see if there was a Jaguar parked in the stable yard at the Old Rectory.

There was. But Paul's cottage was locked up and no lights showed in the dusk. Action was going on somewhere, he had just heard a loud splash. From the swimming pool? There was an open-air one down behind the cottage, but its water proved to be still and deserted. In the garden, then? He tiptoed out on to the terrace behind the house. Down at the far end of the grass walk the last few yards of the left hand border had been stripped of its planting, most of which had been dumped in the lily pool. Paul, muttering and cursing, was wrenching a rose bush out of the ground to throw into the pool after the rest.

Why? Bill thought. Because Fred told him to? Because Fred thought he wasn't in bad enough with his dad already, and needed more action to get him in even worse? If so, why the crafty plot to get me away for the evening, and keep me away while he got on with wrecking the garden? They could have let me go home as per usual and done it then, I don't get this.

He went down the grass walk to where Paul was uprooting a clump of lilies. "Hi there, why are you doing that?" he asked mildly.

"It's obscene, it deserves to be wrecked. It's not gardening, it's showing people how much money you've got."

Bill agreed with him privately, but this was not the moment to say so. "Fred's idea, was it?"

"No, mine. I don't like blond chorus-boys who have it off with my sister."

"I never touched Wanda. Who says?"

"None of your business."

"It was Fred, I bet."

Oh I get it now, Bill thought. Paul must have said something nice about me, and Fred don't like it, he thinks two's company and three's none, so he decides to break it up. He sets Paul up to wreck the garden, and he makes sure I know Paul's played a dirty trick on me.

"Fred don't like you having any friends except for him," he said.

Paul's teeth were chattering. "He's the only friend I have."

There was a pause while Bill decided what to do next. "Your parents in?" he asked.

"What d'you mean, 'my parents'? She's not my mother, and he wouldn't be my father if he could help it."

"Sorry. I meant Mr. and Mrs. Galliant."

"He's out making a speech somewhere, to show everyone he's back in his right mind and the shares can go up again. My stepmother's gone with him."

"Okay then, here's what we do. You and I put all this back in the border before it gets too dark to see, and I don't tell on you to your dad, and when we've tidied it up nice, you and I will have a little talk, okay?"

The "little talk" lasted for two hours. It was rather like trying to de-program someone to get them out of the clutches of a racketeering religious sect.

Teresa Enriquez sat in her stall in the Glyndebourne Festival Theatre, enjoying an admirable performance of Tchaikovsky's *Eugène Onegin*. The set was beautifully designed and lit, the musical ensemble was impeccable. All the details of the production were well thought out and effective without being gimmicky. One of Glyndebourne's discoveries, a pretty young Swedish soprano with a lovely voice, was moving Teresa to tears with a passionate rendering of Tatiana's letter. And the three people sitting on Teresa's right were all asleep.

Strolling through the garden before the performance, she had sensed that there was something odd about the audience. It was well, even expensively dressed in evening clothes. But it was not the sort of jet-set audience she would have expected in view of the prices. There was talk of "the office" between groups of people who obviously knew each other. It was a well-heeled audience, yet in some indefinable way philistine.

The dinner interval came. Teresa had discovered with astonishment that the mad English, instead of sitting sensibly in one of the restaurants in the complex, streamed out into the garden carrying camp stools and picnic tables to swill dry martinis and champagne and eat vast quantities of over-rich food. The idea of a picnic in evening dress on English grass, which by definition would be damp, filled Teresa with horror on hygienic as well as convenience grounds. She had arranged to dine in the Mildmay restaurant with her neighbour in the stalls, a middle-aged German tenor from the cast of *Così fan tutte* whom she had worked with once in San Francisco. She asked him about the three members of the audience who had slept throughout the Letter Song.

"Only at the end they wake, when is applause," she reported, horrified. "And one of them, he.... How is it called? He make noises with the nose."

"It is always so here," the tenor explained. "Until they have eaten their big dinner they sleep. Afterwards, when they have had plenty wine, they are enough awake to laugh when they see on the stage something funny. But a musical joke they cannot hear, unfortunately, because they are not musical. To sing *Così* for them is an agony, they do not know that 'Smanie implacabili' is a most marvellous joke."

"Then why spend they their money to come?"

"Listen, my dear, I tell you. Glyndebourne has no state subsidy. They must beg money from the big industry, and the big industry in return for its money must have tickets to give to the higher personnel, tickets to give to the buyers from abroad, to people who know nothing of opera but come because it is Glyndebourne. So the firms hand out these tickets, *Figaro qui, Figaro là*, and there are many of these awful people in the audience, and they sleep."

Teresa listened with half an ear. The worries driven out of her mind by enjoyment of the performance had come flooding back. She was now very worried indeed by the

112

fact that Richard Galliant's cold English wife whom he detested so much was still living in the house with him. He had not told her of the steps he was taking, if any, to get rid of her. When he came to spend the evening with her he was the same ardent and amusing lover as ever, but gave no sign of willingness to become a husband.

She was also worried about Miguel. That morning a friend of his in Paris had rung in a panic to tell her that according to the émigré grapevine, one of his closest collaborators had been shot dead by frontier guards while trying to cross illegally into the country. Or rather, that was the government version of what would probably turn out to be another murderous drive against the opposition. Alarmed, she had put a call through to Miguel in Miami before leaving for Glyndebourne. According to the man he shared the apartment with, he had left there ten days ago without saying where he was going. Almost certainly he was somewhere in Colombia, trying to cross the frontier.

He was not a very satisfactory husband, but she was used to him. And it began to look as if she might be left with no husband at all.

Celia had dined with friends. Arriving home late, she had to let herself into the cottage in a hurry because the phone was ringing.

"Oh thank goodness you're in at last, dear," said a vaguely familiar voice. "I've been trying you all evening, this is Vi Moseley."

"I'm sorry . . . ?" said Celia, utterly at a loss.

"Lavinia Lure Modes, dear. You came to the showroom to ask about the daturas in our publicity. I've been ringing to warn you. Another one's been stolen."

"Oh no!" said Celia, horrified. "How? Where?"

"From the conservatory this time. Someone broke in in broad daylight and took one while Henry and me were at work."

"Were they seen? Did you get a description?"

"No dear, it's hopeless. The neighbours say someone

came with a van, and they think they remember trousers, but it could still have been a woman. We told the police and gave them your phone number, I hope we did right?"

"Oh. Yes of course. Thank you for warning me."

Damn, Celia thought as she put down the phone, there goes my peace of mind. I'd decided it was over, the remains of the datura had been thrown out on the compost heap. It had done the job and the poisoner had no more use for it. No one was in any danger. But now the thing's beginning all over again, why? Because Galliant has started making public appearances to show there's nothing wrong with him and the shares have stopped going down. The poisoner hasn't got what he wanted yet, so he's decided to give Galliant another dose.

What was she to do? Warn the Galliant household? That would be a fat lot of use. If Mrs. Galliant wasn't doing the poisoning herself she knew who was and was protecting them, otherwise she'd have had the police in long ago. Was Celia to call the police in herself? With no hard evidence to go on? She had been had that way once before, being laughed at and called a lunatic. She'd been proved right in the end, but the experience had left a deep hurt. No, the police had her phone number, let them come to her.

But there was one thing she could and must do, alert Galliant himself to the danger he was in. She put a sheet of paper in her typewriter and tapped out a warning: "The hallucinogenic drug used to poison you came from a tree datura plant stolen from a source in London. That plant has been destroyed, but you should know that another one was stolen today from the same source, presumably as a replacement."

It would have to be unsigned. Not that that mattered, the warning would be just as effective. The thought of sending anyone an anonymous letter made her giggle with embarrassment, but it was necessary for sordid commercial reasons. If she signed it and the guilty Mrs. Galliant came to know of it, she would avenge herself by refusing to pay Celia's enormous bill for the garden.

She slept badly. In the morning she overcame her sense of the ridiculous and forced herself to post her anonymous letter, then set off for Faringfield to put in one more day's work at the Old Rectory.

She was greeted when she arrived by a scene of disarray at the far end of the left hand long border, which Bill and Paul had replanted as best they could in semi-darkness. While Bill helped her restore order, he told her about his evening's adventures and how the border came to be in that condition.

"Could Fred be the one who's poisoning Galliant?" she asked when he had finished.

"He's mad enough, but why would he want to?"

"Goodness knows. Would Paul do the job for him if Fred told him to?"

"I dunno. I tried for hours to talk some sense into him, but in the end he went all hysterical and I had to stop for fear he had a fit."

They worked for some time in silence.

"Oh Celia, I meant to ask you. Right at the start of all this you said you'd smelt a datura somewhere, remember?"

"Oh! How extraordinary. You're right, but I'd forgotten all about that."

"You've not remembered where it was, then? I'm good at jogging your memory, let's have a go. Indoors or outdoors?"

"Indoors, they're tender."

"You're sure? They could have put it out to get the sun, and taken it in again at night."

Celia concentrated. "I still say indoors. I have a vague feeling that the place I was in wasn't very light. And... yes, could I have been a bit out of breath when I smelt it? Suddenly there was this heavy scent, in my throat as well as my nose because I was breathing rather hard."

"You'd been running then?"

She thought about this. "No. I think I was out of breath because I'd been hurrying up some steps, or a staircase, rather a steep one. But it's all horribly vague."

Where could it have been? Bill went on prodding her memory for a time, but only succeeded in making her suspect that she had imagined the whole thing, and had never smelt a datura at all.

An Edwardian stockbroker's villa, Joan Galliant diagnosed, as Morris halted the Rolls in front of it and opened the door for her to get out. She braced herself for battle, and was glad she had come in the Rolls. This was a state visit, for which her Mini Metro would have been inappropriate.

The door of the house was opened by a sallow old woman in black, who addressed her in what she assumed to be Spanish. She proved to have no English, but accepted Joan's visiting card suspiciously and stomped away with it, leaving her standing on the doorstep. Morris caught her eye and giggled. "Do be careful, Madam," he said loudly, "or she'll hex you and turn you into a toad."

There was indeed something witch-like about the crooked finger with which the crone beckoned Joan into the house. But her mistress, who appeared in the drawing-room after the usual interval for titivation, was as modern as her attendant was ancient, with a trim figure, a simple but expensive dress and a handsome face to which everything possible had been done to delay the ravages of time.

"*Buenos dias, Señora,*" Teresa said coldly. "Good afternoon."

Joan recognized the voice at once. She had heard it several times on the telephone, asking for Richard in urgent tones which made it quite clear what the situation was. And now the stupid creature was obviously boiling up for a scene. Any minute now there would be a grand gala performance of the Other Woman confronting the Wife, with full orchestral accompaniment and an odds-on chance of hysterics to follow.

"Do excuse my barging in like this, Mrs. Enriquez," she said. "But I'd heard so much about you from my husband that I thought we ought to get acquainted before we meet at our garden party."

She was definitely Mrs. Enriquez. According to the office at Glyndebourne there was a mister, though he was elsewhere. She was well-preserved and reasonably good looking, but nothing special. Why had Richard fancied her? She was a celebrity, of course, and he was still a bit of a social climber. One had to make allowances for that.

Teresa, meanwhile, was guessing frantically. What had Richard told this abominable wife of his about her? Had he given her notice at last that their marriage was breaking up? Her heart leapt at the thought. But there was another explanation of her ill-mannered visit. Perhaps Richard had told her nothing. Perhaps cold, upper-class Englishwomen spied on their husbands as a matter of course, like sensible women the world over.

"How found you where I live?" she managed to enquire.

"Simple, I rang the Administration at Glyndebourne. As you probably know, my husband is a major contributor to Glyndebourne, so of course they told me." This was part of the truth. The telephone number she had made Mrs. Enriquez leave during one of her heart-throb phone calls had supplied the missing link in the chain.

"Shall we sit down?" she added.

Teresa sank speechless into an armchair.

"Now, Mrs. Enriquez—"

"Excuse please, Señora, I am not 'Mrs. Enriquez.' That name is for the opera. My husband call himself Miguel Gomez Fernandez."

"Oh dear, how frightfully complicated, d'you mind if I call you Teresa? Anyway, let's get out our diaries, because you must come over to dinner one night at Faringfield when you haven't got a rehearsal. No really, Richard and I would be delighted, we won't take 'no' for an answer. How about Monday? You won't be rehearsing that night, because it's the dress rehearsal of *Così fan tutte*."

"Perhaps. I must ask first at Glyndybourny."

"Of course, do check with them and let us know, here's

117

our phone number. Oh, but how stupid of me, you've got it already, I think you rang us once or twice. Do come, you and Richard will have so much to talk about, you're old friends, aren't you? I'm afraid you'll find him a bit under the weather, some sort of allergy the doctor thinks, and it even made him behave a little strangely at times, you may have read about that in the papers. No? Anyway, I had quite a lot of nursing to do, men are such fusspots when they're ill, aren't they? And of course he is getting on in years. It worries me that he has to do so much travelling abroad."

"Why?" Teresa asked, rallying. "He enjoys very much the travel. It makes for him a change when he is bored at home. Perhaps you think he has adventures, perhaps you do not trust him?"

"My dear Teresa, I gave up worrying about that ages ago. He's very good looking and quite unscrupulous, there are messy goings-on with secretaries and creatures like that all the time. I usually have to help him tidy up afterwards, but I wouldn't dream of letting it affect our marriage."

Only the thought of the top Cs in Act II of *The Marriage of Figaro* prevented Teresa from screaming with rage.

❧ EIGHT ❧

Stop talking, you dreadful woman, thought Richard Galliant, so that I can get away, I'm in a hurry. But the silly hag went on and on in her upper class screech, railing and cursing at the West Sussex County Council. This was supposed to be a protest meeting about a controversial planning decision, but it was a hot afternoon and most of the audience was asleep. Being the chairman, Galliant could not slip out unobtrusively before the end.

A few days ago the secretary of the committee had rung, sounding rather nervous, to say that the deputy chairman would be happy to take the meeting if he was "not sufficiently recovered" to do so himself. Normally he would have been glad to get out of a boring chore. But it was another opportunity (he was grasping at all of them nowadays) to appear in public and demonstrate that he was in full possession of his faculties, so he declined the committee's offer with thanks and assured them that he had recovered from his "allergy" and was now perfectly well. He had not foreseen then that just before he left for the meeting a crisis would blow up, consisting of Teresa Enriquez bellowing at him on the telephone like a Latin American fishwife in a rage, and threatening to announce to the press that she had no intention of attending his garden party. What had happened to upset her? He had to find out.

The long-winded woman was still orating. Shut up and sit down, you stupid cow, he thought. To his astonishment, she screeched obediently to a stop and subsided to languid applause. He rose, summed up efficiently, tidied up a confused situation concerning amendments, put the motion to the vote and closed the meeting. Pausing only to buy a peace-offering of hot-house roses, he drove to Teresa's rented love-nest to question her.

Joan, Teresa explained, had "insulted" her. How? By inviting her to dinner. Why was that an insult? In civilized Latin countries, she explained, it was an unheard-of indelicacy to invite one's beloved to dinner with one's wife, only the coarse English would dream of such a thing, had he known that she intended it? He had? Then why in the name of all the saints had he not prevented it?

"I tried to talk her out of it, and I thought I'd succeeded, but it was rather awkward. She knows we're old friends, she wanted to meet you, and she thought we ought to show you some attention while you're here. I tried to ring you and warn you, but you were asleep or rehearsing or something and I got Pilar, who grunted something in Spanish and put the phone down."

"Olt friends? She knows that we are *olt friends*? When you tell her the truth?"

She must trust him and be patient, he explained. These things took time.

"Why time? In Rome you did not say 'time,' in Buenos Aires you did not say 'time.' You said she is cold, she is ugly, she is stupid, my marriage with her is a calamity, I shall end it."

She was perfectly right, Galliant thought, he had said that sort of thing in Rome and in Buenos Aires and several other places too. It had never occurred to him that she would precipitate a crisis at an awkward moment by coming to sing on his doorstep at Glyndebourne. He began to improvise a story about his sensitive and highly strung son Paul who was under psychological stress, and must not be subjected to the shock of a parental divorce just at present. But she went on threatening to put a curse on the garden party and provoke a showdown with Joan, and she obviously meant it. For a time he was very alarmed. It took a lot of eloquence and some heavy love-making to calm her down.

To Celia's relief the job at the Old Rectory was well and truly finished, apart from dead-heading, grass-cutting and any watering that might prove necessary. Even these responsibilities would end after the party in ten days' time. When the others had knocked off she lingered for a last look at her handiwork. As instant gardening jobs went, it was not at all bad, and would not strike one as very vulgar unless one knew how much had been spent on it. An hour ago Galliant had come out into the garden and made complimentary remarks, which seemed to be sincere.

She was turning to go when Fred Watney appeared on the terrace. When he saw her he ran down the grass path towards her, scowling furiously. Seen closer to, he proved to be panic-stricken rather than angry.

"Where's Bill?" he snapped. "Your sidekick with the steroid muscles."

"He's just gone."

This seemed to be the last straw. "Damn. I need help."

"Can I do anything?" Celia asked.

"You? Hell no. I need a weight lifter that can keep his gob shut."

"I can keep my gob shut and I'm stronger than I look. What's the trouble?"

"Paul's flaked out. I got to get him away to the doctor. He's unconscious, it's scary."

"Where is he? Let me see if I can help."

He seemed to think this unlikely, but accepted her offer with panicky bad grace and strode away towards the cottage, with Celia scampering along beside him. "Lucky the family's out," he muttered as they crossed the stable yard. "They'd create like Hell's Angels if they found out."

What the family would have created about became obvious when they reached the cottage. Paul lay slumped in the
armchair unconscious and very pale, with a druggy smile
on his face.

"God knows where he got the stuff," said Fred. "I
don't, honest. I've been trying to keep him clean."

Paul had nothing on but a soaking wet sweatshirt. His
hair was damp too. "He was half in and half out of the
swimming pool when I got here, he could have drowned,"
said Fred. "Dopey and talking silly too. I dragged him in
here and he went all dead-looking like that."

"He's probably in shock," said Celia. "We ought to get
that wet thing off him and wrap him up warm."

"I tried. He's a dead weight. You can't."

"Easy," said Celia, who had nursed the bedridden elderly in her time. "Get a blanket from somewhere."

He produced one from upstairs.

"Now," said Celia. "When I heave him up, spread the
blanket on the chair under him, then get hold of the bottom
of the sweatshirt and pull it over his head. And be quick
about it, because I won't be able to hold him up for long."

Though Paul was scrawnily built he was heavier than
she expected. But she knew the knack and managed to lift
him just enough to let Fred operate. "You'd better call an
ambulance," she suggested when the blanket had been
tucked round Paul.

"No fear, Susie would see it and tell them and they'd
want to know what's wrong. We got to get him in my car
so no one sees."

This was all very well, but it would take time. There
was no way of getting a car up the path to the door of the
cottage.

"If he dies while we're messing about his family won't
thank us," she said.

"No ambulance, the family mustn't know." He sounded
frantic but determined. There was no point in arguing.

"There's a wheelbarrow in the tool shed at the far end of

the vegetable garden," Celia told him. "Fetch it. Hurry, I don't like the look of him."

Fred went. Celia wondered what one did to make junkies under the influence more comfortable, and decided it would be best to leave well alone. After a time Paul stirred in his blanket.

"Is that you, Dad?" he enquired with his eyes shut.

"No," said Celia. "Paul, what have you taken to get you into this state?"

He grunted something unintelligible.

"Answer me, Paul. It's important."

She went on asking, but he had fallen silent again.

Presently he said "Don't let that bitch Wanda come near me."

"Why not, Paul?"

"I hate her . . . I'd like to rip her guts out."

"Really. Why?"

"She sneaks on me to Dad and makes him hate me."

"D'you hate him too?" Celia asked.

"No. Yes. I don't want to hate him but he makes me."

"How does he do that?"

"He keeps telling me I'm rubbish because I'm not different from what I am. I want to make him like me, but he frightens me and I can't help saying stupid things. And then he goes wild at me and I do something stupid to annoy him."

"Paul, listen to me, *You must tell me what it is you've taken.*"

But it was no good. He gave a weary sigh and fell silent again.

After what seemed an age, Fred came back with the wheelbarrow. Under her instructions he wheeled it right into the room. "You're going to have to do the next bit," she told him, "because I'm not strong enough. You saw what I did before, it's quite simple. Brace your knees against his, clasp your hands together behind his back— no, under his armpits—and heave him up. That's right, now swing him round at right angles and dump him in the barrow. Well done, now if we put the blanket over him Susie will think he's a sack of potatoes or something."

Fred's flying saucer, parked in the stable yard, had been designed for fully conscious athletes to crawl into. "We'll never get him into that thing," said Celia. "We'll take my van."

Getting him into the van would have been a matter of moments if Paul had not suddenly come to life and started to fight them, proclaiming that he was being attacked by blue devils with hot knives. After a brisk struggle they managed to force him in at the back, where he lay thrashing about amid miscellaneous gardening equipment. Fred climbed in beside him to hold him down.

"I've been asking him what he's taken, but he won't say," said Celia as she drove off. "Ask him again if you get a chance."

But Paul went on kicking and struggling for a time, then fell back into a coma.

At the junction with the main road Fred said "turn right."

She braked. "But Lewes hospital's casualty department's the nearest."

"We're not going to any public hospital, damn you. I'm a celebrity, the press would fasten on anything about me and drugs. Turn right."

Celia was shocked. Evidently Fred's first priority was his image, not Paul's welfare. "Where do we take him then?"

"There's a special nursing home ten miles up the London road where they all go when this happens."

It meant roughly the same length of journey, so she did not argue. In the intervals of giving directions, Fred embarked on a whining complaint about Bill's behaviour the previous night, but Celia listened with only half an ear. The road was narrow and winding, and she was trying to pass a huge slow-moving truck and trailer. Paul's state alarmed her. The sooner he was under medical care the better.

Meanwhile Fred railed on against Bill. "This is all his silly fault, interfering bastard. Paul didn't want to go, he knew it'd be a bloody calamity, but your Bill talked him into it and now look at him."

Celia had managed at last to pass the truck and could give Fred more of her attention. Where had Bill talked Paul into going with such disastrous results? To a tête-à-tête lunch with his father, Fred explained. "Yesterday his dad came to see Paul, all smarmy and weepy, it happens from time to time, wanting him and Paul to kiss and be friends, so they were to have this lunch together and talk it over man-to-man. Paul phoned me this morning before he went, and I tried to talk him out of it but oh no, your Bill that doesn't know a thing about it had told him he ought to go, so he'd decided he would. But I knew what would happen. 'Don't you go, Paul,' I told him. 'It'll end like it always does with him shouting at you fit to bust, and you'll come away all shook up and hysterical and I'll be kept up all night calming you down.' That's what I told Paul, and that's what happened. Look at him!"

"You mean, he was so upset afterwards that he took an overdose of something?"

"That's right," said Fred. "He felt godawful miserable and he had a snort or two hidden away somewhere."

On thinking about this scenario, Celia decided that there was something wrong with it. "No!" she cried with a sudden flash of insight. "That's not what happened at all. I asked him over and over again what he'd taken, but he wouldn't answer me. Don't you see what that means? He couldn't, because he didn't know. He didn't take anything deliberately. There's been a mix-up and he's eaten his father's lunch."

Understandably, this made no sense to Fred, and Celia did not explain very coherently because she was evolving her theory as she went along. The datura stolen from the Lavinia Lure people had been used to start a new poison campaign against Galliant, and the poisoned plateful intended for him had somehow been given to Paul to eat.

This explanation got a hostile reception from Fred. "Who says Galliant's being poisoned?"

"I do."

"Then why's the family saying it's an allergy?"

"I'm not sure, but datura's a hallucinogen and I imagine they don't want publicity linking them with drugs any more than you do. I expect we'll find that Mr. Galliant had an important public engagement this afternoon. When he's due to make a speech or attend a ceremony, someone puts datura in his food, to make him behave oddly."

"Paul didn't behave oddly, he just flaked out," Fred objected.

"I'm not surprised. Paul's had the dosage that was right for his father, who's much bigger and more solidly built than Paul. It would knock Paul right out. The sooner we get him to this nursing home the better."

Behind her, Paul was showing signs of violent life again. Fred calmed him down none too gently, then said "Why would he eat his dad's dinner? You've no proof it was poisoned. Why d'you think it's this datura stuff?"

"Because of the symptoms. It has to be a hallucinogen because he saw blue devils with hot knives, remember. He'd been in the swimming pool. That's because they get intolerably hot, so they undress and make for water. The datura plant contains atropine, which in large quantities is pretty deadly, that's why I'm breaking the speed limit. But it also contains hyoscine, the stuff they put in seasick pills, which makes you drowsy, and hyoscyamine which makes you excited and aggressive, that's why he's having alternate phases of stupor and frantic activity. Another thing, hyoscine's supposed to be a truth drug of sorts. While you were fetching the wheelbarrow he came to the surface in a dreamy kind of way and I asked him some questions. He replied with some rather startling home truths, that wouldn't have come out normally."

Following Fred's directions, she turned in at a lodge gate and up a drive between lawns backed with evergreens, like the approaches to a crematorium. A country house in the Victorian nightmare gothic style came in sight at the end of it. As soon as she stopped Fred ran inside, and came out with two orderlies and a stretcher. Paul was taken inside and a house surgeon summoned to examine him. Celia suggested that they ought to phone the Galliants and tell them what had happened.

"No," said Fred firmly. "If you're wrong and it's something he's taken, his dad will hammer him into the ground. We got to be sure first."

The house surgeon came hurrying out into the hall. "It's not any of the usual things. His pupils aren't contracted, in fact they're dilated. D'you know what he's taken?"

"Datura," said Celia. "The atropine and the hyoscyamine both have that effect."

"Thorn apple?"

"No, that's the problem. A tropical member of the same family. It hasn't been analysed properly, all we know is that the percentage of atropine depends on the age of the plant."

"What else is there?"

"Hyoscine and hyoscyamine, but it's the atropine you have to worry about."

He nodded. "Have to pump him out."

"Quite. Is there a path lab here with a polariscope?"

"Of course."

"To save them looking it up, atropine is optically inert, hyoscine is laevo-rotatory and the whole mixture shows a light green fluorescence under long-wave ultra-violet."

"You're a doctor?"

"No, a botanist. And take a sealed and witnessed specimen for the police lab."

He made a face. This was the sort of nursing home where police enquiries into the patients' case histories were not always welcome.

When he had gone Celia tried again to persuade Fred that the Galliants ought to be phoned at once, but he was adamant. "We got to be sure first."

Evidently his image had to be protected vis-à-vis the Galliants as well as the press.

Over an hour passed before the house surgeon returned. "Atropine, yes. Hyoscine, yes. So far we haven't identified the hyoscyamine."

"How much atropine?"

"Impossible to tell, but the authorities say it isn't dominant in thorn apple."

"But this is a tropical variety. How is he?"

"Respiration normal. His temperature's a bit high, though, and he's deeply comatose."

"Should his family be told to come?"

He hesitated. "Was it self-administered?"

"No."

"In that case, I think yes."

Celia rang the Old Rectory and asked for Galliant. It was his wife who answered. "I'm sorry, he's not here. Can I do anything?"

Celia told her what had happened. A long silence followed. "You mean, that stupid boy's been experimenting with some damn drug?"

"No. The symptoms are the same as your husband had. They had lunch together, I believe. I think Paul must have eaten something intended for your husband, containing a hallucinogenic drug."

Another pause. "Ah. That's what you think, is it?"

"It's not for me to say. I've asked the hospital to keep a sealed specimen of the stomach contents in case there has to be a police enquiry."

"But look here, this is a family matter, it's nothing to do with the police. Has the hospital called them in already?"

"No. It's not a hospital, it's an expensive-looking private nursing home specializing in withdrawal treatment of drug abusers. I don't think they'd go out of their way to invite police enquiries."

"How the hell did he end up there?"

"Fred Watney knew of it."

"That lout. He would. He's there too, is he?"

"He found Paul, and made me help get him here. Incidentally, he seems to disapprove violently of drug abuse."

"My dear Mrs. Grant, I'm not a complete fool. When he started haunting the place we asked the police about him and drugs and they gave him a clean bill of health. If they hadn't we'd have thrown him out in a flash."

She fell silent. Celia was beginning to wonder if the conversation was over when she surfaced again after a long pause for thought. "Oh well, I suppose I'd better come clean. We said Richard's thing was an allergy because we wanted to stop the run on the shares and make the banks pipe down and stop fussing. But as a matter of fact we've no idea what it is. If you go around telling the press it's not an allergy, it's a drug, the market will assume he's an addict and the banks will call in their loans and a lot of people will be out of jobs, because the firm will go bankrupt. And the first creditor not to get a penny will be you."

"I shan't go around saying any such thing. You seem to have an idea that I'm connected somehow with the press, but I assure you you're wrong."

"Then that's fine and dandy, isn't it, we understand one another. How is Paul?"

"Very drowsy. They did say the relatives ought to be told to come."

"My God! Where is this place?"

Celia explained its whereabouts.

"Right. Tell them I'll be there in half an hour."

"Very well, but did you say your husband wasn't at home? I wonder if he's all right? The two of them did share a meal."

"Oh. Horrors, I never thought of that. But I think I know where he is. I'll ring him before I leave."

Celia saw no reason to hang around at the nursing home till Joan Galliant arrived. But she felt obliged in decency to drive home via Faringfield so that Fred could pick up his car, which he had left in the stable yard at the Old Rectory. They parted coldly and he drove off, leaving Celia to notice, in the beam of her headlights, that the barrow used to transport Paul from the cottage to her van had been abandoned in the middle of the yard. If it was not put away, embarrassing questions would be asked about it in the morning.

She switched off her lights rather than attract Susie's attention and face embarrassing questions now, then started trundling the barrow back towards the shed where it belonged. But a few yards up the path leading to the vegetable garden she halted, terrified. A dim figure, barely visible against the night sky, was standing stock still ahead of her to one side of the path, as if hoping not to be noticed.

"Who's there?" she said in a shocked voice.

The answer came in an even more panic-stricken whisper. "It's me. Anthea."

Celia put down her barrow. "What are you doing here?"

"There's someone in the design studio," Anthea stammered. "With a torch. I want to see who it is when they come out."

"You won't see from here."

"No. I hid here when you drove in. It was terrifying, I didn't know who you were."

"Well, let's get to where we can see," said Celia, and hurried her into the archway leading from the garden to the stable yard. From there they could watch the entrance door to the office block with no risk of being seen.

"Who can it be?" whined Anthea in a panic. "I'm not made for this sort of thing, Celia, it makes me feel quite ill. I wish I was tough and sensible like you."

Celia was feeling frail rather than tough and sensible, and also furious. Anthea, true to her unlimited capacity for tiresome behaviour, was making far too much noise, and would have to be coped with before she alerted the intruder by hiccupping and sobbing. Resisting the temptation to cure her with a good slap in the face, Celia remembered that panicky people were supposed to behave more sensibly if one gave them a job to do, so she explained in a whisper what had happened to Paul, and made her try to remember who had an alibi for the midday period, when someone had poisoned his lunch.

"Oh goodness, let me think," said Anthea scattily. "Celia, who can it be in the studio?"

"If you make less noise we'll find out in due course. Concentrate, now. Was Wanda at home?"

"No. It's her day at the factory in Slough."

"Check tomorrow, will you, that she actually went? Where was Mrs. Galliant while Paul and his father were having lunch alone together?"

"Shopping in Brighton, I think. Or was that yesterday? No, it must have been today, because there was a problem about cars. Joan had taken the Rolls, and Richard had a meeting to chair somewhere, and I had to fix for him to take an office car."

"Well done, Anthea. Now what about Charles?"

"He'd have been at the London office."

"I daresay, but in the morning I want you to check on that too. Did he have any outside engagements and if so did he keep them? How about the designers and the office staff?"

"They're out of it. The house is off limits to them."

"Goodness. The only suspects we're left with are Susie and Morris."

"Not Morris. He drove Mrs. Galliant into Brighton in the Rolls."

"Susie, then. Unless Charles invented an outside engagement and crept down here unobtrusively."

"He wouldn't need to. Any dirty work he or Mrs. G. want done, Susie would do it for them."

They had been waiting for what seemed a long time for the intruder to come out. So far there was no sign of him, and Celia wondered if he was a product of Anthea's fevered imagination.

"Did you actually see whoever it was?" she whispered.

"Yes. I know I'm scatty, but I really did. I was passing and I saw someone walk in from the lane and make for the office block. I thought it might be whoever sells our designs to Pritchard and Colson, so I went in after them, and there was someone with a flashlamp in the studio, moving about."

Celia was still doubtful. She had just decided to give it two more minutes, then go home, when the door of the office block opened slowly. A shadowy figure stole out, looked around furtively, and hurried away out of the yard.

"How surprising," Celia commented when he had gone. "I suppose we'll have to add him to our list of suspects."

It was indeed surprising. Even in the gloom there was no mistaking the stooping, scholarly figure, outlined against the night sky, of Frank Dawson, the firm's accountant.

It was almost eleven when the receptionist at the nursing home called Joan Galliant to the phone to speak to her husband.

"This is damnable," he said. "I've just got home and found your note. How is he?"

"Still unconscious, but they're a bit less worried about him than they were. And Richard, according to the pathologist here, it's datura, the drug that was mentioned in that anonymous letter. The same stuff that upset you."

"Good. Now he'll know how filthy it feels."

"Oh really, Richard, I sometimes think you don't deserve to have a son. Another thing, that sinister little china doll with the perfect complexion and the direct line to the press knows now that you've been fed hallucinogenic drugs."

"Hell. She was there, was she?"

"Very much so, and in a very noticing mood. I tried to persuade her not to tell the world about the drug angle, and I hope I succeeded. I could kill you for leaving me to cope with her on my own."

"Oh hell, I'm sorry. After the meeting something came up—"

"I know damn well what came up, Richard, and where you were. I tried to phone you there, but couldn't get past

132

that awful old creature who gabbled at me in Spanish and put the phone down again. I suppose you were doing your great lover routine upstairs."

"I had to calm Teresa down. She was furious with you, and I don't blame her. What did you tell her about my 'allergy'?"

"As little as possible. We don't want the details of that business going all round Glyndebourne."

"I told you to leave the Teresa problem alone for the present."

"I daresay, but I decided the balloon had better go up now, while she was still rehearsing. We'd be mad to leave the crisis till later. You don't want a Countess Almaviva who's in such a rage that she can't sing in tune? Not after giving Glyndebourne all that money."

"There was no need to have a crisis, damn it."

"Oh yes there was, you couldn't possibly have staved it off till she'd done six countesses and rushed off to Salzburg or somewhere to start chortling all over again. I suppose it wasn't your idea, her coming to perform at Glyndebourne?"

"Good God no!"

"I suspected as much, she was astonished when she saw me. I didn't come up to specification at all as the frigid English frump that you were aching to get rid of. I suppose you made it sound quite convincing in Valparaiso."

"Buenos Aires, to be exact. Among other places. Joan, you really are a prize bitch."

"No I'm not, I just have to tidy up after you from time to time. I shall ring her tomorrow and confirm the dinner invitation. Now you've calmed her down, she'll realize that faces have to be saved all round and she'll come trotting along quite meekly in her best bib and tucker, you wait and see. And I shall ask Mrs. Grant. She obviously thinks she's a lady, and we need to keep on the right side of her. Meeting a celebrity will give her a great lift. One or two men, of course, and—yes, Anthea Clarkson, but I shall put her at the far end of the table. That whorehouse scent of hers gives me a headache."

He laughed. "You really are a bitch. But I love you, and I don't know what I'd do without you."

"Confidentially, my dear Richard, nor do I."

❧ NINE ❧

Teresa Enriquez had spent all day rehearsing and was dog tired. Her voice seemed to be in reasonable shape, and she was fairly sure of getting through without discredit. In any case the last act, which they had been rehearsing, did not make heavy demands on her. The reasons why she was exhausted were quite different.

To accuse the divine Mozart of incompetence was out of the question, but Teresa thought it careless of him and his librettist Da Ponte not to have realized earlier in the composition of their masterwork that a long queue of cast members was building up who had not yet been given a chance to exhibit themselves in an aria, and would mutiny unless their righteous demands were met before the final curtain came down. The action of the last act, with its misunderstandings and disguisings and scurryings in and out of arbours in the Almavivas' garden, had to grind to a halt to accommodate these aggrieved soloists, and the production difficulties did not end there. The audience had to be made to realize who was disguised as whom without making the disguises absurdly unconvincing, who believed whom to be what and at which point Figaro had penetrated his wife's disguise but had gone on pretending to be deceived. They had also to remember, as one long aria followed another, who was hiding in which arbour with whom. Confronted with these difficulties, the eager young producer had reduced himself and the cast to despair.

Her campaign to marry Richard Galliant was not going according to plan. He seemed to be in no hurry to dispose of his estranged wife, who was not nearly as estranged as he had pretended and a much more formidable adversary than she had expected to encounter. It began to look as if her idea of providing for her declining years by marrying him would have to be re-thought.

A disquieting sidelight on Richard Galliant was waiting for her at home. Pilar, grim-faced, had held up in front of her a strong-smelling sheet of newspaper which she said had arrived in the house as wrapping for an outlandish species of fish unheard of in Latin America. But as Pilar pointed out, there was a picture in the middle of it of Señor Ricardo grinning fatuously with his foot on someone's hat, and Pilar wanted to know what the caption meant.

Teresa read the accompanying news story, which disconcerted her. Had not the abominable Mrs. Galliant said something about Richard "behaving strangely at times"? And had she not asked her if she had read about it in the papers? At the time she had discounted that as another deserted wife's lie to put her off Richard, like the parallel allegation about "messy goings-on with secretaries." But it was true. He had behaved very strangely indeed, and it had been reported in the papers. She was horrified. Suddenly he had stopped looking like the steady yet hot-blooded future husband of her imagination. She had no wish to marry a man who got drunk or perhaps had gone mad, and created public scandals. Had he also "messed about" with secretaries? Probably. Marriage to him would be a nightmare, worse than with Miguel.

She took a sleeping pill, an extreme measure reserved for occasions when she was really upset, and woke slowly when the hammering on the front door started at two in the morning. She listened. Pilar came out of her room muttering curses, and opened the landing window. Someone

136

below shouted up to her. Pilar answered, then battered on Teresa's door. "Señora, Señora, wake up. It is the Señor."

Teresa went to the landing window. It was indeed Miguel. What in the name of all the saints was he doing here?

Telling Pilar to let him in, she put on her dressing-gown, made sure there were no traces of Richard Galliant's presence lying about in the bedroom, and went downstairs. Miguel was in the kitchen, with Pilar fussing over him, taking his coat, bringing him coffee. He was jet-lagged, unshaven, still unhealthily overweight. Only his sad eyes reminded Teresa that he had once been handsome.

Why had he come? Something must have gone very wrong in Miami, but all she could get out of him was gloomy monosyllables. Either he was too exhausted to talk, or else the story he had to tell was unsuitable for the ears of Pilar, who was lingering in unashamed curiosity.

"Pilar, go to bed," she snapped.

Pilar obeyed unwillingly. "Now, Miguel, tell me," Teresa said, and prepared to extract from him some pathetic story of fresh troubles at the newspaper or a quarrel among the exiles over the wording of some manifesto that no one would read. But the story was not pathetic, it was hair-raising. An arms dump had been found at a farm only a few miles from Ciudad Antonio. The farmer had named names. Or more probably the Government had told him what names to name; it was a heaven-sent opportunity to put as many members of the opposition as possible where they belonged, behind bars or in their graves. There had been arrests in Ciudad Antonio, and in Miami two prominent émigrés had already been snatched from their apartments.

"*Querida*, I am afraid," he said, clutching at her hand. "There are suspicious people in Miami, people from Ciudad Antonio, circulating among the émigrés. It is they who have organized these disappearances."

He was sure he was on the government hit list. So he had fled to England, thinking he would be safe. But now he was not so sure. "A man I recognized was watching me when I checked in to board the London plane, a man who was a police informer in the days of the military dictatorship."

"But he did not board the plane?"

"No."

"And at London there was nothing suspicious? No one followed you from the airport?"

"No, but there was no need. They knew that I would come to you, and is very easy for them to find out where you are singing."

Teresa wondered how seriously to take this. The émigrés were always working themselves up into a hysterical state about nothing at all. But once or twice what looked like nothing at all had ended in mysterious disappearances or deaths. It all seemed to her rather pointless. As far as she could make out, there was no issue of political principle at stake. The present government in Ciudad Antonio was in power because it was its turn to be in power and make life very uncomfortable for the other lot, consisting of families with whom, for reasons stretching back many generations, they did not get on. But how seriously was Miguel involved?

"This arms cache, you knew nothing of it?" she asked.

"I knew nothing, *querida*, I swear it."

She wondered whether to believe this. Some of the stories he had spun to extract money from her were almost certainly untrue. Had she jetted from capital to capital, slogged her way through opera after opera, to finance the purchase of Armalite rifles, with which to shoot the president of a tiny republic she had never set foot in?

She would try to find out more about that in the morning. Meanwhile there was another aspect of the matter to think about. Miguel knew nothing about her foolish idea of marrying Richard Galliant, and he must never know. His arrival was in a strange way a consolation. It gave her a new role to play, as the respectably married diva with an adoring husband in attendance. They would attend social gatherings together, including the Galliants' dinner and the garden party they were giving in her honour. In the morning she would ring the detestable Mrs. Galliant and explain that her devoted Miguel, unable to bear their separation any longer, had flown over from Miami to be with her, was that not charming of him? And if Mrs. Galliant would be so very gracious as to extend her most kind dinner invitation to include both of them she would be delighted to accept. As an added bonus there would be an opportunity during the dinner, or if not she would damn well make one, to condole cooingly with Mrs. Galliant on a predicament which she herself had never experienced, namely the anguish of having to put up with the philanderings of an unfaithful husband. One, moreover, who added to his offence by making a fool of himself in public.

Miguel's voice broke in on her thoughts. "I should not have come, *querida*, I should have gone to Pablo in Paris. There they would not find me."

His sad eyes searched her face for comfort. He was one of the world's losers, and he had had most of her savings off her. A coward too, he had constructed a whole gallery of terrors out of one man he thought he recognized near the check-in desk at Miami airport. But he was her husband and he was asking her for comfort, so she gave it him.

Celia spent the morning disinfecting and whitewashing a greenhouse, but was interrupted in this agreeable task by a phone call from Joan Galliant, inviting her to a dinner party. She recognized this gesture at once for what it was, a genteel bribe offered as an inducement to keep quiet about Paul's hallucinogenic misadventure. It was delivered with a certain amount of gush to make up for past ruderies, and with heavy emphasis on the celebrity of the chief guest, the world-famous singer Teresa Enriquez. "And she's bringing her husband, but I don't know anything about him except that he lives in Miami. I suppose that makes him a distinguished southern gentleman, or maybe not, we shall see. Anyway, thanks for agreeing to help us entertain them, half past seven on Monday. The men will be in blackers, by the way, so it's long frocks for us."

Celia had scarcely had time to take up the whitewash brush again before she was called back to the phone to speak to Anthea.

"Oh Celia, the most sinister development," Anthea began dramatically. "What shall I do? The Galliants have invited me to dinner."

"They've asked me too," said Celia. "What's the problem? Why d'you think it's sinister?"

"It's hair-raising. *Susie will have done the cooking.*"

"Oh, I see. You think it'll be a Borgia orgy with hallucinogenic soup. I'm sure we can eat without fear, Anthea. The Galliants are dead keen to prevent the media from finding out what happened to Paul. They won't want a repeat performance with a world-famous soprano stripping off in a frenzy and jumping into their swimming pool."

"But the Galliants may not know what Susie's doing to the food."

"Ah, you mean Susie could be playing tricks with it for some obscure Chinese reason of her own."

"Or because Charles is in the plot with her, without his mother knowing," Anthea suggested.

"That seems very unlikely. Besides, if the Galliants aren't tampering with the food themselves and don't know who is, they'll be guarding it like Fort Knox to make sure it remains wholesome."

Anthea began making panic-stricken little noises. "But Celia, why is she giving this party? I'm sure she's setting the stage for some frightful showdown like the last chapter of a detective story."

"Not with this opera singer there, surely? Plus a husband that Joan Galliant hopes will be a distinguished southern gentleman? He comes from Miami, so she's probably in for a surprise from what I remember of the place. Have you ever been there?"

"No!"

"Then don't be too astonished if he turns out to be a

retired furniture salesman from the Bronx or a drug-pushing pimp from some disreputable place in Latin America."

"The idea of this party terrifies me," said Anthea, with an edge in her voice which suggested that she meant it and was not play-acting.

Why had she accepted, Celia wondered, if the prospect terrified her to the point of hysteria? Was it just that very insecure people like her could not bear missing a party? Or was there something more?

"If you're really worried, Anthea, you could be struck down with a diplomatic illness at the last moment. You don't have to go."

"I must. Richard would be horribly hurt if I didn't. Oh Celia, I'll feel safer if you're there too. Promise me you won't cry off at the last moment."

"And miss the riveting experience of dining with the Faringfield mafia behind their wall of silence? I wouldn't dream of it. Which reminds me, you're meant to be finding out if Wanda's and Charles' alibis for the poisoning of Paul's lunch are as solid as they look."

"Oh. Sorry, my mind's getting unhinged, yes I did check on Charles and it was quite interesting. He was supposed to be looking in on the bank in Slough during the morning, to calm them down about the overdraft, I suppose. But I rang them to check if he'd left his hat there, and they said he hadn't been."

"Interesting, but I suppose not conclusive, there could be some other explanation. How about Wanda?"

"She's okay. I know she went to Slough as usual because there was a megafuss while she was there, something about the computer going wrong."

"Really? Tell me more."

"I'm not sure of the details, but I think the computer made a horrid mess instead of printing out a new pattern of hers. The technical people said it was something to do with a magnetic field, and Richard ranted and roared and made all the studio staff turn out their pockets and their handbags."

"In search of a magnet that had been used to send the computer terminal crazy?"

"That's right. He didn't find one, but what he did find in the way of contraceptives and sordid half-eaten Mars Bars was mind-blowing."

"I suppose June Hamilton must be the saboteur," Celia suggested.

"Why her?"

"Didn't Bill tell you? He overheard Paul encouraging her to play some unpleasant trick on Wanda. D'you know anything about her?"

"Yes. Richard thinks she's not good enough, and Charles wants to sack her before she qualifies for redundancy money. Wanda, being Wanda, thinks June will make the grade with more experience and is trying to help her, but June, being a mass of arrogance with a chip on her shoulder, resents being helped and thinks Wanda's stifling her originality and trampling on her genius out of jealousy. The office gossips think June's the one that's been selling our designs to Pritchard and Colson."

"Why, Anthea?"

"Goodness knows, probably out of routine office bitchery. I told you, the place is a snake pit. Celia, promise me you'll come on Monday and give me moral support."

"Of course I'll be there."

"Oh good. But if the starter's a prawn cocktail I shall hide under the table."

For the next few days Celia was very busy and saw nothing of Faringfield and its inhabitants. On the Monday she duly presented herself at the Galliants' front door in a rose pink evening dress which had survived from the grand days of her marriage and was still a knock-out. Morris, transformed for the evening from chauffeur into manservant, let her in.

"That's nice," he said, with apparent reference to the pink dress, though he was also making a clothes-stripping evaluation of its contents. He led her through the house towards the terrace. "You'll find it a bit thundery out there,

Madam's furious with that Miss Clarkson. She was early, got here while Madam was still putting on her face."

He led her through the house and out on to the terrace, where the company so far consisted of Richard Galliant in a bottle-green velvet dinner jacket, Joan Galliant in a cruel shade of electric blue, Wanda looking vague but charming in a floating chiffon of her own design, Charles Langley looking solid and unremarkable and Anthea deathly pale but dressed to kill in skin-tight scarlet sequins.

When Galliant caught sight of Celia he raised both arms in a theatrical attitude of greeting. "Ah, the enchantress who waved her wand, and created a paradise garden for us in the twinkling of an eye."

"Hello, Mrs. Grant," said Joan Galliant. "Champers all right for you, or would you prefer gin or something?"

Celia accepted champagne from a tray proffered by Morris and a further stream of compliments on the garden, complete with references to Gertrude Jekyll, from Galliant.

"Shut up a moment, Richard," his wife interrupted. "There's something I want to tell you all before the others arrive. Recent events may have made you a bit nervous about eating in this house. But if you're afraid of being snapped at by giant hens with punk hair-dos and crocodile teeth like poor Richard, you can forget it, nor will you have to strip off and jump in the lily pool because your skin's burning hot. You needn't shy away from the food, because no Derby favourite's bran mash has been more carefully guarded against nobbling than the dinner you are about to eat. I cooked the whole damn lot myself and put it in the deepers under lock and key, and it's been unfreezing in the sideboard which is also locked, with the key in my handbag. It will be served direct from there course by course under my supervision, beginning with the soup which is in sealed thermos flasks, and I hope you enjoy it."

"Oh thank you Joan, you're marvellous," said Anthea in a twittery voice.

As Joan acknowledged this with a fierce scowl, Celia went over to Anthea to try to steady her with a few well-chosen remarks. But Anthea had moved away, so she changed direction and asked Wanda for news of Paul.

"He's still in the nursing home, Mrs. Grant."

Celia waited for an account of his progress, but none came. Instead, a look of suppressed glee appeared behind Wanda's granny glasses and she added, "Fred says Paul won't be coming back here when they let him out."

"You're glad?" Celia asked. Wanda looked round to see if anyone was eavesdropping, then nodded emphatically.

"I suppose he did bully you rather," said Celia.

"Yes, I don't know why I let him."

Why, Celia wondered, had the worm turned at last? "There's a limit to what one can take from a brother, isn't there?" she prompted.

"Yes!" Wanda shouted, so loud that people turned to look. Checking herself, she added in a fierce undertone: "I found out that he'd interfered with my work. That's unforgivable, *I don't let anyone interfere with my work.*"

Reading between the lines of this remark, Celia decided that her suspicions were confirmed. Paul had persuaded June Hamilton to wield the magnet which had caused the computer breakdown at Slough, and Wanda had found out all about it. Celia began to probe her for the details, but Joan Galliant had evidently seen what was going on and taken alarm, and called Wanda over to help hand round cocktail food. Celia found herself being looked up and down by Charles Langley, but in an impersonal manner which left her feeling fully clothed.

"That's a very nice dress," he said solemnly, as if okaying a life insurance policy whose terms seemed to him satisfactory.

"Thank you," said Celia. If he was a womanizer, he was a very cold and fishlike one.

He turned away towards the edge of the terrace and looked down the long walk between the borders. "You've done a very good job here."

"It's only a matter of spending a great deal of money," said Celia absently. He had one of those flat, boring voices which are an effort to listen to, even if the subject-matter is worth hearing.

"There's something I want to ask you, Mrs. Grant," he went on. "The other day at the nursing home where you so kindly took my step-brother Paul, I complimented their pathologist on having identified the toxic drug so quickly, and he replied that you had told him what to look for. Is that correct?"

"I believe I did make a suggestion, yes."

"It was more than a suggestion, I gather," he droned. "And the same drug was mentioned in an anonymous letter sent to my step-father. Moreover, it looked to me as if the letter and your estimate for the work on the garden were typed on the same typewriter."

"Yes?" Celia murmured ambiguously. His voice might be boring, but there was alarmingly little wrong with his mind.

"I don't understand why you didn't sign the letter," he persisted.

"That's a complicated question," she began, thinking furiously. "You see—"

"Mr. and Mrs. Gomez Fernandez," Morris announced to her enormous relief.

"We will continue this later," said Charles ominously.

Joan Galliant prepared to greet the guests of honour. "Here we go into the starting gate, and I hope the grocer hasn't nobbled the cheese," she muttered. "My God, I never thought of that. We don't want these two flat out in a stupor, do we?"

Galliant introduced everyone round, with a repeat when he came to Celia of his remarks about the enchantress who had waved her wand and created a paradise garden. Unfortunately only the word "enchantress" registered with Teresa, and caused her to draw the wholly wrong conclusion that he was introducing her to a rival for his favour, if not a successor. Worse still, he had described the striking-looking young woman in scarlet sequins as his "personal assistant," and Teresa had decided in a flash that only one kind of personal assistance could be expected of a young woman who smothered herself in scent and dressed like a whore. Unmistakably, this was one of the secretaries involved in "messy goings-on" with Galliant, and her presence at this party was a calculated insult, probably engineered by his intolerable wife. The newspaper had not lied, in fact it had understated the case. They must both be as mad as Lucia di Lammermoor to think of entertaining her in such company.

Meanwhile Celia shied away from Charles Langley to give herself time to think, and attached herself to the soprano's husband, a sad-looking man with bags under his eyes which echoed the curve of his paunch. He came from Miami, she remembered, and asked if it had changed much since she was there ten years ago.

"Unfortunately Miami is full of filthy dirty conspiracies," Gomez announced in a violent Spanish accent, and launched out into a fierce lecture on the iniquitous state of Latin America as seen from Miami, the profoundly mistaken policies advocated by the more misguided émigrés, the struggle to keep his newspaper going as the only voice of freedom left in the country, in the face of a chronic lack of money. And worst of all, those few genuine patriots like himself, who stood firm against tyranny, were in perpetual danger of assassination.

Looking round as she listened, Celia realized that so far the party consisted only of the family and two of its hangers-on, rather low-level company for a world famous celebrity. Soon, however, Morris ushered in reinforcements, five people who had arrived more or less together, and belonged near the top of the West Sussex pecking order: two owners of better-class stately homes and their wives, and a distinguished retired ambassador to whom Celia happened to be related. As she had met both the other couples on many occasions, Joan Galliant's attempt to introduce her was interrupted by glad cries of recognition.

"Customers of yours, Mrs. Grant?" she hissed crossly.

Stung by this, Celia retorted truthfully that the ex-ambassador was her uncle. Meanwhile Galliant was repeating his enchantress-waving-her-wand routine for the benefit of the newcomers, to explain Celia's presence at the party and draw attention to the glorification of his garden.

"What actually happened was that Mr. Galliant waved his cheque book," Celia interrupted, and realized too late that this could have been more charitably phrased. But he had gone on to deliver a lecturette about Gertrude Jekyll acquiring the principles of oil painting from her art teacher and adapting them to the palette of nature's great outdoors. Celia had heard it once too often, and decided that if she was going to behave badly she might as well do the job thoroughly.

"Her teacher Hercules Brabazon was a water colour painter," she interrupted, "I don't think he touched oils in his life."

This was embarrassingly well received by the newcomers, and very badly by Richard Galliant, who decided on a diversion and suggested a general move down into the garden to admire it. As the party strolled down the long grass path between the borders, Teresa grabbed her husband by the arm and took him aside. She had overheard him lecturing Celia on the iniquities of the clique in power in Ciudad Antonio, and disapproved.

"Why?" she scolded. "It is boring for everyone. Can you not for one evening forget your émigré politics and speak of something else?"

"I cannot forget the man at the check-in desk at Miami, the look on his face. And tonight, as we drove out of the gate to come here, a suspicious man was pretending to cut the hedge of the field opposite. I should not have come to this party, all the time I am afraid. Tomorrow I shall go to Pablo in Paris, while I am here with you they know where they can find me and I cannot feel safe. Also, for you it is a risk."

"For me?"

"They shoot at me, and hit you also, perhaps."

Should she ship Miguel off to Paris? All these dangers

seemed to her imaginary. If he was heading for a nervous breakdown he had better have it in Sussex, under her eye . . .

"My dear Celia, what on earth are you doing here, being patronized by these people?" the ambassador asked.

"I might ask you the same question, Uncle Hugo."

"Simple. The County Wildlife Service is dying for lack of funds, he's our last hope. The others are in the same position over their pet charities. If we'd all refused he'd have thought we were looking down our noses at him because of the Princess of Wales and all that. So we all decided to cancel our other engagements and come, so that he keeps the money-box open and doesn't take offence. What d'you think he was trying to do to poor little Di? Was he off his rocker or just drunk?"

"Neither, the background's rather sinister."

He looked at her sharply. "Celia, are you at it again? Is this one of your 'investigations'?"

"Yes, but I got dragged into it very unwillingly. I didn't want to perpetrate this dreadful vulgarity in their garden, and I certainly didn't want to investigate them. Don't blow my cover though, will you?"

"Not if you promise to come to lunch on Sunday and tell me all about it, I'm fascinated. But now I must go and make eyes at our host and hostess in the interests of the County Wildlife Service."

Left alone, Celia started worrying again about Anthea, who was looking very tense and was making no headway at all in an attempted conversation with Wanda Galliant. She advanced to the rescue, but Anthea had moved away abruptly to admire one of the borders. This left her standing a few feet away from Gomez and at the mercy of his émigré politics. She cast around for something else to talk about. Opera, perhaps. She knew nothing about it and rather disliked it, but managed to think up what she hoped was an intelligent question and turned to him to ask it.

The question was never to be asked. Suddenly, the peace of the evening had been shattered. Wanda and

Anthea were screaming. Gomez had leapt from her side into the border and was flat on his stomach in it. Teresa, following suit, was cursing her husband's politics as she realized that his fears were not imaginary, the danger was real. The ambassador was shouting "Lie down, Celia." But it was too late. By the time Celia had worked out that the strange rattling noise she could hear was fire from some kind of machine gun, there was a tearing pain in her shoulder, and blood was running down the front of her pink evening dress.

❧ TEN ❧

It was Celia's standard nightmare, and it went on and on. She was a saxifrage and pot-bound, with her roots squeezed painfully into a three inch pot. People came past and looked at her sitting there on the staging in the greenhouse, people she knew. Why did none of them help? One couldn't expect it of Mrs. Galliant, gardening was one of her blind spots, and nothing much could be expected of Wanda and Anthea, who also came to have a look. But Bill kept wandering past, there was no excuse for him. Why the hell did he not realize that she ought to have been potted on months ago, and take pity on her?

At last something seemed to be happening. She was being wheeled along in some sort of smooth-running trolley. The scene changed to a supermarket, it was probably that type of trolley. The pain had eased, perhaps she had been potted on. Or perhaps she had become human again, since she seemed to be struggling up a narrow, steep staircase, a thing no saxifrage could do. There was something terribly important and rather sinister at the top if it, something that smelt heavy and sweet and gave her a headache. What on earth could it be? She tried to decide, but soon came to the conclusion that she was too sleepy to care.

She came to the surface slowly, in a room which smelt

of hospital but was full of flowers. Memory came back slowly too, of the sound of machine-gun fire and of Gomez lying flat on his stomach between a golden spiræa and a clump of flame-coloured azaleas. One of her arms was bandaged to her chest. Exploring with the other hand, she decided that the wound must be in her left shoulder. Who else had been hurt? She asked a nurse, and was told not to excite herself.

"I shall excite myself into a relapse unless you tell me," she retorted.

The nurse vanished, and fetched a doctor, who told her that she had been lucky. One bullet had hit her in the shoulder and another in her chest, narrowly missing her heart. She would need to take things easy for some time, but there would be no permanent disability.

"Who else was hurt?" she persisted.

"I'm not sure, but your daughter and son-in-law are here. They may know. If you feel strong enough to see them for a few moments, I'll send them in."

"Oh yes! Yes, please."

After a few moments Lucy came in looking worried to death, followed by her nice ugly jug-eared Jim, who was doing well in the Foreign Service but looked more like a prize-fighter than a diplomat.

"Darlings, how nice of you to come," she said.

"Uncle Hugo was there when it happened. He phoned us," said Lucy. "How are you, Mum?"

"Fine, darling, but I must know. Was anyone else hurt besides me?"

"No, you were the only casualty," said Jim. "The police think it was because you were standing next to Gomez. They were aiming for him, of course. But he was half expecting the attack and threw himself down, so they thought they'd got him."

"Goodness, what a surprise," said Celia. "He lectured me on Latin American politics, but I'd decided he was a complete phoney and not nearly important enough to be shot at."

"I expect the altitude makes them trigger-happy," said Jim. "Ciudad Antonio is rather high up in the Andes."

This astonished her. "Really? I'd assumed it was in the wiggly bit between North and South America. Are you sure, Jim?"

"Absolutely. It's jammed in between Colombia and Brazil, right up on the Ecuador border."

He was undoubtedly right. In his job he could not afford to have the normal British blind spot about the geography of Latin America. What he had just told her seemed to Celia important for some reason that she felt too muzzy-headed to work out at present.

"He told me there were trigger-happy people about who wanted to shoot him," she said. "There was something about an arms cache at a farm, and the government arresting the opposition right left and centre. I suppose the Foreign Office knows all about that."

"Probably, but at present I only have to be well informed about Scandinavia."

Celia's shoulder was hurting abominably, but she saw through the haze of pain that Lucy was looking pale and anxious. Summoning up her last reserves of strength, she chattered reassuringly about family matters till it was time for them to go, then sank back exhausted into sleep.

Sleep brought with it a repeat performance of the saxifrage nightmare, including a repeat of the new ending it seemed to have acquired. Once more, she struggled painfully up a steep staircase with a sickly-sweet smell at the top, and woke in terror. Despite the nightmare, the sleep made her feel much more energetic, and she persuaded an obliging nurse to fetch her a newspaper. The story of the shooting at Faringfield spread over two whole columns. There was an almost unrecognizable photo of her, and another of the garden with the scene of her sufferings arrowed and an inset head and shoulders of Gomez, husband of etcetera and a leading member of the opposition to the bloodstained régime in power in Ciudad Antonio. A piece by Our Latin American Expert sketched in a political background of tyranny, intrigue and assassination on much the same lines as the lecture she had received from Gomez that evening. All concerned, from Gomez himself and the Galliants down to one of the girls at Archerscroft, had told the press what a nice person Celia was and how sorry they were. To round off the coverage there was an editorial full of the fiery indignation which is always provoked by filthy foreigners who have the nerve to come and shoot each other for political reasons on law-abiding British soil. In this case the filthy foreigners had aggravated their offence by incompetently shooting an English bystander by mistake. Celia wondered drowsily why killings by foreigners for political reasons on British soil were considered more outrageous than shooting incidents between native Britons in the course of burglaries or domestic misunderstandings. But she could reach no conclusion, and fell asleep again.

Over the next few days she had a procession of visitors. A policeman came, but more by way of a courtesy call than because she was expected to tell him anything useful. According to him, the machine-gunner must have been lying in wait in the shelter belt of trees and shrubs on the far side of the lawn, at a point where he had a field of fire up the vista between the borders towards the house. "And very nice borders, if I may say so, Madam. I believe you were responsible for them."

After he had gone, Teresa Enriquez swept in like a whirlwind, bearing an enormous gilt basket tricked out with bows and full of hideous scarlet roses splashed with bright yellow. She felt so guilty, she said, so embarrassed that Celia should have suffered injuries in the course of a Latin American political quarrel, and her distress was obviously genuine. Celia replied that she was very glad that neither she herself nor Mr. Gomez were dead, and that no one else had been injured.

Teresa raised deploring hands to heaven. "My Miguel, he is prostrated and he much regrets that it is impossible for him to present to you personally his regrets. It is not safe for him to come, you see."

"No, we don't want a repeat performance in the front hall of the hospital," said Celia. "Where is he now?"

"He is at my house. The police guard him. When they are finish asking him their questions, he will go to some friends where our enemies will not find him."

Bill and Anthea came, with a bunch of flower heads from an interesting batch of FI hybrid polyanthus. The sight of Bill sent her into a fever of anxiety about how the business was managing without her.

"Relax, Celia, we're doing fine," he told her. "And everything at Faringfield's okay, I was there this morning to check."

"Everything except that there's a huge panic about Paul," Anthea added. "When he was discharged from the nursing home he refused flatly to go home and holed up incommunicado at Fred's. He won't talk on the phone to anyone from Faringfield, and a letter from Richard was returned unopened."

"I don't blame him, Anthea love," said Bill. "After what happened. Having his place broke into and all his things wrecked was the last straw."

This was news to Celia and she asked for details. Fred, it seemed, had gone to the cottage to collect various belongings of Paul's and found a scene of devastation, with clothes ripped to shreds, the TV screen smashed and fragments of LPs littering the floor. Wanda's work, Celia thought, remembering her hymn of hate against Paul at the Galliants' dinner party. But before she could develop this theory, Bill produced a different one, evolved by Fred, who had rung him and railed at him for setting off a whole chain of disasters by persuading Paul to keep the lunch date with his father.

"Fred reckons it was Paul's dad wrecked the cottage in a fit of temper."

"Oh Bill, what nonsense. Why does he think that?"

"He doesn't. Anything bad that happens, he tells Paul it's his dad done it. He's even persuaded Paul that his dad gave him that dodgy prawn cocktail on purpose."

"For once Fred's right," said Celia. "That's exactly what his father did."

"Oh Celia. Why would he do that?"

"Look at it this way. Why were the Galliants so tight-lipped behind their wall of silence? Why didn't they call in the police and move heaven and earth to find out who was doing the poisoning? It's obvious, surely. They thought they knew. They were convinced that Richard Galliant was being doped by Paul under the pernicious influence of Fred, and they didn't want a public scandal.

"I think the scenario goes something like this. The Galliants want to catch Paul red-handed and force a show-down, or perhaps they want to settle an argument one way or another because he thinks Paul's guilty and she doesn't. So they choose a day when Mr. Galliant has a public engagement in the afternoon, in other words a day when the poisoner is likely to doctor his lunch and make him behave foolishly in public. Wanda is away for the day in Slough, and Joan Galliant takes herself off to shop in Brighton. Galliant invites Paul to a tête-à-tête lunch, pretending that he's having another try at a reconciliation.

"You know the arrangements about the lunches. Susie is over in the staff canteen, laying out the lunches she's taken across the yard from the house, and collecting the money. She's left Mr. Galliant's prawn cocktail and whatever Paul's having ready for them in the kitchen of the Old Rectory. Mr. Galliant gives Paul plenty of time to dope the prawn cocktail—"

"Why a prawn cocktail?" Bill asked. "You'd think he'd throw up like a volcano at the sight of one, after what happened."

"It's the only thing that will disguise the taste. By now Galliant knows it's always the prawn cocktail that's doped, he's eliminated every other possibility and he has to order himself one to set the trap for Paul. They sit down to eat and Galliant says, 'Look here, Paul old boy, your step-mother keeps ordering these prawn cocktails for me because she thinks they're my favourite gastronomic treat, but I'm a bit sick of them actually, though I don't like to tell her so, it might hurt her feelings. So would you mind awfully if we swap? You have the prawn cocktail and I'll have your'—what would it be? Let's say a ham salad."

"Oh Celia, that's neat!" said Bill. "You mean, Paul's supposed to say 'No thanks, I don't fancy prawns today, I'll have some bread and cheese.' And then Galliant ups and shouts 'Why won't you eat it? What's wrong with it? How did you know it was doped? You're trying to poison me, you little bastard.'"

"Exactly. But at this point the scenario goes wrong. Paul starts eating the prawn cocktail without batting an eyelid. How does Galliant deal with that?"

"Oh Celia, what a problem."

"There's only one thing for it. He ought to say: 'Paul, I shouldn't eat that, I think it may be poisoned, and I did wonder if it was you doing the poisoning, but now I know it isn't.' Unfortunately though, Galliant's the sort of man who never admits even to himself that he could ever be wrong about anything. So he says to himself that probably the thing isn't poisoned, and even if it is, it won't do the boy any permanent harm. Remember, he doesn't know that a mildly toxic dose for him is a near-fatal one for Paul who's half his size. So he sits there and watches Paul eat something that nearly kills him."

"You can see why he suspected Paul," said Anthea. "Paul's the only person from outside who'd had the run of the Old Rectory kitchen."

"If it's not Paul, who is it then?" Bill asked.

"We're left with Joan Galliant, Charles and the Morrises," said Celia, "as a foursome or in various small coalitions. Oh, and there's Dawson. He's the joker in the pack. He was in the studio at night, but that ties him up with the design copying, not with the poisoning."

"That's right Celia," said Bill. "He can't be the poisoner, how would he get into the kitchen?"

"It could be done," said Celia, who had been thinking about this.

"Not since they took to locking the back door," said Anthea.

"There must be a key to it in that bunch of Wanda's that's always going missing. He could have got it copied."

"Okay, so he gets in," Bill conceded. "And he finds Mrs. Galliant's in there already scoffing her lunch because she's got a hair appointment at two."

"No," said Celia. "He's looked in through the kitchen and breakfast-room windows beforehand and made sure the coast's clear. You can from the yard. I've tried."

"So she comes in while he's monkeying with the prawn cocktail," Bill objected, "and says 'Ooh Mr. Dawson, whatever are you doing?'"

"He probably hears her coming and hides in a cupboard. Or he says there's been an urgent query from New Zealand on the phone and he's looking for Mr. Galliant, hasn't he come over yet for his lunch?"

"It's midnight in New Zealand at lunchtime here," said Anthea tetchily.

"New York then, don't be difficult," said Celia, and was warming to her theme when the door opened to admit the ward sister. After one glance at Celia's flushed, excited face she turned Bill and Anthea out. The thermometer which she produced revealed a disgraceful state of affairs, and visitors were forbidden till further notice.

By next morning Celia was feeling much better, and chafed under the visiting ban, which prevented her from keeping in touch with the Faringfield situation. But the post brought her food for thought in the shape of a note from her Uncle Hugo, the ex-ambassador. With his condolences and best wishes for her recovery, he enclosed "some mildly scandalous light reading which might amuse you, especially page twenty-two. I didn't blow your cover, but I'm agog with curiosity. Why do the Galliants insist that you're connected somehow with the press? I asked them where they got this extraordinary idea and they wouldn't say."

The light reading was the satirical magazine *Private Eye*, which she seldom saw because the village newsagent considered it a scandal-sheet unworthy of his customers' attention. The cover photo of President Reagan and Mrs. Thatcher had been adorned with balloons coming out of their mouths containing ludicrous remarks. As recommended by her uncle, she turned to page twenty-two. It was in the financial section at the back, which had a well-earned reputation for accurate inside information. Many a financial scandal had first come to public notice in a short paragraph like the one that her uncle had marked for her to read:

> Over-excitable draper Richard Galliant, supremo of Richard Galliant & Co., who caused surprise and embarrassment by attempting to fornicate publicly with a member of the royal family who was doing no one any harm, is in trouble again. Owing to his recent drunken frolics, the shares in the trouble-racked company provoke only nausea when offered for sale, even at rock bottom prices. To the surprise of observers, however, a nausea-free buyer has now appeared in the market who is believed to be none other than Charles Langley, son of Galliant's pouting imperious second wife. It was she who ordered the love-lorn draper to employ her oafish firstborn as the firm's Financial Director, a disastrous appointment which has done nothing to improve the firm's tottering finances. There are two schools of thought among Galliant-watchers about solid citizen Langley's furtive purchases. Are the draper's drunken frolics feigned, in a ploy to buy in the equity cheap before his bankers' panic becomes uncontrollable? Or are stepson Langley and his Borgia mother plying the draper with drink in a plot to snatch control of the firm from him without drawing on their tiny savings bank nest-egg?

Celia read the paragraph through thoughtfully several times, then tore out the page and put it in an envelope addressed to the senior partner of the august firm of stockbrokers who managed her financial affairs. He had been an admirer but was now a good friend, and what were good friends for if not to be made use of? She scribbled a brief covering note:

Dear Harry,
 I am up to my old tricks again. Could you make enquiries and give me some background on the enclosed as soon as possible? Have been shot in the shoulder but am otherwise flourishing, though puzzled by events connected with the above.
Yours as ever,
Celia.

Next day the ban on visitors was relaxed. Wanda Galliant came, mumbling apologies for her mother, whom she apparently expected to find already at Celia's bedside. After making laborious conversation for the regulation ten minutes, she produced a neatly wrapped parcel. "That pretty dress you were wearing at our party was ruined," she said shyly, "so I thought perhaps . . . if you liked it. . . . It is rather your colouring . . . you could have it made up into a caftan or something . . ."

Celia opened the parcel eagerly. Out slithered a dress length of heavy silk printed with a distinctive Wanda Galliant design in shades of pink and grey. Celia thanked her warmly, and wondered yet again how a brilliant creator of beautiful things could be so stupid about everything else.

"One moment, don't go," she said as Wanda turned towards the door, then hesitated. Should she interfere, or shouldn't she? Decidedly, she would.

"Does Paul know it was you that wrecked his cottage?"

Wanda peered at her in alarm through her granny glasses, but said nothing.

"If he doesn't, try not to let him find out," Celia went on. "He's jealous of you because you have a talent and a career, and he has nothing. That's why he's trying to spoil it for you. Don't let him. Keep out of his way."

Wanda stood stock still, with a look of dawning intelligence on her face, as if this explanation had never occurred to her before. Still without saying anything, she turned abruptly and left.

The next to appear was Frank Dawson, full of horticultural enthusiasms and bearing a huge sheaf of magnificent paeonies. He was accompanied by Miss Miller, looking surprisingly contented with life. Her hair had been dealt with professionally and was much improved, and she wore a becoming print dress which was probably new to judge from the way she fingered it. Something must have happened in the Dawson household, but what?

"Frank's had a raise," Miss Miller explained happily, "and not before time too."

Celia congratulated him suitably.

"They must think a lot of Frank," Miss Miller went on, "to give him a raise now when the firm's in such trouble."

"Charles Langley will pull us through it," said Dawson. "I have great confidence in Charles Langley."

"He's a good Financial Director, is he?" asked Celia.

He nodded vigorously. "First class, he's put the company on a sound financial basis at last. Before he came Mr. Galliant was always making muddles, keeping the accounts straight was a nightmare. You have to expect that with an artistic temperament, but I never knew where I was till Mr. Charles came along to keep things in order."

When he and Miss Miller had gone Celia considered the problems raised by their visit. What had Dawson been doing, alone at night with a flashlamp in the studio? There was an obvious answer, but was it the right one? Was his praise of Charles Langley sincere, or was Anthea right in suggesting that underneath, he resented the way Charles had been put in over his head? Why had Charles given him a salary increase at a moment of financial crisis like this? As a bribe, to make Dawson keep his mouth shut about some manoeuvre of Charles's which would be obvious to the firm's accountant but probably to no one else? Or was the story of the raise a fiction, to explain to Miss Miller a sudden access of wealth which made hairdressing and a new dress affordable? In other words, had Dawson, at his wits' end to pacify Miss Miller, been fiddling the books or selling Richard Galliant designs to Pritchard and Colson?

Soon after they left Celia had a visit from Fred Watney, ostensibly to bring her an expensive-looking florist's arrangement and his thanks for her part in the rescue of Paul. But his real aim was different. Since Paul's flight he had no source of information at Faringfield, and he wanted to know who to wreak vengeance on for the wrecking of Paul's cottage. As Celia had no intention of telling him, conversation languished until the door opened again and Teresa Enriquez swept in with yet more flowers and apologetic messages from her husband. "He stay only to hear me sing Countess in *Figaro*, first performance, then he go with his friend to Paris, where he will be safe."

Fred was not one to fade into the background when confronted with another celebrity. "Hi there, you're a singer, are you?" he said. "So am I."

Teresa smiled and prepared to condescend, but he went on. "I saw *Figaro* at Glyndebourne last year, lovely tunes, marvellous book."

"*Le Nozze di Figaro* is a masterwork," said Teresa.

"Yeah, but it looked like bloody hard work to me. There's a bit just before the long interval, twenty minutes of hard slog for everyone without an instrumental or anything to give you a breather, I don't know how they do it."

"That finale!" Teresa warmed to a fellow-artist who understood. "It is a masterpiece, but it is also cruel, cruel. Only today I say to Cherubino—"

"That's the girl who sings the pageboy, right?"

"*Si si*, and I say to her, you are lucky, when you jump from the window to escape from my angry husband, you escape also from that terrible finale which is about to commence."

"Yeah, and you got to be careful too. If you hit a bum note in opera you've had it. In my line of business you can hit ten and they think it's part of the act."

"Your line of business, what is it?" Teresa asked.

"I was into Heavy Metal, but now it's more mainstream,

with a bit of soul. Mind you, that's hard work too, they like to see you jumpin' about and makin' an effort. I don't use an antiperspirant, do you? I think it only makes it worse."

Presently they left together, much more interested in each other than they were in her. Celia was beginning to feel that visitors were a mixed blessing in view of the social effort they required from the visited, when the door opened to admit the one she had been hoping for yet dreading: Joan Galliant.

She had brought a bottle of champagne. "Strengthening stuff, champers, Mrs. Grant. You'll get frightful wind if you drink it all yourself, but you can give the nurses some. Make them break the rules and get them a bit tiddly, and you get much better attention, I always do."

She sat down, every inch the colonel's lady doing her duty by the regiment's wounded, and made the proper enquiries about Celia's health and welfare. But instead of departing when these were over she fixed Celia with a stony eye and said "Now, Mrs. Grant. If this was an ordinary social visit I'd have come earlier, but I thought I'd wait till you were strong enough to answer some quite searching questions. Are you?"

"Certainly, if you don't mind me asking some too."

She waved this aside. "How did you know it was datura and why didn't you sign that anonymous letter?"

"Because the remains of a plant of it turned up in your compost heap, and because you threatened not to pay me for the garden if I showed any interest in your family affairs."

"I see. Could you go into a bit more detail?"

Celia did, then said: "I've answered two questions of yours, and now it's my turn to ask one. Why are you so convinced that I'm connected somehow with the press?"

"Well, aren't you?"

"No, certainly not. Will you please answer my question."

"No, Mrs. Grant, because you know the answer already."

"This is absurd. My Uncle Hugo asked you the same thing, and you refused to answer."

"Yes, because he obviously didn't know, and one doesn't pass on that sort of information to the person's relatives."

Celia stared at her. "What didn't he know? What on earth are you talking about? Let's get this straight, for heaven's sake."

"Very well, if you insist on my putting it into words. I thought it kinder not to tell your uncle that you're Alaric Brooks-Fullerton's mistress, and have been for years."

Celia gathered her wits. Who the hell was Alaric Brooks-Fullerton? Memory threw up the image of a revoltingly pompous man who was always shooting his mouth off in television chat shows, but what was his job? Of course. Editor of the *Evening Express*. Ignoring twinges of pain in her chest, she sat straight up in bed. "Who the hell told you this extraordinary story?"

"I gather it's quite well known in Fleet Street circles, though not to his wife."

"Mrs. Galliant, I shall start screaming and throwing things at you unless you tell me your source at once."

"I suppose I must if you're going to have hysterics. It was Anthea Clarkson, she has access to that sort of information." Her face changed. "You're not telling me it isn't true?"

"Of course it isn't true," Celia spluttered, managing somehow not to scream. "I've never met the man, and if he's as pompous in real life as he is on the TV I don't want to."

Joan Galliant gaped at her. "I suppose I have to believe you, but why on earth would Anthea make up a story like that?"

"Because she's a devious little bitch."

"She must have had some reason, she's a brainy little thing. Let me think. Oh. *Oh!* Don't you see? Damn her, she's even cleverer than I thought. She didn't want you and me to get together and compare notes."

"No, I don't see. Why didn't she?"

"Because little Anthea was afraid I might get confidential and tell you that she was being fucked to high heaven by my stallion of a husband. Whereupon you would pass on this interesting tidbit to your handsome young employee who is obviously her steady."

While Celia thought angrily about this, Joan Galliant suddenly began to laugh. "Well, you had me fooled. You're my idea of a perfect tycoon's mistress, good clear complexion, perfect figure, lots of commonsense hidden under that marvellous helpless look that makes them feel protective. Is all that talent really going to waste? You don't look a bit sex-starved, I was sure you were getting your ration of oats somewhere."

By now Celia was almost too angry to speak. "Mrs. Galliant, you are a liar."

"Oh I say, steady on."

"Anthea has no morals, but she has the glimmerings of common sense. If she was having an affair with your husband, she'd be mad to suggest Archerscroft Nurseries to you when you wanted a firm to deal with the garden."

"She didn't."

Ignoring this, Celia stormed on. "Anthea's totally dependent on Bill Wilkins. She'd never put that relationship at risk, let alone arrange for him to be around a lot at Faringfield if she was having a carry-on with another man there."

"Do calm down, Mrs. Grant, you haven't taken in what I'm saying. Anthea didn't."

"She didn't what?"

"She didn't call you in to deal with the garden. I did."

Celia was dumbfounded. All the facts had to be looked at again from a totally new angle. "I'm sorry," she managed. "Did I in the heat of the moment call you a liar?"

"That's all right." Joan Galliant grinned and picked up

the champagne bottle. "I think we both need a swig at this, don't you? Shocking bad form of me to gulp down my own present to you, but I'll bring you another bottle. Let's get them to chill it for us in the fridge among the corpses and bring it back."

She vanished, leaving Celia still utterly bewildered, and came back a few moments later. "Now Mrs. Grant, where were we?"

"You were saying that you'd called us in to deal with the garden, not Anthea."

"That's right. I fixed it all up while she was in New York on an alleged business trip with Richard. She wasn't at all pleased when she came back and found out what I'd done. You see, I'd noticed this handsome young man who appeared at weekends when Richard wasn't here, and he was obviously servicing Anthea satisfactorily, she looked like a cat that's had cream on Monday mornings after he'd been. I decided that in fairness to Richard, I ought to break it up, so I made some enquiries about him and looked up Archerscroft Nurseries in the phone book, and the rest you know."

"But did the carry-on with your husband break up?" Celia asked.

"Oh yes, it worked like a charm. I waited till poor Richard had stopped seeing giant hens with crocodile teeth, and was back in his right mind. Then one morning when your Mr. Wilkins was working in the garden with his shirt off, I sent Richard out to weigh up the competition, and take a close look at his chest and arm muscles, so that he could decide what would happen if it came to fisticuffs."

"I remember that," said Celia. "Bill said you were standing at the library window watching, and he couldn't understand why you were laughing fit to bust."

"And when Richard came back looking rather thoughtful, I pointed out to him that a girl with a lad like that at stud could only be interested in him for mercenary reasons. Richard saw the point in a flash, it turned out that she wanted a directorship and was hoping, in vain needless to say, to earn one with her anatomy."

A nurse came back with the champagne and two glasses. Joan poured out and raised her glass. "Cheers, Celia. Let's be on first-namers, shall we?"

They drank.

"Don't get me wrong, I'm not a jealous vinegary spoil-sport," Joan went on. "Richard's very presentable for his age, and he's convinced that every woman he meets is aching for him to give her a good blow through the boiler. When a man believes that it often comes true, but I won't stand for him goosing girls on the payroll. When that happens I always break it up. It's bad for staff morale, and it gives them wrong ideas about me. I'm damned if I'll have the workforce thinking he sleeps around with secretaries in desperation because I hate the whole business and shut my eyes and think of England when it's my turn, which is far from being the case."

She poured out more champagne. "There are all sorts of high jinks during his business trips abroad, and one can't object to that, I suppose. But I do resent having to act as a fire brigade when left-overs from these occasions get themselves washed up on these shores and embarrass him with their overtures, like Teresa thingummy with the husband who ought to have been shot and wasn't."

"Goodness me," said Celia.

"Oh, didn't you realize? He'd been goosing her for ages on his business trips abroad, and she turned up here intent on wedding bells, so she had to be disillusioned. That wasn't my most successful dinner party, not by any means, but I did enjoy seeing her take an eyeful of little Anthea in that tarty red frock with the sequins."

This was interesting, but only as a sidelight. Celia decided to get to the heart of the problem.

"I can't get over Anthea's cleverness," she said. "Her story about me and the media put you off me, and the way you behaved as a result put me off you. Of course, you didn't want me or anyone else to realize that you suspected Paul of poisoning his father."

Joan choked on her champagne. "Oops! Who told you that, Celia?"

"No one, I worked it out. You were wrong, of course. You knew that when Mr. Galliant switched their lunches and Paul ate the prawn cocktail."

This time the choking lasted several minutes. When Joan had recovered she said: "Don't tell me you worked that out by yourself, because I don't believe it."

"I did, as a matter of fact. It seemed the logical conclusion to draw from the facts."

"But look here, you say we know now Paul's innocent. We don't. Richard thought he was guilty and that Paul decided to gobble the thing up and take the consequences, because otherwise he would be suspected."

"Surely that's a bit far fetched?" Celia objected.

"It would be if I could think of anyone else to suspect."

"Isn't there anyone?" said Celia.

"No, it has to be Paul. No one else was allowed in there."

"One moment," said Celia. "What are the prawn cocktails served in?"

"A glass bowl on a stem, like you have grapefruit in. Cheap and nasty but convenient."

"When your husband has one, is it put in anything different?"

"No, that was the whole point. No one knew till the last moment which one Susie was going to put out for him. That's why Paul's the odds-on favourite in the suspicion stakes. You're quite right, we decided to have a showdown. Richard sold Paul the idea that it was silly not to be on speakers with one's son, so why didn't they have lunch together. Come lunchtime, Richard sets up an observation post as planned at the bathroom window, because you can see down from there into the stable yard. At zero hour, Susie pushes her food-trolley over to the office block and dead on cue, Paul comes across the yard and into the back door—"

"Was he carrying anything?"

"Not so's you'd notice, Richard says, but the young all wear these blouse things with huge zip-up pockets, you can't tell. Anyway, Richard gives him a few minutes to nobble the prawn cocktail, then he goes down and they fetch themselves beer from the fridge, but it's all a bit tense, because Paul's terrified of Richard as well as hating him. As they settle down in the breakfast room to eat, Richard makes a face at his prawn cocktail and says Susie keeps making them for him because she thinks it's his great gastronomic turn-on, but in fact he's sick of them though he can't hurt her feelings by saying so. And would Paul mind swapping it for his quiche? Paul looked a bit astonished, but in the end he said 'yes' and down went the prawn cocktail."

"All of it? He didn't mess it about and leave half the greenery?"

"No heel taps at all, because if he'd fiddled with it Richard would have suspected. If you've got to get something down that you don't like, you shovel it in quick and try not to think about it."

"And your husband sat there and watched him eat it? Knowing or at least suspecting what it contained?"

Joan made a face. "Richard's a genius and I dote on him, but he hasn't really grasped that other people actually exist, except as objects created to serve his convenience. All he thought was, serve the little bastard right for what he's been doing to me, I want him to know how filthy it feels. He didn't foresee, of course, that a dose meant for a great ox like him would pack a much more dangerous punch if taken by a bantam-weight like Paul."

"But Joan, if I'd eaten the thing, I'd go off as soon as I could and put my fingers down my throat and heave it up, wouldn't you? Why didn't he?"

"I wondered about that, but he didn't know about the dosage either. He probably thought 'I'll try it for kicks, and go and sleep it off at old pal Fred's fun palace where no one will see me when I strip off and dance the fandango in the swimming pool.' He's quite capable of it, he smokes cannabis although I pretend not to notice. I daren't tell Richard that, he'd kill the wretched child with a horsewhip or something."

On thinking it over, Celia decided that she was not convinced. "I still don't see why you're ruling out everyone except Paul. What about Susie, for instance?"

Suddenly Joan Galliant showed faint signs of a genuine emotion. "No, I absolutely refuse to believe that. She's been with me twenty years and I'm as devoted to her as I'm sure she is to me."

No doubt, Celia thought. But was Susie even more devoted to the interests of the son of the house, Charles Langley? According to Anthea Susie would do any amount of dirty work for him.

"So who else is there?" Joan went on. "We didn't cotton on to how the trick was worked till after the Princess of Wales lark, but since then we've kept the kitchen door locked, Susie even locks it when she goes across the yard with the trolley."

"Who has keys?"

"Richard and Wanda and I and the Morrises."

"Not Paul?"

"Certainly not. But of course we left the door unlocked for him to come in that day and nobble Richard's prawn cocktail. Have some more champers."

"No, thank you," said Celia, thinking hard.

"You've gone very quiet," Joan remarked.

"I'm wondering about the mentality of a son who hated his father enough to make him look a fool in public and ruin his business. Or is there another motive?"

Joan put down her glass. "Are you sure you're not working for the media? You're asking some damn penetrating questions."

"No, it just happens that I have a logical mind, and I don't see why Paul would want to ruin his father."

"He doesn't want to, Celia," Joan said. "But we think he gets money from his cow of a mother, which means that he's under her thumb."

"Ah. You suspect Paul of supplying his mother's firm with copies of Richard Galliant designs."

"We're damn sure it's him, but we can't make out how he does it. That's not all. Nobody believes this story of ours about an allergy, that's why the shares have been bumping along the floor. But last week someone started buying them up steadily, and I bet it was Pritchard and Colson."

Celia was about to ask her next question when a nurse came in and tried to eject Joan Galliant on the ground that visiting hours were over. A brisk battle of words followed, which the nurse won.

"Oh very well, do stop fussing nurse, I'm going." Joan paused in the doorway. "I'm very impressed, Celia. You're much too brainy to be a gardener."

The nurse scolded Celia for exhausting herself with too many visitors and removed the empty champagne bottle with a look of disgust, leaving Celia with only herself to answer the questions which crowded into her mind. How much, for instance, did she believe of what she had just heard? Did Joan Galliant really believe Paul was guilty, or was she just building up a case against him to distract Celia's attention from the case against Charles, herself and Susie? Was there a case against Anthea? Probably not, why would she want to poison a man she was sleeping with and hoping to wheedle a directorship out of? But perhaps she was not having an affair with Galliant, was that a malicious invention of Joan's? There were practical questions too. How easily could someone slip into the house while Susie was away? Would they be seen by someone at a window in the office block across the yard? The job could be done in seconds if the person brought a ready-poisoned prawn cocktail with him, to substitute for the one Susie had put out, and there was no problem about the container, canteen crockery was always going missing. The timing would be tricky if he was not to collide with Paul when he came to collect his lunches. If the poisoner was not a member of the family, he had taken formidable risks each time he administered a dose. It was tempting to go on suspecting Paul. . . . Her head ached from the champagne, but the questions went on churning through it. Betrayed yet again by the thermometer she was sedated into a stupor from which she emerged in the morning feeling woolly-headed and very sorry for herself indeed.

Bill Wilkins turned off the main road into the lane leading to Faringfield. It was weeks since he had felt so cheerful. The sun was shining, and Anthea had stopped keeping him at arm's length. She had agreed to let him spend Saturday afternoon and Sunday with her, which must mean that whatever had gone wrong with their relationship had righted itself. She was more affectionate, perhaps a little less tense, though she always lived on her nerves. If things went well this weekend, he would try to make her tell him what the trouble had been.

But before he could relax at Anthea's there was one chore to attend to. He drove on past her cottage and halted outside Frank Dawson's cottage at the far end of the green. The overpowering scent from its garden confirmed that he was at the right address. Celia had given him a vivid description of Dawson's sea of paeonies, and he was hoping for a sight of them.

He walked up the front path, carrying two seedlings of Celia's much-coveted *Helleborus corsicus x niger* "Roger Grant," which she was swapping for some seedlings of Dawson's paeonies. There was no reply to his knock, on a Saturday afternoon Dawson was probably working in the garden. He explored round to the back of the house, and there, set out in long beds, were the paeonies. The earlier varieties were just past their peak, here and there petals from an over-full bloom were falling silently to the ground. It was a stunning sight, and he stood there taking it in for

171

several minutes before it occurred to him to wonder where Dawson was.

"Is anyone at home?" he called.

There had to be someone. Celia had told him all about the unhappy Dawson household which centred round a helpless invalid who could not be left. If Dawson was not at home Miss Miller must be. The long window of a living room was open and he looked in. It was empty.

He looked down the garden again. Half way down it was a terrace overlooking the paeonies, with a kind of arbour on it, backing against the boundary hedge. He went closer. In it, lying on two day-beds, were Dawson and his invalid wife, having their afternoon siesta. He had probably been reading to her when he fell asleep. It looked as if he had let the book drop over his face. Bill tiptoed away, intending to leave the hellebore seedlings in the shade by the back door with a scribbled note.

Then it occurred to him that the thing over Dawson's face was an odd shape for a book, and too shiny. He went back for a closer look, and took violent alarm.

"Mr. Dawson!" he shouted; stupidly, for he had seen the cellophane bag which told him that there could be no answer. He knew about this, he had read about it in an article on euthanasia. Putting a plastic bag over one's head and suffocating was one of the ways of committing suicide.

Mrs. Dawson was not asleep. Her forehead was quite cold. He must have suffocated her first, it was a suicide pact. They had decided to end their lives together, on the terrace overlooking the sea of paeonies.

Fighting down nausea, Bill went to search for a telephone. On the way back to the house he decided that he never wanted to see a paeony again.

❦ ELEVEN ❦

"Poor Dawson," said Anthea when Bill told her what had happened. "But I'm not falling about with surprise. The Miller woman must have driven him over the edge at last."

"Him doing it in the garden among all them paeonies made it worse somehow. He was saying goodbye to them, it looked like."

"I suppose they were his big turn-on," Anthea mused. "Or were they just an excuse for getting away from those two women? Where was Miller, by the way, while the death-throes were happening?"

"Away somewhere. It's Saturday afternoon. They'd have to give her time off at weekends when he's home. The police are still there, waiting to break it to her when she comes back."

"I wonder what she'll do with herself without him?" said Anthea. "Poor old harridan, I feel damn sorry for her. In fact I'm sorry for all three of them. Miller was in a big panic about whether she'd be made an honest woman of when Mrs. Dawson died, and the more she panicked the more shrewish she became. I suppose she couldn't help it. Dawson had to ignore her lack of allure and fake the heart-throbs, because no way could he find anyone else to do the nursing. I'm sorriest for the poor bloody wife, who had to watch all this and get on with the only thing she was really good at, namely dying inch by inch."

"You could call it a mercy killing then," said Bill. "And he'd decided he'd have to go with her."

"No, I think everything suddenly got to be too much for him and he couldn't see any future for her without him, so he took her along too. Now listen, Gorgeous. This is our first weekend together since Easter and I want us to relax and enjoy each other and not think any more about sad things like the Dawsons."

"Okay love, but they've let Celia have a phone now. I must ring her, tell her what's happened."

So he killed himself and her, Celia thought after Bill had phoned. She was not really surprised, the strain of someone else's terminal illness was something she knew about, Roger's had lasted almost a year. But she had little time to brood before the phone beside her bed rang again. This time it was Harry Winterbourne, her friend and stockbroker, whom she had asked for information about the story in *Private Eye*. At first she could get nothing out of him but agitated demands to know what she had been up to. "How typical of you, Celia," he said. "I saw in *The Times* that you'd wandered into the line of fire during an argument between Latin Americans, and I thought oh dear, she would. I do wish you'd take more care of yourself."

Celia stopped him fussing as best she could and wished, by no means for the first time, that she was a large, red-faced lady whose ability to look after herself was obvious at first sight, and not a small, helpless-looking one who made sixty-year-old stockbrokers become idiotically protective. It took her a long time to calm him down and make him answer her queries.

"To start with, Celia, that piece in *Private Eye* is almost a week old. The day after it came out, Richard Galliant Limited asked the Stock Exchange to suspend trading in their shares."

"Because of what *Private Eye* said about them?"

"No, it's what any responsible board of directors would have done in the circumstances. They were open to the accusation of having driven the share price down by deliberately alarming the market about the company's viability. Quite a number of shares had changed hands and were being registered in the name of nominees, and they didn't know what was going on."

"But could the whole thing be a plot to buy their own shares cheap?"

"If it is, they're breaking the law. They can't buy their own shares without their shareholders' consent, and they haven't asked for it. Anyway, they're heavily in debt to two merchant banks, I doubt if they've got the cash to spare."

"Supposing Charles Langley bought the shares with private money of his own?"

"Risky. Their annual report's due next month, and any change in directors' shareholdings has to be declared in it. Everyone would know what he'd been up to."

"But if he went on pretending not to have any shares? There are these nominees for him to hide behind."

"My dear Celia! That would be a criminal offence."

"Suppose he doesn't mind committing any number of criminal offences? Supposing he's committed one already?"

"Good gracious, what sort of an offence?"

"There's a theory that he had to leave the firm he worked for in the City under a cloud after an insider trading scandal, and that he's buying the shares with the illgotten nest egg resulting from this wicked transaction."

"Celia, your imagination is running riot."

"All sorts of things are running riot here, but not my imagination. On the contrary, it is boggling at the things that happen."

"Mine boggles at what you have just said. I naturally checked on Charles Langley at the merchant bank he worked for before he joined Galliant's. He was one of their bright boys, they were sorry to lose him when he accepted the Galliant job."

"Could he have left under a cloud they didn't know about?"

"Certainly not, what happened was this. Galliant's owed them a lot of money, and the financial control there seemed to be very slack and they were worried. So they told Richard Galliant that he'd have to accept a nominee from the bank as Financial Director if he didn't want them to call in the loan. They'd intended to put in someone pretty junior, and they were rather upset when Charles Langley said he'd like it, because they were nursing him for one of their own top jobs. They were astonished too, it was a big step down for him salarywise and so on, but I gather he's developed a conscience. Wanted to get away from juggling with money, and into a place where people actually made things."

"Is that what they told you? They didn't explain what really happened? Charles Langley's mother is Richard Galliant's second wife. I think she decided that Galliant was too much of a handful for her to cope with alone, so she dragged Charles in to help."

"No, Celia, you've got this wrong. Langley was in the firm for a year before he introduced Galliant to his mother, it was quite a romance. Half the merchant bank was at the wedding."

This conversation left Celia very thoughtful. Somehow the jumble of miscellaneous information that she had collected must fit together into a pattern, in her experience it usually did. But several of the pieces were the wrong shape, it was impossible to imagine a pattern that they could be fitted into. What was she to do, throw out the awkward pieces and make a neat pattern of the ones that fitted? To yield to that temptation was always the surest way to the wrong answer. The awkward pieces had to be turned round and round, looked at from different angles, fiddled with till they suddenly proved to be the key to the whole puzzle. Somehow, the thing must make sense.

It must make sense. . . . The words became a meaningless incantation that hammered obsessively through her brain: It must make sense, it must make sense, it must make sense. But it did not, and the more she repeated the stupid little catch-phrase, the more incapable she became of connected thought. By the evening she was frustrated to the point of tears and so tense that the ward sister threatened her with a visit from the hospital psychiatrist. To avoid this fate, she allowed herself to be sedated into a state in which she no longer wanted to think about anything at all.

It was Sunday afternoon before she woke from a snooze with a reasonably clear head, to find Charles Langley sitting in her bedside chair reading a newspaper. Though it was Sunday he was wearing a collar and tie and his no-nonsense haircut was so neatly brushed that he looked slightly unreal.

"Oh good, you're awake," he said in his usual flat, slow voice. "They didn't want to let me see you, but I said it was important."

"Is it?" Celia asked, confused.

"Well, yes. I thought we might put our heads together."

She stared at him, wondering what this would lead to.

"You see, Mother was very impressed with your grasp of our family problems," he explained. "She said you were too brainy to be a gardener, and that set me thinking . . ."

He went on to explain his thought processes. Prompted by his mother's remark, his orderly mind had thrown up the memory of an Old Marlburian dinner he had attended back in the previous autumn, at which his neighbour at table had told him an interesting story that seemed to him relevant to the matter in hand. "It was about a woman gardener with a first class brain who had sorted out an extraordinary business in his mother's garden at a house near Guildford called Monk's Mead.* So I rang him last night to find out the name of the gardener in question. He

---

*See *The Mantrap Garden* by the same author.

thinks the world of you, Mrs. Grant, and I expect you remember him: Adam Lindsay."

"Oh. Yes, of course."

"Lindsay says you've a lot of experience of this sort of thing," Langley went on. "So I thought if we pooled your results so far with mine, we might get somewhere."

Celia refrained from pointing out that her "results" would have been more impressive if the family had not brought up heavy artillery whenever she showed her head above the parapet of their wall of silence. Instead, she asked him what seemed to her the test question. "D'you think Paul's guilty?"

"I can see why Richard thinks so. He has the opportunity, and he's quite capable of eating something he'd poisoned himself rather than lose face. But the case against him isn't cast iron. And I don't see what his motive would be."

"Avenging his mother's sufferings at the hands of his father?"

Charles produced a neat, businesslike smile. "If you ask me, Dorothy and Richard thoroughly enjoyed inflicting sufferings on each other."

"But isn't Paul on her side?"

"Oh no. He loathes her."

"Really? Why?"

"Because she makes up to him and tries to use him as a weapon against his father."

"Doesn't he loathe his father too?"

"Paul's a very complicated chap, you see. For years his parents used him as a battering ram in their fights with each other, and now I think he's got so that he enjoys banging his head hard against a brick wall. Perversely, he doesn't loathe his father. He adores him."

Celia looked at him with heightened respect. "You mean, Paul rejects the parent who accepts him and makes a fuss of him, and longs to be accepted by the parent who rejects him."

"That's right, and the more brutally his father treats him

the more he longs to be accepted and the worse he behaves."

"To the point of administering toxic substances to his father to make him look foolish in public?"

"No. On my reading of Paul's character that's unthinkable."

"Are you sure your reading's right?"

"It's not just speculation. He talks to me, surprising though it may seem. I think he approves of me because I fill the slot that Richard was trying to push Paul into. I'm the businesslike, not too imaginative member of the family who attends to the detail that a genius can't be expected to bother with."

"Has Paul actually discussed the poisoning problem with you?"

"Once, just after the Princess of Wales episode. He wanted to know what I thought was going on. He was in a panic, terribly upset to see his father held up to public ridicule. I duly reported this approach to Richard, who replied 'That's what the little creep would say if he was doing it.'"

After a pause for thought Celia said: "I see why his father suspects him. He's the only outsider who had no problem of access to their kitchen and breakfast room. But I've been wondering how possible it would be for someone else to slip in undetected."

"Ah. Exactly my line of thought, Mrs. Grant."

"There are coal cellars and so on in that porch outside the back door. Could they serve as hiding places for someone waiting for the right moment?"

"Again, we're thinking along the same lines. There's an outside W.C. under that porch, which is no longer operational, I suppose it was intended for the use of the parson's servants. No one would think of going in there, a poisoner waiting in it for his moment would be perfectly safe. Moreover, there is a gap above the door for ventilation, and I established by experiment that a person of average height standing on the seat would see Susie's trolley when she set out with it to the office block."

Celia was delighted with him. The contrast between his boring voice and his sharp enquiring mind added to her enjoyment. "Oh well done, Mr. Langley. Let's see now, what does that give us? Some time before Susie sets off, the poisoner slips into the porch and hides in the W.C. Can he be seen doing it from the offices on the far side of the stable yard?"

"Probably not. The parked cars would block the line of sight. And he'd be hidden from any observer in a first floor office by the overhanging porch."

"Very well then. He waits in the outside W.C. for Susie to go, then dashes into the house and switches Mr. Galliant's prawn cocktail with a ready-doctored one he's brought with him. It would only take a moment."

"How does he know it's a prawn cocktail and not a ham salad or a bit of quiche?" Langley objected.

"Ah. That is a difficulty. But Susie's posted up her menu on the office notice-board the night before, so he knows what's on offer. And if he's fairly senior in the firm he's had business lunches with Mr. Galliant and knows what he's likely to choose. Perhaps he can check by looking in through the breakfast room window to see what Susie's laid out, but there's no harm done if Mr. Galliant's chosen something else and the drugged prawn cocktail has to be taken away. Is there somewhere for him to hide if he's interrupted?"

Langley nodded. "The usual rabbit-warren of sculleries and pantries and walk-in cupboards that you get in a house that age."

"Well, there you are. It's a tenable theory, Mr. Langley."

"Yes. The problem is, who?"

"A paid emissary of the first Mrs. Galliant?"

He made a face. "Isn't that carrying revenge on one's ex-husband a bit far?"

"I wasn't thinking of revenge. I assumed it was her or

180

her firm that was buying up your shares and hiding behind nominees."

"Why? She can't buy control of the firm, because my stepfather owns forty-one per cent and he gave another ten per cent to my mother as a wedding present. What would she or Pritchard and Colson want with a minority shareholding in Galliant's? Another thing. This person had bought up about fifteen per cent of the equity before we asked the Stock Exchange to stop trading in our shares. But anyone owning more than a five per cent shareholding has to reveal his identity to the company's board of directors, so if it is one person and not several, he's breaking the law. You see what that points to?"

"Yes! It's a short-term holding, is that right? He's hoping to get rid of the shares again at a profit before the law catches up with him."

Charles nodded gravely. "And who's in the best position to do that? Obviously, the person who's driving the shares down, and intends to make a killing when they go up again. All he has to do is to stop doctoring Richard's food and wait for the market to register the fact that the 'allergy' is a thing of the past. If it's someone in the company he knows that when our annual report comes out in July the figures will look good and the shares will shoot up. He can't lose."

But who was the mysterious buyer? They discussed various possibilities without hitting on anything probable.

"How about Anthea Clarkson?" Celia suggested. "She's told me a lot of lies about you and your mother. Unless she's been telling them for fun, she's up to something."

"Why would she want to poison Richard and make him look ridiculous?" Charles objected. "She was having an affair with him in the hope that he would give her a directorship."

"I know, that's the snag. But Anthea Clarkson is the sort of frightened person who needs a very fat bank balance to feel safe. She'd do far worse things than that to a lover if there was money in it."

"But where would she get the cash to buy up Galliant shares?"

"She may have an ill-gotten nest egg. I have a feeling that she left her job in London under a cloud."

Langley sat up sharply. "How did you know that?"

"I don't, I'm only guessing. But she talked about her change of job rather defensively, as if it was a step down."

"You're right, it was. She was quite high in management at a very reputable investment trust. I rang them and asked them about her, and they were very cagey, as if something had gone badly wrong."

"Could it have been insider trading?"

"Oh. Yes, it could. If they let her get away with it to avoid a scandal, she'd have a lump sum to buy Galliant shares with."

Celia's conscience began to prick her. Because I happen to dislike Anthea, she told herself, that's no reason for making accusations against her that I can't prove. And I don't want them to be true, it would mean frightful hurt for Bill. Shying away from this painful thought, she said: "Could the poisoner have been Dawson? He had a desperate domestic problem that only money could solve, and he's the sort who would kill himself if it went wrong."

"What d'you mean, 'went wrong'?" Langley asked.

"Suppose someone found out what he was doing, and blackmailed him, he'd panic and take the drastic way out."

"That is a possibility, yes."

If there is a blackmailer, I bet it's Anthea, Celia thought, despite her resolution not to be unfair to her. Anthea had caught Dawson red-handed in the studio at night with a torch, and she was not the sort of girl to let an opportunity slip.

Langley was looking at her with an odd expression, as if wondering whether or not to say what he was thinking. "Changing the subject completely, Mrs. Grant, had it occurred to you that perhaps the shots that wounded you were meant for you all the time, and not for Mr. Gomez?"

"Of course. I considered that possibility and decided it

didn't make sense. Who among our acquaintance possesses a machine gun?"

"I know it sounds fantastic, but someone might have got alarmed because they thought that you were getting to know too much."

"One mustn't exaggerate one's own importance. Besides, who knew that Mr. Gomez was on some unspeakable Latin American hit list, so that I could seem to have been shot in mistake for him? They'd need to know well in advance that he was dining with the Galliants that night, otherwise they wouldn't have time to set the thing up. Besides, I hadn't found out anything that made sense, and nobody knew that I . . . was interested in this sort of probem."

"And very good at them, I must add. You're wrong, though. One person knows all about your exploits in this field: we're back at Anthea Clarkson."

She digested this unwelcome thought. "She'd need an accomplice to do the shooting."

"Or she could be somebody's accomplice. You said yourself, she'd do almost anything for money."

"No," said Celia firmly. "Anthea's silly and self-centred but she's not as wicked as that."

"Now, Mr. Wilkins, just as a matter of routine," said Detective-Sergeant Bailey, "would you mind telling me what your movements were between, say, eleven yesterday morning and the time you arrived at Mr. Dawson's house?"

"Okay, if I must," said Bill. He and Anthea were furious. Bailey had interrupted a lazy Sunday afternoon cuddle on the lawn behind the cottage.

"Thank you, Mr. Wilkins, I'm sorry to trouble you."

Bill collected his thoughts. "Until twelve I was catching up with odd jobs at the nursery—"

"Anyone see you there?"

"Yes. Two of the girls came in to help."

"And after that?"

"I went home and changed and packed to come over here."

"No lunch, Mr. Wilkins?"

"I stopped at a pub on the way for a beer and a sandwich."

"Ah. Where was that?"

"The Bell at Ringmer."

"Talk to anyone there you know?"

"No, it was full of foreigners come to sing at Glyndebourne."

"I see. And you arrived here when?"

"At about two thirty. I checked that everything was okay in the garden over at the Old Rectory and had a word with Mrs. Galliant, she was sitting out on the terrace. Then I went to the Dawsons' to deliver some plants that he wanted from the nursery."

"That would be when roughly, Mr. Wilkins?"

"Five—ten minutes before I rang the police."

Anthea had listened to this questioning in growing agitation. "What is all this? Why does he need an alibi? D'you mean, it wasn't a suicide pact?"

"We're not ruling out foul play at present, Mrs. Wilkins."

She was not Mrs. Wilkins, but let that pass. "He was very unhappy, you know. His wife was dying slowly, and there were problems about the nursing, and everything got on top of him."

Detective-Sergeant Bailey consulted his notebook. "Miss Miller, that's the nurse-companion, says he was quite cheerful when she left to catch the bus to Brighton. Unusually so, he'd just had a raise in salary that pleased him a lot."

Anthea started to say something, then checked herself.

"Yes, Mrs. Wilkins?" said Bailey.

"Nothing. I was only going to say that I'm not Mrs. Wilkins."

When Bailey had apologized for his mistake and checked that neither of them had seen or heard anything suspicious, he left. Walking back across the green to the Dawsons', he ran through the facts he had gathered so far. Someone wearing gloves had handled the plastic bag which had suffocated Dawson, and in two places the glove-wearer's traces were superimposed on Dawson's fingerprints. Fibres of some kind under his fingernails suggested that there had been a struggle. A piece of lint in his mouth smelt faintly of ether, and the pathologist reported that he had been anaesthetized before the plastic bag was put over his head. Mrs. Dawson had presented no problem, being far too weak to raise a finger while her husband was being murdered. Afterwards she had been smothered at leisure with her own pillow.

Having established so much, Bailey had turned his attention to the boundary hedge which divided the garden from a patch of rough woodland beyond. Broken twigs suggested that someone had pushed through it at the back of the terrace where the Dawsons were taking their afternoon nap. It would have been perfectly easy to creep up on them from behind, take them by surprise as they slept, clap an ether-soaked pad over Dawson's face, smother his wife and set the thing up to look like a suicide pact. But it was not a suicide pact, and only an optimist would have hoped to pass it off as one.

Back at the cottage Bill had his arm round Anthea's shoulders. She was shivering a little. "I said we wouldn't think about them, Gorgeous, but I can't get them out of my mind. Especially her, Mrs. Dawson. I went over there once or twice to chat her up and you'd be amazed at the books she read and the wise things she said about them. She was very brave, she kept up appearances and made the best of her awful life. She shouldn't have died like that."

"Anthea love, what were you going to tell that policeman but decided not to?"

"I suddenly thought, no I mustn't say that, it will make him connect up the Dawson thing with the Galliant drugging scandal, and we'll have a replay of that in the Sunday papers and the company's future will be even more knife-edge and I'll be that much nearer to not having a job."

"But love, what was it you decided not to say?"

"Jim Dawson didn't have a pay increase. He asked for one. I was there when Richard discussed it with Charles Langley, and they turned it down."

"Could Miss Miller have got it wrong?"

"Why should she? It's very important to her."

"Suppose he got hold of some extra money from somewhere, but he hadn't come by it honestly. He had to explain to her where he got it from, so he invented this story. See what I mean?"

"Of course I see what you mean, damn you. Gorgeous, I'm afraid."

After Charles Langley left Celia, she fell asleep again. Looking back weeks later on her behaviour at that time, she was at a loss to explain why that particular Sunday afternoon snooze should have proved the turning point. It was dreamless, but she woke with a perfectly clear head, and the knowledge that the narrow staircase of her dreams, with the sickly sweet scent at the top, was the staircase at Anthea's rented cottage.

She could see herself now, asking to use the bathroom; going upstairs, trying the wrong door, an ill-fitting one which proved to be locked. When she went down again Anthea explained that it was the door of a bedroom in which the owner of the cottage kept possessions she did not want her tenants to use. She had wondered at the time why the upstairs of the cottage reeked of a heavy flower scent and not of Anthea's overpowering Paris concoction, but had been too polite to ask.

And afterwards, the mental block had made her suppress the memory of the datura in the locked bedroom. She had been so anxious not to be unfair to Anthea. She was not in love with Bill, which would have been ridiculous and disgusting at her age, but she had to prove it to herself by not thinking nasty thoughts about his girlfriend. She did not want him hurt, she had refused to face the truth because she must always give Anthea the benefit of the doubt. Once one faced the truth about Anthea, everything fell into place, the pattern became clear. But Bill was going to be hurt, because there was no more doubt to give Anthea the benefit of.

She braced herself for an ordeal. He and Anthea had promised to call in on her on their way to Glyndebourne for the opening night of *The Marriage of Figaro*. What on earth was she to say to them?

They arrived dressed to kill. Anthea was wearing a caftan made up in a Wanda Galliant printed silk and not, to Celia's relief, the tarty scarlet number she had appeared in at the Galliants' dinner party. Bill looked handsomer than ever in evening clothes. It was heartbreaking, they made a stunning couple. Heads would turn when they joined the parade through Glyndebourne's beautiful garden before curtain time, Celia had seen it happen elsewhere.

He is going to be hurt, she told herself. How long could she put it off? Only a matter of hours, she realized, when he confirmed hints she had heard on the midday news that the police regarded the Dawsons' apparent "suicide pact" as a double murder. To her alarm, Bill was thinking along lines which would lead him to the conclusion she herself had already reached.

"Knew something, Celia, didn't he? A thing someone didn't want him to know. Where did he get that money he said was a salary raise? Some naughty way, because he lied to Miss Miller about it. Blackmail's the only way I can see, and he'd forgotten that the people you blackmail can get naughty too."

"His wife was killed too," said Anthea. She had gone haggard beneath her make-up.

"They was having their afternoon snooze together in their garden," said Bill. "You'd have to kill her as well, or she'd see who you was and tell on you."

"Dawson could have backed a successful horse," said Celia with a desperate attempt at lightness, "and lied to

Miss Miller because she disapproved of gambling."

Bill frowned obstinately. "Bookies don't kill you for winning money off of them. People do when they've been poisoning their boss and stealing the firm's designs and someone who's found them out puts his begging bowl under their nose and says 'money, give me money.'"

Celia had only one thought, to head him off, postpone the crisis, prevent Anthea from taking alarm. Even on a Sunday evening, someone competent would be on duty at Lewes police station, she would get on the phone as soon as Bill and Anthea left for Glyndebourne.

Meanwhile, Bill must be pointed in the wrong direction. "People who take drugs kill at the drop of a hat," she said.

"Oh Celia, you mean Paul? He's off hard drugs, why d'you fix on him?"

Concentrating grimly, Celia began to improvise a case against Paul. There was no guarantee that he was off drugs, they only had Fred's word for it, and addicts were amazingly clever at concealment. He had sold Galliant designs to his mother's firm because he needed the money. His mother, who hated Galliant as much as he did, had evolved a scheme for driving the share price down and gaining control of the company, and when she asked Paul to poison his father he was only too willing.

"Hey wait, Celia," he interrupted. "If he'd monkeyed with that prawn cocktail, why did he agree to eat it?"

Simple, Celia argued. To avoid being exposed as the poisoner who had tried to ruin his father's firm. But that did not satisfy Bill. Why did Paul not use an emetic as soon as he could, before the poison took effect? Celia dealt with that as best she could, but he faced her at once with another hurdle. Had she noticed that there was a disused outside lavatory under the back porch of the Old Rectory? Could not someone have slipped in there to wait till the coast was clear? It would be the work of a moment to run into the kitchen and switch the prawn cocktail with a doctored one. That would be too risky, Celia retorted. What if Paul arrived to collect his lunch while the poisoner was in the kitchen? The only suspect who did not run that risk was Paul himself.

She waited. Would he realize about the kitchen window and work out that the poisoner would see Paul coming in time to hide? Apparently not. He was looking baffled and unconvinced. Had she given him enough red herrings to think about to stop him from realizing the truth? If so, she could breathe again.

Anthea was looking a little less haggard, rather smug in fact. "We ought to be going, Gorgeous," she said, "or we'll be late for the opera. Sorry, Celia."

Bill stood up. "Let's hope it's only the opera we're going to, and not another machine gun target practice thrown in."

"Are you expecting one?" Celia asked.

"Gomez is going to be there. The one they shot at before."

"Who told you that?" said Anthea sharply.

"Fred Watney. I think he heard it from you, Celia."

"He was here visiting me when Mrs. Gomez mentioned it, I think," Celia murmured. This was dangerous territory, she must get him away from it at once.

But it was too late. "There was a bit in the Sunday paper," said Bill, "on account of them shooting you by mistake. All about how the people thrown out of the Latin American countries sat in Miami plotting and trying to get arms to start revolutions, they seem a wild lot there. Anthea was in Miami for a bit last year, after she finished with her job in London. But she says she didn't see anything of that."

"It was a temporary job, Gorgeous, filling in before I started at Galliant's." Anthea's voice was tightly controlled, but her hands were trembling. "And I was much too busy with it to gape at squalid little people plotting in cafés."

She was staring at Bill, with a cruel expression on her face that Celia had never seen before. And well she might, for what Bill had just said must have shocked her to the

189

marrow. He had just brought her slap up against the fact that he had all the pieces of the jigsaw in his mind, including the key one that made sense of all the others, and that it was only a matter of time before he puzzled out the truth. He was in terrible danger, something must be done at once.

Celia longed for them to go. Presently they did. The moment the door closed behind them she grabbed the telephone and rang Lewes police station.

❧ TWELVE ❧

The garden at Glyndebourne was looking its spectacular best. This being a Sunday and a first night, the performance started early so that the critics could get their notices into Monday's papers. By four o'clock the first arrivals were having tea in one of its many flower-filled enclosures or strolling on the great lawn which, thanks to a hidden ditch, seemed to merge into the pasture-land beyond and sweep up without a break towards the ridge of the South Downs. The tea and the stroll in the garden and round the lake were part of the ritual which made Glyndebourne a social occasion like Gold Cup Day at Ascot, rather than a mere visit to the opera.

Cars were arriving all the time in the field which served as a car park. Most of them contained elaborate picnics with folding tables and chairs as well as salmon and strawberries and champagne, to be eaten in the garden during the long dinner interval. The one in the Galliants' Rolls-Royce was no exception. As usual they were doing some business entertaining, and had decided to ignore Glyndebourne's admirable restaurant and expose their foreign guests to the full blast of British eccentricity and the British climate. Morris was under strict instructions to guard the picnic with his life against poisoners until the moment of serving.

"Let me see now, Richard," said Joan Galliant as Morris eased the Rolls into a parking space. "Is this the one where the men disguise themselves as Albanians and the girls get horizontal with the wrong lover?"

"No, do pull yourself together. That's *Così fan tutte*."

"Oh, then it must be the one where the girl who's supposed to be a boy dresses up as a girl and jumps out of a window. And in the end the girls are disguised as each other and no one can remember who's pretending to be what or why."

"My dear girl, it's perfectly simple. The Countess is disguised as Susanna to trap the Count, and the Count falls for it and makes love to Susanna, and Figaro pretends to think Susanna is the Countess and makes love to her to make her jealous. And then they go off to one of the garden pavilions to make love properly, only Barbarina and Cherubino and Marcellina are in there already—"

"Oh do shut up, Richard. You realize that one of us is going to have to explain all that through an interpreter to a trade delegation of Japanese?"

"It's not worth the effort, Madam," said Morris as he held the door open for her. "After all that singin' in Italian, the Japanese will be too exhausted to care, even if the gents pair off with each other."

Joan climbed out and began tottering towards the opera house on high heels. She was in full evening dress and wearing far more jewellery than she thought proper on a fine Sunday afternoon, but Galliant insisted on a display that would impress the Japanese.

Just ahead of them were Bill and Anthea.

"Yes, I gave her a couple of tickets," Galliant admitted when Joan pointed them out.

"Oh, why?"

"She asked for them, and I felt a bit sorry for her."

"I don't see why. She was only letting you goose her for what she could get out of it, and that young man will give her all the healthy exercise she needs. . . . Oh look, there's Charles with our Japanese."

Bill was puzzled by Anthea's mood. She had insisted on arriving early but would not explain why. Now that they were here, she hurried into the walled garden beyond the foyer and looked round eagerly.

"You looking for someone, Anthea love?"

"Yes . . . I can't see him anywhere."

"Anyone I know?"

He had to repeat the question several times before she answered. "No . . . It's just someone I know's going to be here that I did business with, there's something I have to settle with him."

But the mysterious business contact was nowhere to be seen. Not in the formal garden between the clipped yew hedges, nor on the great lawn outside the garden front of the house, nor in the dell at the head of the lake where Bill, tired of carrying their rug and picnic basket, insisted on dumping them ready for the dinner interval. The search went on, down the path to the bottom end of the lake where it vanished into woodland, back on the main lawn up on to the terrace and into the house through the Organ Room and into the foyer.

"Maybe he didn't come after all," Bill suggested.

"He must have, I checked with him this morning."

"Anthea love, we're here to have fun, don't let's spoil it. Is it that important?"

"Of course it is, damn you, he owes me a lot of money. Come on, let's have another look."

He tried to dissuade her but she insisted. The crowd of opera-goers was moving about all the time, they must repeat the whole search in case they had missed the quarry. Presently the starting bell began ringing, but the man who owed Anthea money had not been found.

Celia was out of luck. According to Lewes police station, Inspector Grainger, who had dealt with the enquiries after the shooting at the Galliants' dinner party, was out on a case and not available. Could anyone else help? Baffled by Celia's attempt to explain the emergency, the CID desk officer contacted Inspector Grainger on his car telephone. Unable to make any sense of a secondhand version of Celia's remarks, he offered to come to the hospital at once, but he was miles away on the Kent border and by the time he arrived it might be too late. Desperate, Celia arranged to save time by meeting him at Glyndebourne, and called loudly for a taxi to be ordered to take her there.

This unleashed an enormous fuss. The senior staff nurse was fetched, then a house surgeon. She must not discharge herself, it was much too soon, they would not be responsible for the consequences. But she stuck to her point: if they detained her, they would be responsible for a lot more consequences than they imagined. In the end they gave way under protest, much to her relief. She had to get to Glyndebourne in time, and she made the driver hurry. The vision haunted her of Bill, with Anthea beside him, strolling across the Glyndebourne lawns in the field of fire of some marksman hidden in nearby thicket.

As the taxi sped through Uckfield, Celia sorted out the whirl of ideas in her head, ready to present them in an orderly and coherent fashion to Inspector Grainger. She was horrified with herself for having let matters get to this pass, when she ought to have seen the solution staring her in the face days earlier. Her failure to remember where she had smelt the datura was the result of a mental block on thoughts critical of Anthea, but that was no excuse. Ignorance of Latin American geography was even less excusable. She had blithely assumed that Ciudad Antonio was in Central America. It was not, it was a small state in the High Andes, almost an enclave in Colombia. This was the area where the tree daturas were endemic, and where primitive peoples had made sophisticated use of them for hundreds of years in religious rites as hallucinogens. Anyone from that area would turn naturally to the datura if he wanted a drug with hallucinogenic properties, and would know how to use it.

According to Gomez, he and the other exiles from Ciudad Antonio were perpetually short of money to keep the pot of political agitation boiling. Almost certainly, his newspaper, and perhaps other enterprises, were financed by his wife's enormous earnings as a singer.

For several years Teresa Gomez had been carrying on an intermittent love affair with Richard Galliant, which she had reason to expect would end in him divorcing his wife and marrying her. When she accepted the engagement to sing at Glyndebourne, a few miles from where Galliant lived, the exiles must have suspected that her main purpose in spending several weeks in England was to bring the love affair to a head and make Galliant marry her.

If she succeeded, the flow of funds to Miami from their operatic milch-cow would be cut off.

How to prevent this? By discrediting Galliant, making him look ridiculous and putting Teresa off him. How was that to be done? With datura. Administered by whom? By an alluring girl whom they would persuade to dangle herself in front of him. Being the sort of man he was, he would fall for it at once.

Where in Miami was a suitable girl to be found? Difficult. Perhaps in one of the British firms with offices in Miami.

Anthea had left her London job under a cloud and taken a stopgap one in Miami. She must have seemed to them like an answer to the wickedest prayer imaginable. She was almost too highly qualified for the role, and how was she to be paid in view of the state of the émigré exchequer? Simple. She could be promised enormous sums, and when the time came there would be unexpected difficulties.

Even if it occurred to Anthea to wonder when and with what she would be paid, she must have seen distinct gains to herself in what was proposed. In view of her business qualifications, she might well persuade the victim to take her on to his staff, and a job out of London, where her lapse from virtue over insider trading was not known, was what she needed. More important, she could foresee a moment when Galliant shares would be available at giveaway price, and the moment when they began to climb again would be under her exclusive control, because she would be starting and stopping the administration of the hallucinogen. There might be other pickings in a firm like that, such as selling exclusive designs to competitors. She wanted money, because money was safety. Her winnings in London from using her inside knowledge to buy shares had given her a start, but she wanted more and she wanted it fast. One way or another, this seemed to be a way of laying hands on a lot of it, especially if her paymasters kept their word.

But then things had started to go wrong. Having Archerscroft Nurseries at work in the garden at the Old Rectory had proved even more inconvenient from Anthea's point of view than Joan Galliant had intended; it had forced Anthea to tell Celia an elaborate set of lies to put her off the scent. Her encounter with Jim Dawson at night in the design studio had been even more inconvenient, Celia suspected. It looked as if he had caught Anthea there redhanded, copying Wanda's latest design to sell to Pritchard and Colson. Her quick thinking had hidden the truth from Celia, who had arrived at a very awkward moment. But Dawson needed money even more urgently than she did. He had probably proved a very determined blackmailer. The alternative to facing a lifetime of being blackmailed was to kill him.

Celia cursed herself for not having managed things better when Bill and Anthea called on her at the hospital on their way to Glyndebourne. By making out a case against Paul as the poisoner, she had probably convinced Anthea that she was on the wrong track, and not dangerous enough to need shooting. But she had failed to convince Bill. He was not very far from the truth. His dogged mind would worry at the facts till he found it. He knew how long Anthea had spent working in Miami. But in answer to a casual question from Celia, she had denied in a panic that she had ever been there. Sooner or later he and Celia would compare notes and wonder why. For that reason if for no other, he had to be silenced now.

Gomez was at Glyndebourne. He would stroll in the garden during the interval. So would Bill and Anthea. It would be easy for Anthea to make sure they went close enough to Gomez for another "attempt on his life" like the one at Faringfield, with Bill as the victim.

As the taxi sped through Ringmer and turned left up the flank of the South Downs, Celia wondered how long it would take her to explain the danger and get it acted upon. Would Inspector Grainger be there, or would she have to wait for him? As the taxi dived down into Glyndebourne's wooded hollow and turned into the drive, she saw to her enormous relief that a police car was standing in front of the manor house. Inspector Grainger stepped out of it, and she braced herself for a testing exercise in crisis management.

Teresa Enriquez sat in front of her dressing-room mirror, a prey to first-night nerves. Distant applause from the auditorium marked the end of the overture. Down on the stage Susanna would be trying on her bridal bonnet while Figaro measured the room, the first act was under way. The second would follow it without an interval, and then she would have to make her difficult first apearance with the stage to herself, a not very responsive audience to face, and one of the most beautiful and well-known arias in the whole operatic repertory to sing. From then on she would have no respite, apart from a bare minute off the stage between the *terzetto*, with its high runs, and the demanding Act Two finale. Only rigid self-control kept her from breaking her strict rule and opening the half bottle of champagne, mysteriously labelled "Mrs. Christie's champagne"* which she had found in her dressing-room with a message of first-night good wishes from the management.

*Mrs. Christie, the soprano Audrey Mildmay, sang Susanna in *Figaro* at the opening performance in the opera house in 1934. She combined her membership of successive Glyndebourne casts with the duties of a hostess, and the first night champagne she provided for the artists became a tradition which continued after her death in 1953.

Three, even two years ago she would have sailed through the part triumphantly. How much longer would she be able to get through it all?

She seized the champagne bottle. "Pilar, take this and put it away somewhere."

Pilar obeyed, with a cheerfulness which Teresa found offensive in view of the reason for it. While the love affair with Richard Galliant was still on, she had behaved differently, scowling and muttering under her breath, or praying loudly to the Virgin, a habit she had when she wanted to register a protest. For Teresa to take a non-Catholic lover was bad enough. And despite Pilar's sketchy English, she had probably grasped that Teresa was hoping to commit the grievous sin of divorce. But now the sulks were over. As she dressed Teresa and fitted her into her wig, she chatted cheerfully as she had done in opera houses all over the world, to stave off first-night nerves.

Teresa was still furious with Galliant, who had not even come to her defence on that disastrous evening, when Joan Galliant made it offensively clear that having a husband who got shot at at dinner parties was a shocking breach of good form. Meanwhile her relations with Miguel were getting worse and worse. There had been phone calls for him from an angry-sounding Englishwoman, who was she? Pablo had arrived from Paris. He and Miguel had spent hours shut up together in gloomy conspiratorial conference, from which they emerged at intervals to ask her ever more insistently, but in vain, for yet more money for the cause.

A sudden thought came to her. "Pilar. Bring me my jewel case."

Her imposing jewels were her last line of defence against poverty and old age. Normally she would never have brought them to the theatre, but after her last refusal of money she had caught Miguel trying the drawers in her bedroom and knew at once what he was looking for. They were supposed to leave for Glyndebourne with her, but she had to be early and they had made an excuse to come on later, with the obvious intention of ransacking the house for her jewel case, so she had brought it with her. She checked that everything was still in it and locked it in the drawer of her dressing table. What was she to do with the key? There was no pocket in her crinoline, so she put it in her handbag while Pilar was not looking.

Someone knocked on the door. Surely it was not time for her call yet? A low rumble of laughter had just come from the auditorium, the Count must have discovered the pageboy Cherubino hiding in the armchair half way through the first act.

The knock was repeated. Pilar was trying to keep someone out of the dressing room, explaining in Spanish that the Señora saw no one during a performance. But the intruder pushed past her. It was the front of house manager.

"I'm sorry, Madame, the police are here. There is a security scare. Inspector Grainger insists on speaking to you at once."

She recognized the police officer who had questioned her and Miguel about the shooting at Mrs. Galliant's disastrous dinner party, and her heart sank. What had happened now?

"We have reason to believe," siad Grainger, "that another shooting incident is likely to occur here along the same lines as the previous one. I'm sorry to have to trouble you when you're about to perform, so I'll be as brief as possible. I understand that you have a house guest, a friend of your husband's who arrived yesterday from Paris and is returning there with him tomorrow. Would you describe him please? What does he look like and what was he wearing when you last saw him?"

"This you can ask my husband," said Teresa feverishly, with half her mind on the opening phrases of "Porgi amor."

"We don't know where Mr. Gomez is," the house manager put in. "He's not in his seat in the artists' box."

"Because now I do not sing," Teresa explained. "Only in the Second Act I sing, then he will come."

"We can't wait for him, I'm afraid, Madame," the house

manager said urgently. "Please do as the inspector asks, there's no time to lose."

The inspector began firing questions at her. Name? Pablo Trueba Garcia. Hair? Black, curly, with grey sideburns. Eyes? She could not remember. Height? Perhaps one metre eighty. Build? A two-handed gesture indicated a thin man with a pot belly. Moustache or beard? Neither.

"Does he have a dinner jacket with him?" Grainger asked.

She looked bewildered.

"A tuxedo," the house manager explained. "A *smoking*."

At this she lost her temper. "Am I the good God that I should know? Am I a spy of the police, that I should search in his baggages? I am an artist. Go. Go, you ruin my performance."

Grainger withdrew gloomily. He had suffered a piece of appalling bad luck. The plain clothes detective-constable detailed to give Gomez police protection against another "assassination attempt" had not known that the gents at Glyndebourne had an exit into the garden as well as the one near the foyer. Gomez had given him the slip, and was nowhere to be found. Bill Wilkins and his girl were somewhere in the auditorium, they must be intercepted before they left it at the interval. He hurried away to attend to that.

"Two minutes, Miss Enriquez," the call boy shouted. Down on the stage, the first act came to an end and the stage hands put the finishing touches to the second-act set, representing her state bedroom. She crossed herself, uttered a quick prayer, and started down the passage.

Suddenly Miguel was in front of her, blocking her path to the stage. "*Querida*, my life is in danger, I must leave for France tonight," he hissed. "Please, I must have money."

She brushed past him. "I have told you, no. I cannot give more."

"But *querida*—"

The stage staff were signalling to her violently. The curtain was up. The orchestra had started on its long prelude to her aria, during which she was supposed to stroll disconsolately on to the stage, so that the audience could get used to the sight of her before she launched into "Porgi amor." She made it in a run with three bars to spare, shut everything but the key of E flat major out of her mind, and began to sing.

The *Times'* music critic sat up sharply in his stall and made a mental note. As he put it in his notice next morning, "Miss Enriquez asserted her authority over the role from her first entrance. Instead of offering us the usual staid matron, patiently awaiting the end of the prelude before singing of her deep sorrow, she entered trippingly at the last moment, a light-hearted young girl in sad mood, but by no means as inconsolable as her opening aria suggests. This is surely what Mozart intended . . ."

"God of Love," Teresa sang, "give me some consolation for my pain, my sighs, give me back my beloved, or let me die." Her beloved was so unsatisfactory that she did not want him back, her husband was an inefficient money-grubbing conspirator in danger of his life, Pilar was gloating, the police had burst into her dressing-room, the whole situation was *brutissima* and she was very angry. But she found to her surprise that she was singing very well indeed.

Celia and Inspector Grainger were in the box office. The clerk had the evening's booking plan in front of him, trying to locate the seats occupied by Bill and Anthea.

"The friend from Paris is called Pablo Trueba Garcia," the Inspector told Celia while the clerk searched. "She gave me a description of him, but it could apply to almost anyone and she won't say whether or not he has a dinner jacket with him. If he has, we'll never pick him out from all the people picnicking in the garden."

"If he hasn't, he'll be conspicuous," Celia reasoned. "Too conspicuous to come out in the open, he'll be hiding somewhere in a thicket. You'll need men to search."

He nodded. "There's my sergeant, and a detective-constable who was supposed to be giving Gomez police protection. I've sent for more men, but on a Sunday night it takes time."

Since the start of the second act Miguel Gomez had been standing in the wings, watching Teresa's performance. On the stage, Count Almaviva had just heard the noise in the Countess's locked dressing-room where her half-undressed page, who was hiding from him in there, knocked over a chair. Teresa braced herself, and made a perfect run up to a firm C in alt as she begged the Count not to make a public scandal out of this embarrassing circumstance. The repeat twelve bars later was just as good, the sight of Miguel scowling at her from the wings had fuelled her anger and the effect on her voice was miraculous.

The *terzetto* ended and she let herself be led offstage on the Count's arm, as he went to fetch tools to break open the dressing-room door. The moment she was out of sight of the audience Miguel was upon her. "Teresa *querida*, please—"

She called the stage manager. "Please to take away my husband, he make me nervous."

"But Teresa—" Miguel began.

"If he stay, I sing bad," she insisted. "Go, Miguel."

Before she knew where she was, the page Cherubino had come jumping through the window to escape from the Count's fury, and she was due back on stage, to find her way through the high point of Mozart's operatic achievement, a miracle of wit and musical invention: the arduous twenty-minute finale in which eight of the main characters battled their way through a series of comic predicaments and brought the curtain down on the second act of the opera.

"Ah Signore, quel furore . . ." she began, and found to her astonishment that she was not dreading the ardours that lay ahead, her own fury had unlocked something in her voice and she had begun to trust it again. She would get rid of Miguel, forget about Richard Galliant. She did not need either of them, as long as she had her voice.

In the box office, the clerk was still poring over the booking plan. "If they're in corporate patrons' seats as guests of Mr. Galliant," he said, "we wouldn't have a note of their names."

"Where are the corporate patrons' seats?" Grainger asked.

"Oh, we don't put them all together. There's a block here . . . and here . . . and here."

This was clearly a hopeless line of enquiry. "How long till the curtain comes down?" Grainger asked.

The house manager listened to the music. Presently the audience laughed. "They're half way through the finale, that was the drunken gardener with the pot of carnations. Another ten minutes and we'll be down."

"How many exits are there to the auditorium?" Grainger asked.

"Four. Six if you include the balcony."

"Too many to cover. Where's the best view of the audience?"

"From the stage box. I'll let you and Mrs. Grant in there as soon as we're down and I'll have the house lights up at once, so that she can spot them and point them out to you."

The stage manager came through on the house telephone. "We've located Mr. Gomez. He was making a nuisance of himself in the wings."

"Where is he now?" Grainger asked.

"In his wife's dressing room."

"Fine," said Grainger. "Try to keep him there, will you, till we can come and deal with him?"

As soon as the curtain came down Anthea stood up and began pushing past people to make her way out, so energetically that Bill had had trouble following her. He caught up in the courtyard leading to the garden.

"Oh, there you are, Gorgeous," she said, hurrying on. "Go and start unpacking the picnic, d'you mind? I'll be with you as soon as I can, I must see this man."

"The one that owes you money?" Bill asked. "Can't it wait?"

"No, damn you. He said he'd be here, he promised. And tomorrow he goes off abroad."

As she shot away, a man who was not in evening clothes cut through the crowd towards him. "Mr. Wilkins? I'm a police officer. Would you come with me, please? Mrs. Grant is here, and she has something very important to tell you."

Must he? Bill objected. He was with Anthea, she would be joining him in a moment, they were all set to eat, what was all this anyway?

"Please don't worry about Miss Clarkson, we'll be attending to that."

"What d'you mean, attending to it?"

"Mr. Wilkins, I can't explain here. It's for your own safety, please don't make my job more difficult, just come with me."

Mystified, Bill followed him through the foyer at the back of the theatre and across the drive into an office where Celia was waiting for him.

"Oh Celia, you didn't ought to be here," he said when he saw her drawn face. "You should be in bed."

"Sit down, Bill," she said in a voice that was barely under control. "I don't know how to begin to say this, it will upset you a lot... Perhaps I'll start with a question. You remember, I said I associated smelling the scent of a datura with walking up a staircase and being out of breath? D'you remember if you repeated that to Anthea?"

"Oh yes, Celia, I did. I thought she might have an idea what staircase it was, but she didn't."

"Bill, I'm sorry about this, but she wasn't telling the truth. It was her own staircase at the cottage."

He went white and utterly numb. She started to explain, but he interrupted. "Oh no, Celia. You dunno what you're saying. Anthea's not bad. She's frightened, but she's not bad."

"Most of the bad things people do are done because they're frightened, and Anthea was very frightened. When she realized that I had this vague association with a staircase, she was terrified that I'd remember which staircase it was, and she decided that something must be done about it. Before and during the Galliants' dinner party she was in a state of abject panic, and while we were having drinks in the garden I couldn't make out why she moved away whenever I went anywhere near her. She knew, you see, that I was going to be shot, she'd arranged it with Gomez, and she didn't want to be anywhere near the firing line."

"Celia, you're raving. She doesn't know Gomez."

"Then why did she tell me she'd never been to Miami, when you know perfectly well that she has?"

"I don't want to hear no more of this," Bill shouted fiercely. "I want to talk to Anthea."

"By all means, but where is she? The police were supposed to bring her here with you."

"She went off to look in the garden for a man she says owes her money."

"Who? What man?" Celia asked, startled.

"I dunno, she didn't say. Someone who's going off abroad tomorrow, so she must see him tonight."

Celia was too horrified to speak. The silly, greedy little tramp. Gomez had promised her a huge reward for her services, and could not pay. She was dunning him for money that he had not got, probably making wild threats to expose him. If Gomez had any sense he would get rid of her before she told his wife what he had done.

And I'm a fool too, Celia thought. I saw the threat lurking in the garden, but I picked the wrong victim.

"Bill. Go at once and find Anthea and bring her here before she gets killed. Use force if you have to, but get her out of that garden. Make the police help. The man who owes her money is Gomez. Don't let her go anywhere near him, or we'll have a repeat performance of what happened to me at Faringfield, and this time his friend from Paris may take better aim."

Gomez was no longer in his wife's dressing room. When Grainger put his head round the door he was screamed at in Spanish by the dresser and told firmly to go by her mistress. "Probably in the auditorium," said the stage manager. "I think he went out through the pass door."

All over the garden people were picnicking luxuriously, with wine coolers on the grass beside folding tables with elegant tablecloths and in some cases even a candlestick, though it was still light and the moon was only a pale disk hanging above the sweep of the Downs in the evening sky. As Anthea ran on past the feasting groups, some of them wondered who the dark striking-looking girl was who seemed to be in great distress, looking for someone she could not find. But Anthea took no notice, she was obsessed with her only aim: to find Gomez before it was too late. Nothing else mattered, not even the fact that Bill would be wondering where on earth she was.

"What can she be up to, one would think it was the Olympic Games," said Joan Galliant as Anthea hurried past the Galliants and their Japanese. But Anthea sped on without noticing them. Gomez had promised to meet her here, where was he? Not in the Dell, not in the formal garden, not among the picnickers spread over the great lawn, not in the marquee provided for picnicking in bad weather, not in either of the restaurants. Down on the grass beside the lake, perhaps. She had looked there once before, but she would look again . . .

When Teresa Enriquez returned from the stage for the long interval she was pleased with her performance, and determined to give her husband a piece of her mind. But he was not there. Pilar did not know where he had gone or perhaps would not say, for she had suffered a baffling change of mood and sat crouched in a corner muttering, as if afflicted by the Evil Eye. As Teresa dusted more powder over her face and chest, a possible explanation of her dresser's state of living death occurred to her. She tried the locked drawer containing her jewel case. It was still locked. She took the key out of her handbag and opened the drawer to check. Her jewel case had gone, and Pilar's face wore an expression of guilty defiance.

In half an hour I have to sing "Dovo sono," Teresa thought, therefore I must not scream at her. But Pilar was doing the screaming, yelling abuse at her for being unfaithful to the Señor, for not giving him the money he needed to uphold the cause of the fatherland. Conserving her voice for "Dove sono" with supreme self-control, Teresa slapped her hard across the face twice without uttering a syllable. As Pilar went on screaming abuse, a rap came on the door. "Is anything wrong, Miss Enriquez?"

"No, it is only my dresser who has the hysterics."

Correction, she thought. It is only my dressser who is in the pay of my husband and had been spying on me for years, and now she has handed over to him my jewellery, which is my last defence against an old age of poverty and despair. She summoned the stage manager. "That policeman who was here, I wish him to come again to arrest quickly my husband."

"Very well, Madame," said the stage manager without batting an eyelid. His responsibility was to see that the performance went smoothly. If that involved humouring *divas* who had quarrelled with their husbands, that was part of the job.

Grainger's sergeant was parading through the garden, on the lookout for anything suspicious. But the theatre held almost eight hundred, roughly half of them men in dinner jackets, and the gunman was almost certainly wearing one. How was he to know who to suspect?

Bill Wilkins rushed up to him. "Have you seen Anthea Clarkson anywhere?"

"Who?"

"The girl I was with when you came up to me just now. It's her they want to kill, not me."

"I didn't see her, what does she look like?"

Grainger had caught up at last with Gomez, who had slipped out through the Organ Room on to the terrace, and down the steps on to the great lawn. Grainger hurried after him, but was held up by a slow-moving elderly couple hobbling down the steps. Gomez had reached a gap in the yew hedge on the far side of the lawn before Grainger caught up with him.

"Mr. Gomez, when we agreed that you should attend your wife's performance, you were told that we accepted no responsibility for your safety if you came out into the garden. Please go back into the building at once."

"Oh, I think I am not in any danger here." He walked on through the opening in the hedge. Beyond it lay a glade surrounded by woodland, with undergrowth for a gunman to hide in.

Grainger grabbed his arm. "I'm sorry. I insist on your coming in."

"No, you have no right. This is not a police state."

"If you're taking that line, Mr. Gomez, I shall have to ask you to accompany me for questioning, under suspicion of having caused a public mischief by wasting police time, though there may be more serious charges to follow. According to the Foreign Office there has been no recent change in the political situation in Ciudad Antonio, and no reason to suppose that anyone would make an attempt on your life."

There was an alarming bulge in Gomez's side pocket. Grainger gripped him in an arm lock and pulled out a flat oblong case. Anti-climax. When he opened it he found jewellery, not the expected gun.

"Is this your property, or your wife's?"

"That is a private affair between us. It is not your business."

"Mr. Gomez, I am going to take you to an office which the management has put at my disposal where we can talk.

208

I don't want to embarrass you by holding on to you as we pass through the crowd, but I want you to go back through the Organ Room into the foyer and out of it at the other end, when I will give you more directions. I shall be walking very close behind you, and if you make the slightest attempt to escape you will find yourself flat on the ground with me on top of you, is that understood? Very well, let's go."

But before they could move a voice behind Grainger called out, "Oh there you are, Miguel, I've found you at last."

Grainger spun round. "Stop, Miss Clarkson. Don't come any nearer."

"Anthea, stop, don't go near him," shouted Bill, pounding across the lawn with the sergeant on his heels.

Anthea halted, framed in the gap in the hedge. Her expression changed as it dawned on her what was about to happen. Seconds later, the killer opened fire.

❧ THIRTEEN ❧

The audience was back in the theatre, most of it unaware
that anything out of the ordinary had happened. Out in the
garden Bill's and Anthea's picnic lay untouched in the Dell
at the head of the lake. The killer had crashed away
through the woodland between the garden and the lane, and
road blocks had been set up on all the routes away from
Glyndebourne. Gomez was awaiting interrogation in the
catering manager's office. On the stage, the Count was
puzzling away in *recitativo secco* about the amorous
pageboy who had proved not to be hiding in his wife's
dressing-room after all, and over various other things
that baffled him. When Teresa's cue came, she sailed
through her second big aria on a wave of anger. "Where,"
she enquired in C major, "are the beautiful moments of
sweetness and delight?" Where indeed, with her jewellery
gone? She could kill Pilar for giving it to Miguel, and
would divorce him as soon as her lawyer told her which
country to do it in. On the other hand, she was in magnificent voice and got a big round of applause at the end.
While she was disguising herself as Susanna for the last
act, helped by a sullen Pilar, a message arrived from Inspector Grainger to say that her jewellery was safe and he
would like to question her about her husband's activities

after the performance. In cheerful mood, she repulsed Cherubino's amorous advances in D major, forgave her husband in G major, and acknowledged a great number of enthusiastic curtain calls.

"Now, Richard. There's something we've got to attend to," said Joan Galliant as they settled into the Rolls to drive home. "First thing tomorrow morning, you're going to cancel that hellish garden party."

"Oh no, surely not? We have to put a bold face on our troubles; show that I'm back in full possession of my faculties and nothing's wrong."

"On the contrary, to give this party will convince the whole of Sussex you're out of your mind. Last time we entertained, someone got shot. Your chief accountant has been murdered, probably by your personal assistant, who in her turn has copped it from the chap who wants to kill Gomez but can't aim straight and always hits someone else. Gomez is 'helping the police with their enquiries,' which may well mean that they know he's guilty but can't prove anything. When they release him from their clutches he will emerge with a very bad smell trailing after him. You now propose to give a party with his canary of a wife, who is also your discarded mistress, as guest of honour. He will insist on coming with her to—what was your phrase? —put a bold face on it and show there's nothing wrong. When he appears nobody will dare to go near him for fear of being shot. Do you really want to put the whole county of Sussex to the trouble of inventing excuses for not attending this embarrassing and perhaps dangerous occasion?"

"She's right, Mr. Galliant," said Morris from behind the wheel. "There'll be no one there except gatecrashers, and most of them crime reporters. We can't have you and Madam all mixed up with the tit-and-bum bathing beauties on page two."

"I suppose we could postpone it," Galliant murmured.

"If you ask me, Richard," said his wife, "you ought to

211

spend less time sucking up to a lot of well-heeled bores, and more attending to what's happening to the firm. I've no head for business as you know, but as far as I can see the only people you need to convince that you're in possession of your faculties are the banks, so that they stop threatening to call in their loans. Wouldn't it make sense to go up today and explain to them exactly what happened? We know now, thanks to Mrs. Grant."

"I suppose I could do that. I'll think about it."

"Good. And there's something else that's been worrying me for some time. I'm not arty, and I know Wanda's a brilliant designer. But she has a very personal style, and people won't buy it if they don't happen to like that sort of thing. Aren't you afraid of losing customers unless you widen the range?"

He took alarm at once. "D'you really think so?"

"Well I do think Wanda makes the juniors work within her own styling, instead of striking out on their own. Richard, why don't you go back to doing some of the design work yourself? You do it so well."

"D'you really think the range is too narrow?"

"It's not for me to say, it was just an idea I had . . ."

After dropping the worrying idea into his head, Joan Galliant decided she had said enough for the moment, and pretended to fall asleep. He really enjoyed the design side, and he was very good at it. He had only started sleeping around because he was bored, and the same applied to his attempt to make it socially in Sussex. She studied his profile fondly through half-closed lids. She had married him partly because he was a very attractive man, and partly because her frustrated flair for management craved an outlet. The next item on her agenda was to reconcile him to Paul, but that would have to wait till things had settled down a little.

Celia had only a confused memory of how she got back to the nursing home and into the blessed comfort of bed. She remembered collapsing in awful pain just after Grainger had told her that Anthea was dead, and she remembered lying on a stretcher with Bill looking down on her with a face of stone, as if he would never forgive her for getting it wrong and letting Anthea die. Lying in bed with the blinds down, she was disgusted with herself. Why had she not realized in time that the danger was to Anthea, not Bill? She could imagine his state of mind. He was a one-woman man, and would he ever get over the loss of Anthea? Or rather the loss of the illusions about Anthea that he had built up over the years? He would blame Celia for her death, that was certain, the partnership between them would never be the same again. She drifted off into a repeat of the saxifrage nightmare, complete with the agonized climb up the staircase. But this time Bill was standing at the top, looking down at her with the white face and quivering nostrils which meant that he had lost his temper and that anything might happen, because he was completely out of control.

Visitors came, stayed for a few minutes talking in hushed tones, then went: Lucy and Jim, Richard and Joan Galliant, Inspector Grainger. But not Bill. Three days had passed. Still he did not come, and when the door opened again to admit only Charles Langley, she could not hold back her disappointment.

"Why doesn't Bill Wilkins come to see me?"

Langley considered the question. "He'll be in Nottingham, I imagine."

Why Nottingham, Celia wondered, then remembered. Anthea's parents lived there.

"Oh. Yes, of course," she said. "For the funeral."

"It's tomorrow. He made most of the arrangements, I believe. He went there at once, to break the news to Miss Clarkson's family."

I should have thought of that, Celia told herself. But he would have left a message or sent flowers if he hadn't been furious with me.

"If I'd been more quick-witted, she'd still be alive," she lamented.

"Oh no. You couldn't have foreseen it."

"I could, and should have. I was pretty sure she'd killed Dawson because he was blackmailing her, but it was only a guess—"

"A correct guess, Mrs. Grant. The police say she'd been realizing investments over the past few weeks and withdrawing the proceeds from her current account in amounts which correspond to sums paid into Dawson's bank a few days later. They also say the fibres under Dawson's fingernails came from a pullover they found in her wardrobe."

"Oh, I wish I'd known all that. I didn't think it through because I wasn't sure she'd killed him. I'd have foreseen how she'd react when the police decided it wasn't a double suicide and started looking for suspects. She'd panic. And when she panicked her first thought was always that she must have money. I was sure Gomez had promised her a huge fee for her part in the operation against Galliant, she wouldn't have taken it on otherwise. But Gomez hasn't any money, according to what he told me at that awful party. When none was forthcoming she probably behaved quite hysterically, because I imagine she intended to vanish abroad with it before she was arrested for murder. Gomez must have foreseen that she'd implicate him if she was arrested, so he decided to get rid of her."

"How did she persuade Gomez that he ought to get rid of you?"

"That was panic again. She was afraid I'd remember whose staircase it was that I'd smelt the datura at the top of, and when I asked her casually if she'd ever been to Miami, she decided I was much nearer the truth than I was. I suppose she told Gomez I'd worked the whole thing out and was liable to tell his wife all about it unless something was done."

Langley nodded. "Even when she was in a panic she was a very convincing liar."

"Yes, I've known her for years, and I didn't realize how vulnerable she was till very recently, or what she was capable of when she was frightened. The panic was hidden

214

behind a very hard-boiled exterior. Gomez must have had a disagreeable surprise when she suddenly disintegrated. Has he been arrested?"

"No. They've taken his passport and made him report to the police daily, but they're having trouble making a case against him. According to his passport he's been in Europe since the end of February, dividing his time between London and Paris, but that's not a criminal offence."

"He'd have to be around, though. To locate a source of *Datura suaveolens* and steal one, and mastermind Anthea's operation; and to keep in touch with Pilar when Teresa Enriquez arrived to start rehearsing."

"Yes," said Langley. "It would be quite easy for him to get a confederate in Miami to post letters to his wife that he'd written in advance."

"Surely they can get him for his part in Anthea's murder?"

"Apparently not. He and Pablo are telling two different sets of lies which contradict each other."

"Oh. So they caught Pablo?"

"Yes, at a road block just outside Ringmer. According to Gomez, Pablo was sent by his political enemies to shoot him, and gained his confidence by pretending to be a fellow-victim of the Ciudad Antonio terror. Pablo says he never went near Glyndebourne and doesn't know anything about any murder, but Gomez was up to his neck in drug-pushing and probably had urgent reasons for killing Anthea Clarkson."

"Then why was he staying in England as Gomez's house guest?"

"He says Gomez invited him over to discuss a very shady business deal, which he virtuously rejected. According to a more reliable source, namely Interpol, Pablo is a not very successful criminal who got across one of the Colombian syndicates, and had to hide out in Paris. It looks as if he helped Gomez plan the plot to poison Galliant in return for a share of Miss Enriquez's future earnings. But Grainger thinks he'll have trouble getting a conviction against either of them without Anthea to interrogate."

"If I'd been quicker, she'd still be alive," Celia murmured.

Langley looked at her knowingly. "You keep harping on that, but I shouldn't worry. It was for the best, he'll thank you in the end."

"Who will?" she asked weakly.

"Your Mr. Wilkins. That's what's worrying you, isn't it?"

She nodded, astonished by his perceptiveness.

"It was a shame about Anthea Clarkson," he went on. "She had so much going for her. She was good-looking and intelligent and she could have had a brilliant business career. Why on earth did she take to crime?" He thought for a moment, then added: "I suppose she came to grief because like many women, she didn't have the emotional stability you need as ballast for a first class brain."

Celia stared at his neatly brushed hair and clean, ordinary face. You bloody sexist, she thought. But she was feeling too ill to quarrel with him, so she shut her eyes. When she opened them he had gone.

She slept. When she woke up she was still angry. Do I lack emotional stability? she asked herself. Would a man be less upset than I am if he'd failed to prevent a colleague's girlfriend from being killed?

She was still grieving when a nurse wheeled in a telephone on a trolley. "You're not supposed to take calls," she explained, "but it's a Mr. Wilkins and he insisted."

Celia grabbed the phone. "Bill?"

"Oh Celia. I'm in Nottingham, Charles Langley just phoned. He says you're blaming yourself, but that's silly, you're not to. You done your best, you got nothing to reproach yourself with."

She clutched the phone and tried to stammer an answer. Tears of relief were streaming down her cheeks. But she was damned if she was going to let herself sound emotionally unstable.

216

ABOUT THE AUTHOR

JOHN SHERWOOD is a well-known British mystery author who lives in Kent, England.

STIMULATE YOUR MIND WITH THE CONAN FLAGG MYSTERY SERIES FROM M.K. WREN